EXIT INTERVIEW

Born and raised in the charming city of Kolkata, **Amrita Mukherjee**'s formal education took off at South Point School, after which she graduated with a first class in Sociology from Presidency College and topped it off with another first class in the masters programme from Calcutta University.

As a journalist, for the last fifteen years, she has been closely associated with the world of entertainment and Page 3 journalism, working with top publications like *The Times of India* and *Hindustan Times* in Kolkata, and was also the features editor at ITP Publishing Group in Dubai.

A strong believer in alternative journalism, she has been practising it, with good results, in her blog: www.amritaspeaks.com.

Presently, she is a media activist and freelance journalist, writing for Indian and international publications and websites.

This book is her first attempt at fiction writing.

EXIT !NTERVIEW

Amrita Mukherjee

RUPA

Published by
Rupa Publications India Pvt. Ltd 2015
7/16, Ansari Road, Daryaganj
New Delhi 110002

Sales Centres:

Allahabad Bengaluru Chennai
Hyderabad Jaipur Kathmandu
Kolkata Mumbai

This is a work of fiction. Names, characters, places and incidents are
either the product of the author's imagination or are used fictitiously
and any resemblance to any actual person, living or dead, events or
locales is entirely coincidental.

ISBN : 978-81-291-3500-1

First impression 2015

10 9 8 7 6 5 4 3 2 1

The moral right of the author has been asserted.

Printed by HT Media Ltd., Noida

*Dedicated to my brother, late Anirban Mukherjee,
who always said I would write one day*

Contents

∾

Prologue

∾

Rasha Roy sat on the terrace of her office with her laptop open in front of her. Her fingers were frozen on the keys and her brain failed to frame any words. She had no clue how long she had been sitting there in that state. Her eyes were fixed on the beautiful blue waters of the Arabian Sea at a distance. The wind played with her lovely curls, sometimes blocking her vision. But she didn't make any effort to flick the hair away from her face. She just sat there like a statue of calmness.

The leather and bamboo outdoor furniture interspersed with green plants and gazebos gave her office terrace the feel of a roof-top restaurant in a five-star hotel. She could see some of her colleagues sitting and smoking away leisurely on the white leather couches under the wooden shades in one corner of the terrace. A group was having an animated meeting in another section of the lounging area. While some employees were having lunch sitting on the high stools and tall round glass top tables, she preferred to sit in a remote corner lost in her thoughts. She always made the most of the cool February weather in Dubai and worked on the terrace. Had it been any other day, she would have been enjoying the lovely view of the majestic Burj Al Arab hotel on one side and the sea on the other, but today was different.

She had just had a meeting with her boss who had told her, in the sweetest possible words, that she was the most disorganized, incompetent, arrogant worker in the department—a journalist who could not write, who could not give wings to her thoughts, whose copy had to be edited and re-edited and who could not speak proper English even, to start with.

'You don't have the right diction, Rasha!' That's what her editorial director, Sabrina Kapadia, had told her. 'And on top of that, you have

that I-am-the-best attitude that you refuse to give up,' she had added.

Rasha found herself tongue-tied in front of her boss. This was solely because she didn't know what to believe in, her English marksheets from her convent school back in Kolkata or her boss's conclusion on her skills in the language.

Sabrina uncrossed her booted-legs, closed the page of her diary—an extremely girlie one with a pink butterfly bookmark sticking out of it—where she had scribbled some points, probably the things she had planned to tell Rasha. She asked Rasha to have a glass of water and finish the article. Then she left with a contemptuous gait. But Rasha just sat there for hours, her mind a cauldron of thoughts. She tried to absorb the insult and maintain a calm exterior, and kept telling the tears to stay away. But the stubborn droplets just kept welling up. With furtive glances, Rasha tried to see if anyone was looking at her. No one was. Suddenly, she remembered the shades that had so far been sitting pretty on her head. She dropped them on her eyes and let the river flow.

Part 1
Touch Down in Dubai

• • •

RASHA HATED SHEDDING tears and making a public spectacle of it. And she definitely hated the questions: 'Why are you crying? Are you okay?' If ever she gave in to an emotional outburst, only the pillow in her bed came to know about it. But on this Emirates flight to Dubai, that had taken off from Kolkata, she just didn't seem to care that everyone was looking at her. She was not shedding silent tears; she was actually on the verge of howling.

The view from the sky couldn't have been more beautiful. Dawn had painted the horizon red; and with every mile, the crimson gave way to a beautiful yellow. The layers of crimson, yellow and azure were almost a reflection of the rainbow of thoughts that were fleeting through Rasha's mind. She was happy to be flying towards her all-new life in a new city with her boyfriend, but she just couldn't get rid of the sorrow that worked 24x7 like a cement churner inside her stomach and erupted like a volcano in her eyes.

In her twenty-eight years on this Earth, she had never been away from her parents and her elder sister Rania. Although she had always loathed the curfew hours imposed on her by her progressive-yet-society-fearing Bengali parents and she had had endless debates and fights with them over it, she couldn't deny that there was no life for her without them. Rasha was a problem child in many ways. Rebellious and non-conformist, with a mind of her own, she questioned every society norm that didn't come within the purview of her logic. To her father's immense embarrassment, she got through high school wearing her father's T-shirts and horrendously baggy sand-blasted jeans.

Then when she was doing her masters in Criminology at Calcutta University, she caught on to this trend of night-clubbing that had become a rage in Kolkata in the late 90s. Rasha found herself to be a part of a new generation sucked into a whole new universe that came alive in the dark of the night inside the four walls of a discotheque. It was an easy-to-fit-in space where everything began and ended with revelry. Rasha was careful, however, to set her own limits inside that psychedelic arena—which meant no making out, no skimpy outfits, no unknown dance partners, only a bit of liquor, a pack of cigarettes and an occasional joint. But to her utter dismay, when she went home late in the night, her fun came to an end with a big full stop. As soon she got off her friend's car or bike, she would see the drapes in her parents' room drawn back, signalling that her mom was standing there in the dark waiting for her. Instantly, she would brace herself for another altercation with her parents. They would tell her that only 'bad' girls came home late and she would argue that everyone went out clubbing and she was not doing anything wrong. She would reason she was with friends whom her parents knew and she just had a few sips of beer and she was definitely not drunk. Although her parents would finally get tired and go to sleep, Rasha knew that all her arguments were in vain. The sequence of events would be the same the next night she went out clubbing. But that didn't mean she wouldn't go out. She loved dancing at the disco and she would just go ahead and let her hair down. It was her parents who would have to stop the endless worrying.

The scenario at home, however, would change completely the following Sunday morning. Rasha would leave her bed finally at eleven o'clock, and her mom would be waiting for her with a smile and a cup of coffee. Dad would chat happily at the breakfast table. Her elder sister Rania would join them. Although Rania had no comments to make about the events of the night before, Rasha knew she did not approve of her lifestyle either. Five years older to her, Rania had been the kind of girl who had never ruffled feathers at home except for the fact that she didn't want to marry. Her parents initially coaxed her, lined up suitors at her door, but she was steadfast in her resolve. She never told her parents or even Rasha the reason for her decision, but she made sure she stuck to it. Rasha was not that close to Rania when it came to sharing her secrets. She would rather share it with her mom than her elder-and-somewhat-sombre sister. But there was an invisible thread of love and protection that connected the two of them. Sometimes words were not said but things were understood.

So when Rasha decided to move to Dubai, Rania knew that more than being with her boyfriend, Arun, she wanted to explore a new world. That's why when their parents vehemently opposed Rasha's plans to go to Dubai saying that they couldn't imagine her getting into a live-in relationship, Rania stood by her sister and said that she would miss the opportunity of a lifetime if she didn't go. Whether she lived in or lived apart was inconsequential because her parents' friends and relatives would not be there in Dubai to see what she was up to.

'Ma, why are you so worried? Rita mashi, Urvashi mamima or Bhombol kaku are not going to be her next-door neighbours in Dubai like they are here. They won't be able to keep track of when Rasha is coming home and with whom or, for that matter, if she is living in with someone,' Rania said with authority at the dinner table one night. The word 'living in' did strange things to their parents. While their father's ears instantly took on a tomato hue, their mother choked on the water she was drinking. She started coughing violently.

'I hope you realize that Rasha is an adult who can take care of herself,' said Rania.

What she intended to imply but couldn't say directly to her

parents was: *If she wants to have a sex life she will have it. You won't be able to stop her.*

The tomato streak now travelled from Rania's father's ears to his cheeks and her mom looked at Rania like she had, at last, spotted the Brutus in her family. Rania now gently stroked her back to ease the coughing but her mom's expression did not change. Meanwhile, her dad decided to shift all his attention to the mutton he was eating. He focussed his attention to sucking the marrow out of a bone making a strange whistling noise.

Rasha stiffled a giggle. Her mom completely ignored her and continued.

'But Rita was saying that all women have to wear burqas there and are not allowed to leave home after 6:00 p.m.'

'Gosh, there you go. It's one of the most modern cities in the world. I will show you pictures on the net tomorrow. And, Ma, please stop taking advice from your neighbours. They are still living in the 60s,' said Rania.

That night at the dinner table Rasha had told her elder sister a silent 'thank you', but she never had the heart to tell her the real reason for leaving Kolkata. She did not want her sister to lose her sleep.

Rania always felt that a bright student like her sister, who had been top of her class from school through university, should have pursued higher studies abroad or, at least, should have gone for a PhD somewhere in India. Instead, the journalism bug had bitten her so hard in her tenth standard that the first thing she did was to take up a job as a trainee sub-editor even before her Masters results were out. Rania, who was an average student doing okay in an average job as a receptionist in a large IT firm, had loathed the idea of her brilliant sibling taking up a job for Rs 3,300 in a sinking newspaper as a trainee in the editorial department. But there was nothing she could do about it. Her sister always had her way.

~

Rania came to see Rasha off at the airport along with her parents. Rasha felt she looked more solemn than usual. Although they never had a relationship where they would whisper about boyfriends late into the night, Rasha knew she would miss her elder sister, who, so often, stood by her decisions.

'Rashu, you are meant for bigger things. I hope Dubai will prove to be that platform. And please be easy on Arun. He is a nice guy. You can be really stubborn at times, don't give him grief,' were her parting words.

Rasha had coached her mom for fifteen days prior to the date of leaving that she did not want any scenes at the airport and that she was just four-and-a-half hours away, which was the time it took by train from Kolkata to Jamshedpur—her maternal uncle's home and their weekend destination. When the time of departure came, her mom remained emotionless, as did her sister and father, but Rasha just couldn't hold back her tears and burst out crying.

'Now what are you doing?' said her mom with a forced grin.

Rasha knew exactly what it took her mom to manage that smile and how much she would be missing her younger daughter—the-hard-to-deal-with rebel, her best friend. But she kept that smile on her face till Rasha faded into the immigration section.

Rasha's tears, however, showed no signs of abating. No matter how much she tried to console herself—thinking of Dubai, the land of gold and dreams, of meeting Arun after six long months—her mind went back again and again to her apartment in Gariahat. The images of the place where she had lived for twenty-eight years of her life engulfed her—the bed where she slept hugging her mom tight, the terrace where she played as a child and had physical brawls with the boys of the apartment building, the balcony where she would spend endless hours studying and eyeing the boy on the bicycle, who would come for her and stand patiently in front of her apartment building everyday at 5:00 p.m... She looked out of the window of the plane. The crimson and yellow gave way to blue, but all she saw in the horizon was her mother's face.

Wiping away her tears, she hoped she had taken the right decision, to dislodge herself from her family. She hoped her decision would keep her family safe.

2

WHEN THE FLIGHT captain announced that the plane would be landing soon, Rasha managed to gather herself. She washed her face in the washroom, sprayed some perfume and fixed her hair. She looked around. The people on the flight were mostly Bengalis talking in their mother tongue. From their conversations, Rasha gathered that some lived in Dubai, some were transiting to other Gulf countries and the rest to the US or London. As she settled in her seat, she noticed that it was particularly comfortable. Although her state of mind did not allow her to relish the breakfast of eggs and sausages served on the flight, she had noticed that the food was warm.

Rasha took out the small mirror from her purse to put on some lipstick. Then out came her Lakmé kajal—the only make-up item she couldn't imagine her life without. To hide her puffy eyes, she applied the kajal generously. She then added a dash of blush to her cheeks. She was meeting Arun after a long time and she was determined to look radiant. She closed her eyes and leaned on the backrest. Immediately, she saw an empty white room and heard unknown male voices in her mind. She sat up alert, her eyes wide open.

I am having nightmares even when I am awake, she thought. *Daymares. Should I call them daymares?* she fumbled in her mind, trying hard to distract herself.

The middle-aged man sitting next to her, who was so far following her every sniffle, every sigh, finally mustered the courage to ask, '*Apni bangali?*' ('Are you Bengali?')

Rasha wasn't in the mood for a conversation, but she politely answered, 'Yes.'

'Me too. I live in Bahrain. I have a business there. You are a very friendly girl. I saw you talking to that stranger.'

'I never talked to anyone,' Rasha quickly retorted.

'That dark gentleman you were talking to. You were very friendly,' the man repeated with a smile that seemed to have a whole lot of meaning.

Rasha then remembered. She had spoken to Arindam Rakshit, who was her cousin's childhood friend and worked at the airport. He was the epitome of handsomeness—tall, dark and good looking. She bumped into him whenever she was flying and they exchanged pleasantries. This time she was handing him her cousin's new mobile number. Rasha looked at the man. He was running his tongue on his lips like he was about to dig into the tastiest ice cream on earth. She tried hard to hide her irritation. But there was something in his dying-to-talk-to-you expression that made Rasha give in to her devilish side.

'Oh him? He is my ex-husband.'

'Really? You are divorced?'

'Thrice.'

'Thrice!' he exclaimed.

The man looked horrified like he had spotted a dead body. Rasha was pleased.

'I…I am sorry,' he muttered.

'No it's alright. I am getting married again. That's why I am going to Dubai,' said Rasha.

'Again?' the man looked at her with disbelief. He started sipping his whisky, not too keen on the conversation anymore. But Rasha wanted to talk. The man was proving to be great for her mood.

'Oh! I am so excited. I am going to shop in Dubai for my

wedding and then my husband is gifting me a brand new Rolls Royce on the wedding.'

His attention sprung back to her with the mention of a Rolls Royce.

'What does your husband do?' he asked.

'He is a big businessman. He's got sprawling villas, a fleet of cars, a private jet and all that...'

'How old would he be?'

Now Rasha looked at the man demurely. 'He is not that young you know. He is sixty-two.'

The last words did something to the co-passenger from Bahrain. He tried to speak but the words were lost in his mouth. Then he just nodded and went back to his drink. Rasha had to really make an effort to hold back the laughter that was rumbling inside her. She turned to the window.

2

The plane had dropped altitude and she could see the ocean of sand below her. She could see the desert shrubs sprouting here and there; and then came rows and rows of houses systematically placed with the roads criss-crossing through them. For a second, she couldn't recognize the patches of blue in some of the houses. Then she realized those were swimming pools. Most of the houses were painted white and gleamed in the sun. Everything looked so clean and neatly arranged. It was such a stark contrast to the place from where her flight had taken off. From air, Kolkata looked like a cumbersome and crude amalgam of buildings garnished with beautiful patches of green and water bodies. In Kolkata there was anything but order, and here there was anything but chaos. She liked Dubai instantly and only for a moment missed the bedlam that was home.

She sniffed her handkerchief, which she had borrowed from

her mom at the airport. It smelled of Yardley, her mom's favourite perfume. She tucked it into the pocket of her jeans. Rasha was naturally stylish and liked to dress smartly, but never in her life had she taken so much trouble to dress up, that too, on a flight. She had bought a new pair of Bare jeans from Pantaloons that accentuated her shapely hips. She always wore clothes that set-off her hour-glass figure, but thanks to her semi-conservative upbringing, she could never bring herself to wear anything too tight or too revealing. So her style was tucked-in shirts and straight-cut jeans. She felt it went perfectly with the image of a journalist. Today, she had chosen an Allen Solly shirt in her favourite shade of pink, flat shoes from Inc.5—she hated high heels and never felt its need because she was 5.6 feet tall—and the black corduroy jacket from Giordano that Arun had gifted on her birthday. Her shoulder-length curly hair was pulled back in a ponytail and the two small silver eardrops, gifted to her by Rania, dangled gaily from her earlobes. The earrings seemed to have that sprightly demeanour that Rasha's long strides down the vestibule seemed to lack at the moment.

As soon as she was off the escalator, she spotted a woman with a pleasant smile wearing a yellow coat, standing with a placard with Rasha's name on it. She gave her a huge bunch of red roses with a small card tucked inside it in Arun's handwriting. The card read: 'Welcome to Dubai'. She could feel the excitement of meeting Arun finally pushing away the gloom of the entire flight. She thought of what she would do when she met him. She just hoped she didn't break down into tears again. Her emotions were not in the best of state after all.

'There's a trolley for your hand luggage, you can put it here,' the woman said.

Rasha was carrying only a small bag and her handbag. She put her bag in the trolley, but kept her handbag with the passport and visa in it, firmly slung on her shoulders. Rasha was glad for her comfy shoes because there seemed to be a long walk ahead of her. But thanks to the Marhaba service (meaning 'welcome' in Arabic), represented by the woman in yellow by her side, Rasha was entitled to a buggy ride. Arun had specially hired their services to receive Rasha and take her through the formalities of passport control and baggage claim. The buggy was driven by a woman in a niqab, which means only her eyes were visible through the slit in the black veil. She deftly veered the vehicle down the polished, wide corridors of the huge and bustling Dubai International Airport.

As a child, Rasha's father had always told her that if she ventured out alone, she would be kidnapped and sold off for camel racing in the Middle East. That was just about all the knowledge he had about this part of the world. In fact, her father, who had travelled to the US and the UK, was pretty much opposed to her going to the UAE because he firmly believed that it was a place where harsh Muslim laws prevailed, where women were not allowed to work and were kept in veils inside their homes. Rasha thought her father would have been pleasantly surprised to see this lady so adeptly steering the buggy through the crowded airport.

She was struck by the sheer grandeur of the airport. The large spaces, carefully laid out lounging areas, the strategic lighting and almost all the brands in the world showing off their wares at the mile-long duty-free area, were bound to amaze even the most well-travelled passenger. Rasha felt that if she sat there for an hour, she would actually see the entire world pass by because there were people from almost all nationalities at the airport. One of the largest airports in the world boasting more than six thousand weekly flights with 130 airline companies operating to 220 destinations across the continents with the help of 58,000 employees, Dubai airport was a world in itself and Rasha quickly saw why.

As she disembarked the buggy and walked into passport control, she was ushered to a desk where she handed her passport and visa to an abaya-clad woman. Her headscarf, or sheyla, was neatly pinned on her head and Rasha noticed she had a beautiful face. Her eyes were lined with heavy kohl and it was clear that she had taken great care to do her makeup. Rasha made a mental note that she had never seen a woman at the Kolkata passport control.

The lady looked at her passport and smiled. 'Kemon accho? (How are you?)' she asked in Bengali.

Now it was Rasha's turn to be surprised out of her wits. 'How do you know Bengali?' she asked the Emirati lady.

'Sourav Ganguly. I am a great fan of Sourav Ganguly. I want to go to Kolkata one day just to meet him,' she beamed. She stamped Rasha's passport. Reporter Rasha would have liked to prolong the conversation, but there were too many people standing behind her in the queue.

She walked out of the airport into the sea of people holding placards. She could feel her heart thumping. She clutched the roses in her hand and scanned the faces to spot Arun. Her eyes failed to spot his face. She did the exercise again, but he wasn't there.

'Madam, have you found him?' the Marhaba lady asked.

Rasha said a dejected no.

~

Where could he be? He is not the sort to get late, she thought. Not one to jump to conclusions, Rasha tried hard to stay calm, but she could feel her excitement giving way to worry. *What could have happened?* she mused. She switched on her mobile, but the roaming on her Kolkata number had not yet been activated so she couldn't call him. Her flight was late and on top of that she had been standing there for ten long minutes and there was no sign of him.

'Madam, let's go to our office at the other end. We can call from there.'

Rasha nodded and followed the lady in yellow. As she entered the office, she could see the back of a man sitting at the desk. As the man turned around, she could feel her knees buckling under her.

'I told these guys to bring you straight to the office. I don't know why you were waiting there for so long,' said Arun.

Rasha hugged him. As she turned to kiss him on the cheeks, he turned away.

'Better do all this at home,' he said, glancing apprehensively in all directions. He picked up her handbag.

Rasha was slightly taken aback at his stiffness, but ignored it and followed him out of the Marhaba office. A Volvo limousine belonging to Emirates was waiting outside for them. After her luggage was loaded in the car, they got in and Arun asked the driver to go to Karama.

'This is a limousine, Rasha,' said Arun.

'Really?' she said stretching her leg and feeling the long space in the rear.

'I have never been in a limo.'

'I know that. That's why I mentioned. I knew you would miss the interiors in your excitement and then later accuse me of not pointing it out.' He smiled.

Rasha noticed that Arun had lost a few kilos but looked toned. He also had a visible stubble.

'I thought you would not come. Maybe your dad finally decided not to let you come,' he said after Rasha had finished her limo inspection.

Rasha felt at ease now because Arun always joked about her controlling parents, especially her dad. When Rasha told her parents about her desire to get married to Arun in a few years, they approved quite readily. Rasha remembered that her dad had actually asked for Arun's address and phone number and kept it with him when Rasha 'formally' went out with him for the first time. Arun pulled Rasha's leg mercilessly after that.

'Did he think I would have eloped with you? I could have given him the wrong address and number,' he always said.

'Will you please let me take my first look at Dubai?' Rasha told Arun in a slightly rebuking tone, completely ignoring his take on her dad.

What she saw she just loved. Spic-and-span, broad roads, snazzy cars and flamboyant buildings were such a contrast to the lane-less narrow littered roads of Kolkata. The spunk and newness of Dubai struck her and she immediately understood why Arun wanted so desperately to come back to Dubai after he experienced the city for three days when he was called over for an interview. Rasha's eyes took in the beautiful flowers in dark pink, white and yellow lining the sidewalks of the city. She wondered how much effort and expense went into making the city look so dazzling and refreshing.

~

Arun had taken an apartment in Karama. He had told Rasha it was not as upmarket as Jumeirah or Marina, but it was a nice Indian neighbourhood, where all amenities were within easy reach. It was also a foodies' paradise. If you were in the mood for Indian, Chinese, Thai or Pakistani cuisine, all you had to do was step out of the house in your pyjamas and chappals. A foodie to the core, Rasha had no qualms admitting to Arun over the phone that she was already salivating.

Right now, Rasha had no clue where their limousine was heading. Arun gave the driver directions before finally asking him to stop in front of a building with a pleasant pink colour and long balconies with ornate iron balustrades painted white. Some of the balconies had potted plants and pink flowers hung over the balustrades. The visage of the building looked pretty as a picture.

'That's our home,' said Arun pointing to the long balcony on the third floor. Looking up, Rasha felt the throbbing of her veins.

This would be her own home where she would be the one deciding what to cook, when to wash the clothes, what colour the curtains would be and no one would be waiting with the drapes drawn back when she would return home late in the night.

Thinking of the curtains, she remembered her mom. 'Oh! Arun, I need to call home to tell them I have arrived safely.'

'I have already sent Rania a text. Get inside, settle down, then you can talk to them at leisure,' said Arun.

Rasha thought: *that's so Arun, always responsible*. And she smiled lovingly at him.

Arun opened the door of the apartment for her and she immediately fell in love with it. There was a small square area linking all the rooms. The kitchen, not too large but spacious enough to accommodate the refrigerator, was neatly done up with white cupboards. An arched door from the square space led to the hall which was pretty huge. The bedroom was smaller than the hall, but was spacious. The sun-bathed balcony connected the hall and the bedroom. There was a large bathroom with a bathtub. Rasha immediately visualized herself taking long bubble baths in there like the Bollywood heroines in Lux adverts! In fact, she had always wanted a bathtub at home, but their bathroom in Kolkata was too small for her to even dream of installing one. There was another small bathroom, more like a powder room, fitted with only a WC and washbasin.

'This is what you call the perfect 1BHK, one-and-a half bathroom apartment in Dubai,' announced Arun. The hall was completely empty except for curtains, a TV, two chairs and a single mattress on the floor. The bedroom only had a double mattress on the floor, curtains and another TV. The kitchen had the cooking range, refrigerator and microwave oven. That was all the apartment had.

'I have left the apartment as bare as possible so that you can do up the place the way you like,' Arun said.

'So you were that sure I would join you?' asked Rasha sarcastically.

'You know bare minimum works for me. But aren't you glad it's like this?'

Arun subtly avoided a direct answer to Rasha's question. He knew it wasn't the right time. He took Rasha in his arms and gave her a long kiss. Rasha could feel her body melting in his arms. It seemed almost like an eternity that she had been away from Arun. Once they had had enough of each other, they relaxed on the mattress in the bedroom.

'But, Arun, why did you not let me kiss you at the airport? I was very surprised at your reaction.'

Arun smiled. 'Although Dubai is extremely liberal, you must remember you are in a Muslim country. This is the month of Ramadan and the month of abstinence. Any kind of physical intimacy in public is not approved of. One can end up with a fine or even land up in jail. So it's best to keep your emotions in check and respect the law of the land,' he said. Before Rasha could ask him any more questions, Arun opened the suitcase lying on the floor and took out something.

'Close your eyes,' he said. Rasha did as she was told. A beautiful diamond pendant with seven small diamonds set in circular rings of white and yellow gold sat pretty on her neck.

'Oh! Gosh! Arun!' Rasha gushed. She was moist-eyed again and gave him a tight hug.

3

RASHA WAS STANDING in a long queue on the ground floor corridor of Presidency College. Although she had been standing there for an hour waiting to pick up the admission form, except for a niggling pain in her knees, the wait didn't seem to affect her at all. She was just looking at every brick of the building, hoping and praying that she would get admission to Presidency College. The college had become a part of her family legacy. Anybody who was worth his salt from her mom's side—be it her uncle who was holding an enviable post at the World Bank or her aunt who was a respected scientist in the US or her cousin who had just graduated with record marks in English and immediately got himself a place in Oxford University with full scholarship—had gone to Presidency College.

During Rasha's growing-up years, the discussion at family get-togethers would invariably veer towards Presidency College. And she would be fascinated to hear the exploits of his uncle, who sat next to Nobel Laureate Amartya Sen in class, or her aunt chirping about her classmate, actress-filmmaker Aparna Sen, or her cousin talking about their endless adda in the college canteen and the fascinating library.

From where Rasha was standing, she could see the first floor balcony of the main college building. The thought that freedom fighter Netaji Subhash Chandra Bose had probably stood there during his college days did something to her adrenaline glands.

'Do you have your marksheet and money ready? You are after ten people now,' a pleasant voice nudged Rasha out of her daydream.

'Yes,' she replied, showing her marksheet to the tall boy standing in front of her. Rasha thought he would be about six feet tall. He was quite dark and had short hair that seemed to stand up on his head. His eyes sparkled so did the tiny stud on his left ear. He was wearing a khaddar kurta, which looked washed and worn too often. The big sneakers he was wearing looked quite odd with the jeans and kurta. A white paper was pinned on his kurta. The paper read: Arun Mitra, III Year, Volunteer.

He quickly moved on to the boy standing in front of Rasha. The boy was wearing a shabby shirt and trouser and was accompanied by an elderly gentleman in a dhoti. Both looked nervous. Arun Mitra perused his marksheet.

'You have got 85 per cent in Higher Secondary exams, that's amazing,' said Arun as he handed back the marksheet to the boy.

The boy looked hesitant. 'Dada, I live in the village Lakshmikantapur. I went to four colleges today and finished all my money buying admission forms. I heard Presidency College gives away free forms to the needy, so I am standing here with that hope.'

Arun patted the boy on his back, 'We do. But the quota for the day is over.'

The boy's face fell.

'Don't lose heart. I am there for you.' Arun took out twenty rupees from his kurta pocket and handed it to the boy.

'The change...'

'We will have tea together in the canteen, with the change, when you get admission to this college.'

The boy smiled gratefully.

Rasha could feel her eyes welling up after witnessing the tall boy's kind gesture.

Rasha made every effort to look ordinary on the first day of college. Ragging wasn't menacing in Presidency College. Her aunts and uncles even told her that it was, at times, enjoyable, but she wasn't taking any risks. She wasn't going to stand out in a crowd on the first day. So she made every effort to look plain in an ill-fitting salwar kurta and wore her oiled hair in a boring plait. She wore the specs that she usually used at home. She managed to duck in the back benches and remain inconspicuous when the seniors made her class dance and sing to their tunes. Ragging lasted half an hour and Rasha heaved a sigh of relief when the seniors, following tradition, took them to the canteen for a treat of samosas and hot chai.

Like everything in Presidency, she had fantasized about the canteen too where generations of brilliant students and famous alumni had had their intellectual discussions. However, the sooty high walls and the dim lighting didn't appeal to her much. But the students didn't seem to mind it at all. They were cheerfully chatting away inside the canteen. Rasha found the sun-lit balcony outside a bit more attractive and planned to have her tea there after a quick trip to the washroom.

She asked a senior where she could find a washroom.

'It's in the next room. Just go across the badminton court and you will find it.'

Rasha found it strange that a badminton court was inside a room. She hesitantly opened the giant door and saw a crowd sitting on the floor while a mixed doubles match was on its way. The room was so big and the ceiling was so high that Rasha immediately knew why it was a chosen place for badminton. She walked by the sidelines of the court and crossed the room to another giant door that she assumed was the women's washroom. She closed the door behind her and tried to lift the huge iron latch that had to be pushed up to bolt the door. She struggled with the latch and her bladder at the same time. After a long struggle, the long, heavy iron latch finally gave way and thundered to the floor. She had no choice but to walk out of the bathroom. Everyone at the court was laughing now and the girl who had asked her to use that washroom had joined them too. Rasha could feel her ears hot against her face and she frantically looked across the room for a face that sympathized with her plight. There was one. Arun Mitra was sitting cross-legged on the floor with a cigarette in his hand—his face devoid of any expression.

∾

Second day onwards, the freshers were safe in Presidency College. Traditionally, only the first day of college was reserved for ragging. So, the deliberately gawky, spectacled, ill-dressed Rasha Roy was quickly dumped into the wardrobe and out emerged a stylish fresher in a white double-breasted shirt and a fitted denim pencil skirt. In matching canvas pumps, wearing her contact lenses, Rasha was determined to forget the embarrassment of her first day in college and start afresh. And yes, she intended to find out about Arun Mitra—the man who didn't laugh at her. Few seniors from Rasha's school were in the same college now. She hunted one of them down during the break. Her excuse was that she wanted to know how to conduct herself in the college. Third-year Political Science student Meera Attal was in splits when Rasha told her what had happened the day before.

'Rasha, that girl framed you. She knew you will not be able to handle that bolt. There's a technique to do it, I will teach you,' laughed Meera.

'A bathroom bolt in this college has a technique?' Rasha grimaced. 'But that guy, Arun Mitra, was very sweet, you know. He was the only one who didn't laugh,' she added.

Meera started laughing again.

'Now what?'

'He probably didn't even know you were in the room.'

'What? Why?'

'He was stoned. He is big on marijuana.'

'Marijuana?'

'Don't tell me you are so naïve. Many people here do marijuana.'

'Do you?'

'Sometimes. Gives a nice high. You should try.'

Rasha gulped.

'Relax. It's like smoking a cigarette. Just tell them to make a light joint for you. You will enjoy it.'

'So Arun is actually a marijuana addict?' asked Rasha.

'Umm…I don't know if I can say he is an addict, but he seems to like it since he is always smoking a joint.'

'Gosh! And I thought he was different.'

'He is! He is very different.'

'How?'

'Teachers in Presy usually categorize students as notorious and meritorious. But Arun is the only one who is called nototorious—notorious and meritorious. He is super brilliant. He is majoring in Economics and always tops his class. He represents the college in debates, and badminton and table tennis tournaments and always comes back with a prize. He heads the Social Work Committee and is responsible for running the Night School. Professors love him for his intellect and attitude, although they know he is always carrying a joint with him. Sadly, his girlfriend has everything but a brain.'

'He has a girlfriend?'

'Aha…now someone is very interested.'

'Okay, you don't have to tell me about his girlfriend, I am really not interested,' said Rasha.

'Come on, I was just joking. GF is uninteresting; I would prefer to talk about Arun.'

'Okay.' Rasha deliberately shrugged her shoulders to show she was not interested anymore. But Meera continued.

'Last year, Arun landed in major trouble with the police,' said Meera with a mysterious look.

'Why? Now don't tell me he is into smuggling marijuana too.'

'No, no.' Meera started laughing again.

'Then?'

'You will notice there is a dilapidated building next to our college. Most of the men living in that building earn their living by playing musical instruments in those bands that are hired during durga puja processions or weddings. Through the college library window, Arun spotted one of those men beating his wife black-and-blue. He just hopped over and beat up that guy. Obviously, the man complained to the police and they came to college to arrest him. The principal used his contacts in high places to stop the arrest. But he was unhappy with Arun for being so headstrong. Arun was even suspended for ten days. If you are ever harassed by any guy on or off the campus, call Arun; he will fix him.'

'By beating the guy black-and-blue?'

'Not always. There was this guy tailing me from Dhakuria bus stop where I take the public bus to college. He was horrible. He would be in a lungi, always stood next to me in the bus, uttered horrible things under his breath and tried to touch me. I was so scared of him. I tolerated him for a week. I couldn't tell my father because he was anyway against me joining a college that was so far away from home. He would probably have taken that opportunity to put me in some hopeless college near home. So, I reported the incident to the general secretary of the students union. He put me on to Arun. One day, Arun got into the same bus with me, but we behaved like strangers. He stood next to the man all through the journey and when I got off near college, he just took the man aside and told him something. I don't know what he said, but thankfully I saw the last of that man.'

'Interesting!' said Rasha.

'Yeah, he is a character.'

'Indeed! A stoned knight in shining armour,' smiled Rasha.

∾

Rasha enjoyed Presidency College immensely. But when she was not attending classes or chatting in the canteen, she saw herself checking out what Arun was up to. She found it strange that she was actually doing that a lot, but she couldn't help herself. Most of the time he would be playing cricket with the children of the fourth-class staff in college, or studying in the library, or looking for volunteers to teach in the night school, or sometimes sitting on the lush grounds with a joint, staring up at the sky.

One particular day, Rasha was sitting in the extended sill of one of the tall windows of the college when a cricket ball landed at her feet. Instead of just throwing it to the batsman, Rasha did the entire exercise of bowling and bowled the guy.

Arun clapped. 'That's fabulous. You play cricket?'

'Yes, sometimes with the boys of our locality.' Rasha was now quite sure that she did that because she was looking for his attention.

'Come play with us. An able player in our team will help,' said Arun.

Rasha felt like she had just been given the Arjuna Award for her outstanding achievement in cricket. She held the bat tight. Her enthusiasm touched the ball which flew into the first floor window, and the next moment, they heard a crash. Rasha's face was drained off all colour. She had hit the ball through the window of the History department.

Arun smiled. 'I will handle this. Don't worry.'

Rasha didn't dare to go anywhere near cricket or the History department for the next six months. She didn't dare face Arun either. She found out he had taken the blame and the flak from the teachers. She didn't know if she should thank him or apologize to him. So, she stayed away from him. Once or twice she spotted him in the canteen with Salina Choudhary, his girlfriend according to the rumour mill in the college. Salina was pretty, but seemed dumb, and had nothing in common with Arun. While he was always in his khaddar kurtas, Salina wore minis and contoured jeans. She had every strand of her hair in place while Arun looked he had not even combed his hair in the morning. He wanted to go to Oxford after graduation and she wanted to open her own beauty salon!

∾

'I just wanted to tell you there is no need to feel bad about breaking that window pane the other day,' said Arun.

Rasha was sitting in the college canteen sipping tea. She hadn't realized that Arun had silently crept into the chair next to her.

'But I put you in a spot, didn't I?' Rasha asked.

'Let me share a secret with you. I broke the glass in the first year, then again in second year. In my third year, you did it. But by then, my teachers were used to me doing it.'

His smile was infectious.

Rasha laughed. 'I am relieved to know that.'

'I did something worse in my few days in IIT. I smashed the windowpane while a class was going on. Thankfully, no one was hurt.'

Rasha wasn't listening to the incident anymore; the word IIT had filled her with curiosity.

'What were you doing in IIT?'

'I was doing Electrical Engineering from IIT Kharagpur. Within a month, I realized it was not for me. I quit within three months.'

'You got through IIT, then you quit? I can't believe this.'

'I am used to this reaction,' sighed Arun.

'Then what did you do?'

'For the rest of the year, I did what I like doing best and then took admission here in the next session.'

'What do you like doing best?'

'I am off to Oxford next month. If you stay in touch with me, I will tell you.'

'Congrats! That's great. We can stay in touch over email,' said Rasha.

'That's fine. But I want to meet you in person too.'

Arun's sparkling eyes were staring intensely at Rasha. She shifted in her seat. She felt joy sweeping through her body. She wanted to ask him why he wanted to meet her when they had only spoken twice in the entire year in college.

'Okay, I will try,' she said instead.

'I promise I will meet you and tell you what I like doing most,' he repeated.

~

After she finished college, Rasha took up a job in the newspaper *Kolkata Daily*. By then, Arun had moved from Oxford to London Business School to do his MBA. He kept his promise; and every time he came down to Kolkata for his holidays, he called her and they would go out for pizza at Roof Top on Lee Road or hit his favourite momo joint on Sambhunath Pandit Street. Rasha started looking forward to Arun's Kolkata visits.

They never discussed Salina nor did Rasha ever ask him what he liked doing best, something that he had promised to tell her when they met. She presumed his answer would be playing cricket. He would talk about his life in the UK and he would tell her about the girls he had met in the UK and how his blind dates always ended in a fiasco. Meanwhile, Rasha would finish the momos on her own plate and keep eyeing the ones still left on Arun's.

'Can you imagine I even landed up with a girl, who was actually a guy before he changed his sex?' said Arun passing on a momo from his plate to Rasha's, as if it was the most natural thing to do.

She told him about her break-up with her boyfriend of three years. Then she told him about the guys she had met after that. Tears streamed down Arun's face as he laughed hysterically when Rasha told her about her latest date—a very handsome guy, who had a big job in a multinational company and who was obsessive about his collection of gold chains and innumerable gold rings.

'On our second date, he was hinting that he wanted to propose to me,' Rasha told Arun.

'I was already a bit put off by his constant talk about jewellery, but he took me completely by surprise when he said, "Rasha, I just have one request. Please don't send me those horrible forwards on email. Last time you sent me that forward of a girl's face changing into a skeleton, I could not sleep through the night. You should keep in mind I live alone and I am really scared of ghosts."' That was Rasha's second and the last date with him.

Rasha had also liked a friend's brother. They had met at a common friend's place and had a few drinks. On their way back, Rasha poured a peg of rum in a bottle of Coke and topped it with cola. She got on a cycle rickshaw with the bottle in her hand and the guy sat next to her drenched in paranoia.

'But I don't blame the guy. You are one of a kind,' said Arun. Such comments from Arun did something to Rasha.

Once out of college, Arun was a very different person. Along with his ear stud, he had said goodbye to his marijuana joints and mud-stained sneakers. Shirts and T-shirts had taken the place of khaddar kurtas. He definitely brushed his hair and, at times, even used hair gel to keep his unruly mop in place. His aftershave smelled exhilarating to Rasha.

Their friendship grew over email and phone calls. Thereafter, Arun came back to Kolkata, took up a job and they promised each other that they would definitely meet on the first Friday of every month. Rasha liked the fact that unlike most guys, who kept her perpetually waiting at metro stations, movie halls or restaurants, Arun was always on time for their Friday meetings, or were those dates? Rasha wasn't sure.

Rasha once asked Arun to help her out with his corporate contacts at the Royal Calcutta Golf Club so that she could do an article on the caddie-turned-successful golfers. Arun got her all the contacts and even offered to accompany her to the golf club. He was supposed to wait for her at the metro station. Rasha was late by an hour. Mobile phones had not caught on so much then, so they both didn't own one. When Rasha finally boarded the metro, she could already visualize Arun having turned into a fire-breathing dragon and she thought of ways to save herself from his wrath. Instead, he just sat there on the steps of the metro station, his face placid like the waters of a fjord and he gave her a warm smile as he got up to greet her.

'I am so sorry, Arun. I landed in a bit of a spot with this writer I was interviewing,' said Rasha.

'I guessed that something must be wrong. I was hoping it was nothing serious. I am happy to see you are okay,' he said gleefully.

Rasha heaved a sigh of relief. 'You know what happened was at once so serious and hilarious,' she said.

'I am all ears, but let's start walking to the Golf Club,' said Arun.

'I was asked to interview this writer and I hadn't read anything he has written. I did my research on the net, but I was still nervous when I rang the bell to his house,' she said.

'An elderly lady opened the door and I blurted out, "Is Mr Pradip Mukherjee at home?" The lady looked irritated. "This is

Prabir Mukherjee's home." In my nervousness, I had uttered the wrong name.'

'Trust you,' laughed Arun.

'This was only the beginning. Then the writer started asking me what I thought of his work and I had to honestly tell him that I hadn't read any of his books. He looked disappointed. Then he started talking about how he fell in love with a girl of twenty-three when he was fifty-five. I felt extremely uncomfortable when he started giving me intimate details about his affair and his wife hovered around us. He showed me the photographs of his two grown-up daughters on his book shelf next to which was his girlfriend's snap. I tried hard to veer the conversation back to his literary career, but he kept saying, "Don't you think this makes a better story?"'

'That makes a good scoop, doesn't it?' asked Arun.

'Not really. He showed me the clippings of a dozen Bengali newspapers where he has talked about this girl. Nevertheless, I managed to get the conversation back on track, but it took me a lot of time.'

'I get it,' said Arun.

'Wait, I have not delivered the punchline yet.'

'There's more left?'

'He finally started telling me how this girl used to meet him at the Press Club and sit on his lap and kiss him openly. Then he said, "I don't know why I wanted to talk to you about her? Do you remind me of her? How would you feel if you kissed someone who was fifty-five?"'

'What cheek!' exclaimed Arun.

'By then, I had got up and my bag was slung on my shoulders. I said, "I would feel I was kissing my father or even my grandfather maybe."'

Arun was in splits. 'Poor guy. He should have done his research on fireball Rasha Roy before he agreed to do the interview.'

That day, after the interviews got over, Rasha and Arun took a long walk on the lush green golf course, enjoying the winding path, the canopies of green over their head and talking about everything under the sun. Both of them never realized how time had passed. Rasha felt that her comfort level with Arun had grown beyond normal and she had really begun to like his confident persona. What she liked most about him was the fact that he let her be. Although by then they had become the best of friends, Arun never tried to pry into her personal life. He was happy with the information Rasha shared with him about herself and never asked for more. She absolutely loved this attitude of his.

∾

It was during one such session over pizzas at Roof Top when Rasha revealed that she was under pressure to get married.

'My sister does not want to get married, so my parents have turned their attention to me. But I will definitely not marry till I find my kind of a guy,' Rasha said.

'And I will only get married after you get married,' said Arun.

'Why?'

'Because you will not be meeting me as often and I will get bored and I will have to start looking for new company. So I might as well get married then.'

Rasha laughed. 'Then marry me. You will not get bored your entire life.'

'I don't have any problems doing that if you are ready to marry me.'

Arun had said the words in zest, but Rasha stopped in her tracks.

'Are you serious?'

'Yes, I am.'

'Wait! Wait! Do you mean to say you want to marry me?'

'Yes, if you are okay with it.'

Rasha thought for a second.

'What about Salina? Isn't she the one you are interested in?'

Strangely, this was the first time Rasha had mentioned her since they left college.

'Rasha, you must be mad not to see that you are the one I am interested in. I haven't been in touch with her since we left college.'

Rasha came up with an unnatural giggle. Her heart was racing, her palms were sweating and she could feel a buzz inside her head.

As they left the restaurant and got into a cab, they held hands for the first time.

'Are you in a hurry to get married?' she asked Arun.

'Not at all, it's entirely up to you.'

'Okay! I want to fund my own wedding so I need to have a bank balance before I decide to take the plunge. It will take some time. Can you wait?'

'If we don't look at a lavish wedding, you won't need a fat bank balance. So you wouldn't need much time to build it either. '

Rasha squeezed his hand and smiled. He dropped her home.

Rasha was still smiling when Arun pulled down the window of the cab and doled out another example of his witty self. 'By the way, I heard Salina's opened a beauty salon on Lansdowne Road. You can get your wedding make-up done there. I am sure she would love to deck you up for your D-day and might even give you a discount.'

He was long gone when Rasha found herself still standing alone on the sidewalk laughing. She felt a sense of pride that the no-more-doped knight in shining armour was hers now.

Suddenly, the cab came back with Arun hanging out of the window.

'Now that you have agreed to marry me, I will tell you what I was doing that whole year I dropped out of IIT. I was volunteering at Mother Teresa's Missionaries of Charity. I just hope you were not thinking I was playing cricket. Good night, love.'

Both sets of parents approved of their respective choices, but they decided to wait a year before they got married. Meanwhile, Arun landed a job in Dubai. Rasha had no plans of joining him in Dubai so soon because she was busy with her own job in Kolkata. But the turn of events were such that she had to take a decision. She decided to give life a fresh start in Dubai.

Interlude

• • •

Sabrina reappeared on the terrace. Rasha noticed her jawline had relaxed and it seemed as if she wanted to talk to her. Instead Sabrina changed direction at the last minute and went to the smoking area of the terrace and lit a cigarette. Sabrina could probably feel Rasha's glare from under the shades and decided it was better not to talk to her. It was past lunch hour, but Rasha noticed that Sabrina had the same nail polish on. Usually the colour changed after lunch. Her post lunch 'business meetings' were mostly trips to the next door salon for varnishing and revarnishing her talons. In case the business meeting, which usually lasted for two hours, didn't materialize, she always had a doctor's appointment in the afternoon. But from the changed colour on her toes, everyone knew who the doctor was. It was an open secret within the team.

Two months ago, Rasha had decided that she would not take things lying down and show Sabrina what she was actually made of. But even then, she felt she was fighting a battle she had lost from the very beginning. Going any further would be futile.

Finally, her fingers moved on the key. She wrote:

Dear Ms Sabrina,

Please accept my resignation from the post of Lifestyle Editor of Silver Screen. I will be grateful if you take my pending annual leave into account and release me at the earliest.

Thanks,
Rasha Roy

PS: Bitch…just remember, every dog has his day.

She took a long look at the last line and deleted it.

After writing her resignation letter, she continued sitting alone in one corner of the terrace, holding a cup of coffee. As the sun dipped into the sea, creating a glorious sunset, images of Kolkata wafted back to her like the aroma of the coffee she was holding in her hand.

Part 2
Kolkata Unfolds

• • •

4

RASHA WAS TYPING at a frenetic pace, sitting at her work station. The entertainment pages were to be sent to print at 6:00 p.m. and it was already 4:00 p.m. She was still waiting for a quote. But she wanted to get her story ready first and weave in the quote when it came. Her boss had told her that he wanted the story as the breaking news on the front page even if it was Armageddon that day. She had been following it up for the last two days and was constantly hitting a wall. Just when she had almost given up, magic happened.

She had discovered through a source that a big Hollywood film was being shot in Kolkata and had both Hollywood and Bollywood stars on board. But the whole project was such a hush-hush affair that despite tapping her sources really hard, she could not get a whiff of where the sets were located, or even where the stars were staying. Finally, she managed to squeeze out a bit of information from one of the twenty phone calls she made. Bollywood veteran Raj Puri was the lead actor in the project, she was told. She knew a socialite in Kolkata who was good friends with him and would be able to connect her with Raj Puri. Fortunately, the lady really liked Rasha. So when she called her, the lady was ready to help.

'He is staying at the Park Hotel. I don't have his mobile number, but I can give you his room number. His wife is travelling with him, so if he is not there, she can help you out. She is a good friend of mine. I will put in a word for you,' she said.

Rasha thanked her and hung up. 'Finally, a breakthrough!'

she exclaimed in joy. Rasha called up the room and Raj Puri's wife answered.

'He's gone for a shoot.'

'No, I don't know the location where they are shooting.'

'No, I don't know when he will come back to the hotel.'

'Yes, she told me you will call.'

'No, I don't have any details about the film.'

'What's your name? I will tell him you called.'

Click! She hung up. Rasha called up the room at least five more times. Every time his wife picked up and said she had no information about her husband and hung up.

None of the staff photographers were in office that day because the assignment book was choc-a-bloc with events and they were all busy. Only a freelance photographer was drumming his fingers on the desk with his eyes fixed on the assignment book, hoping for work to overflow to his kitty.

'Indra, can you do me a favour?' Rasha asked in a polite but firm tone. 'Can you go and sit at the lobby of Park Hotel all day today? All you have to do is take pictures of Raj Puri if you see him walking in or out. I would have loved to accompany you, but I have to concentrate on the pages and get everything ready because boss is in meetings all day today.'

Rasha knew Indra often got his angles wrong and sometimes his pictures came out hazy, but he was diligent and that was exactly what was needed for this assignment. Indra sat there all day, but there was no sign of Raj Puri. Rasha's frustration grew. She hated going up to her boss and telling him that she hadn't managed to get the story. She started making phone calls but to no avail. Crestfallen and unhappy, Rasha left office and took a cab wondering how would she face her boss the next day. Her mobile rang and a baritone boomed at the other end.

'I heard you have been looking for me all day today. Silly girl, why didn't you leave your number?'

'Who is this?' Rasha asked feebly.

'On top of that you are asking who I am? Don't you know who you have been calling all day? This is Raj Puri!'

Rasha's phone almost fell out of her hand. She couldn't imagine a veteran, award-winning actor like Raj Puri would call her back. This was a moment that dreams were made of, but Rasha's phone betrayed her just then. The battery had been low for some time and this was the precise moment it decided to go dead. She immediately got out of the cab, entered a phone booth, called up Park Hotel and asked for Raj Puri's room.

He came on the line. 'I am sorry my phone went dead.' Then without wasting any time, she went straight to the point. 'Can I interview you right now?'

One thing Rasha had learned in her profession was to get the story then and there. Celebs were an unpredictable lot. The next day their phone might go on ringing for an eternity or they might not be in a mood to talk or they might just give you time a week later, by which time every newspaper would have had the story.

'Yes, shoot,' he said.

Rasha took out her pen and paper and sat on the stool in the cramped phone booth. There was a small fan over her head which wasn't working and she was sweating profusely in the heat, but she was the embodiment of concentration. She had to get her story.

Raj Puri told her everything about the project—how he came on board the film, which was being made by an Oscar-winning director from Hollywood. He told her how Kolkata was the mainstay of the story and which areas of Kolkata they were shooting in. He also told her the name of the Bengali actress who was playing a pivotal role in the film.

After talking to him for twenty minutes, Rasha finally asked him, 'How did you get my number?'

'My wife told me you called a number of times today, but you hadn't left any number.'

Rasha almost thought aloud, *how could I? She hung up on me every time.*

'I met this photographer at the lobby of the hotel, who was from *Our Times*, the newspaper you have been calling from. I asked him for your number. I came up to my room and called you.'

Rasha didn't know how to thank Raj Puri, or for that matter his wife for passing on the information to him or Indra for staying put at the hotel lobby.

She called up her boss, Surit Basu, from the same booth. 'Boss I have got the story. It will be in tomorrow morning.'

She could hear a chuckle at the other end. 'That's why I always put my chief reporter on the job. Good show.'

Next day, she called up the Bengali actress for her quotes saying that she had already spoken to Raj Puri.

'I have to take permission from the director of the film. Can you please call me later?' she said.

Rasha kept calling her, but she didn't answer her phone till 4:00 p.m. Rasha wasn't worried because she had confirmation that she was doing the film, so her story stood.

She turned around and saw the lead headline on page 1:

Headline: **Hollywood team shoots in Kolkata**

Intro: **Raj Puri says he is enjoying working in the city with Oscar-winning director**

On the top, there was a red flash that read: **Exclusive.**

Rasha gave the page on the computer a satisfied look and started reading her story one last time before she gave it to her boss to take a look.

Surit Basu had a fairly large room with a glass door. He sat facing the door so the entire team could read each of his expressions, but could not hear the conversations that went on inside. Rasha glanced and saw Surit da, as they all called him in the very-Bengali-informal way one called an elder brother, busy looking at mobile phones brought in by a dealer. He wanted to buy a new state-of-the-art one, and judging from his expression from the other side of the glass door, Rasha knew that he was pretty confused. Rasha's mobile rang.

The actress's name was flashing. 'Hi ! Rasha, I saw your missed calls. Sorry I was shooting. Tell me what you want to know.'

'Have you talked to your director?'

'No, I haven't had the time. But if Raj Puri's spoken to you, then I guess I can talk too. You said you are carrying the story on your front page, right? I thought it will not look nice without my quote since I am in the film too. Are you carrying my picture?'

'Yes, we will carry it if we get your quote.'

'Carry a nice one, please. In the last one, I was looking a bit fat.'

Indra had got a lively picture of Raj Puri posing with his entire Hollywood team including the director. She thought she would use the actress as a small inset. That way, the designer would not have to tinker too much with the page, which was almost done. As she hung up, she saw a text message on her mobile from Surit da.

'Why is Surit da sending me a message sitting right here?' she thought.

She looked up, but his room was empty and then she looked back at the text message.

It read: I have put in my resignation. I have left the office and please don't call me right now. I have to gather my thoughts.

Rasha felt like she had been struck by lightning and although she was sitting upright in her chair, her body felt like it was lying face down in mud as torrential rain lashed against her skin. She couldn't move. She sat like that for almost ten minutes. Then she called Surit da's number.

He picked up the phone. 'Right now, I am sitting on a bench in front of the Ganges. Bye!' He hung up.

Looking at the faces of her colleagues, Rasha knew that they had also heard what had happened. Whether Surit da had sent them the same SMS or they had come to know from somewhere else, Rasha couldn't tell.

At that moment, a thousand thoughts raced through her head, Rasha didn't know why would someone as talented and important as Surit Basu leave his job like that? What had happened?

~

Rasha had joined *Our Times* two years back. One out of every five people she met forbade her to join a department headed by Surit Basu.

'He's a drunkard, a womanizer and does everything apart from journalism,' was the refrain that ran through most opinions.

One person even said, 'With your kind of attitude, I can see Surit Basu getting a slap from you in a month's time. Do you know he tried to force himself on a girl recently in the middle of the office?'

'Force himself?' Rasha was wide-eyed.

The girl, who was telling her all this, had incidentally never worked with Surit Basu. She fumbled for a second for the right words and then clarified, 'I mean he tried to hold her hand forcibly. It became a huge issue.'

'Why didn't *Our Times* ask him to leave?'

'He knows the right people in the right places I guess,' the girl glared.

Rasha just shrugged. Despite the warnings, she decided to form her own opinion about Surit Basu at their first meeting. And she had to admit that it was not all that bad. She was a regular reader of *Our Times* and felt the newspaper was a great mix of serious, investigative and entertaining journalism, and most importantly, it presented news in an interesting and eye-catching manner. She wanted to be a part of the newspaper. She had called up Surit Basu and asked for an appointment. Without showing any call-me-later attitude that was so typical of most editors, he had asked her to meet him the next day.

Rasha had heard that he was in his forties. But no one told her that he had a complexion that could put the extremely fair Kapoor clan of Bollywood to shame. His cheeks were so pink that Rasha actually wondered if he had applied blush. Although the skin on his face was childlike, his hair had turned salt-and-pepper. His dark, intelligent eyes, aquiline nose and shapely black eyebrows gave him an imposing persona. He seemed a sophisticated, erudite and articulate man, the kind who didn't have to try too hard to get the attention of women. He was dressed in a pin-stripe formal shirt and brown cotton trousers, and wore D&G reading glasses.

His desk was neatly arranged with A4s lying on one side and files on the other. A pleasant departure from the disarray on an editor's desk she was so used to. The book case on his left had some fat books on newspaper designing, a couple of books on journalism and then there were a whole lot of magazines from her favourite *Time* to *Filmfare*.

After pleasantries were exchanged, he came straight to the point. 'So why are you here?'

'I want to work in *Our Times*,' Rasha blurted out.

'Why?'

'I find your newspaper very interesting.'

'Where are you working now?'

'I have been with the *Indian Chronicle* for two years now, after a year with *Kolkata Daily*.'

'What's your beat?'

'Entertainment, but if I see a good story, I chase it. It can be any story,' Rasha tried to sound confident.

'I don't know if you have seen the lead story in the *Indian Chronicle* today. It's about the robbery and kidnapping of a five-year old boy in Park Circus,' she added.

Surit Basu, who was till then looking at the computer more and less at Rasha, looked up.

'That's your story? That's an *Indian Chronicle* exclusive. How did you manage it?'

Rasha had learned the tricks of her trade well. She knew the last thing you did in journalism was give out your source, but in this case, since this could actually turn into a full-time job, she decided to be truthful.

'My school friend lives next door to where the incident took place. I was in office when she called me at 11:00 p.m. last night. So I took the office car and went to the spot. The editor held back the pages. I came back, filed the story and then the newspaper went to press.'

'No wonder it's your exclusive,' said Basu with interest.

Rasha was beaming inside. She knew it was a great story. The maid servant had spiked the lassi with drugs. She and her gang had not only scooted with all the jewellery and cash in the house, but they had also taken with them the five-year-old boy with the hope of arm-twisting his rich businessman father into shelling out some more cash. Rasha knew she had a big story when she had got the call the night before. Now she was glad she could flaunt it to Surit Basu.

'By the way, never ask me if I have read a newspaper in the morning. I read all the newspapers before I come to work and you will be expected to do the same,' he said.

Rasha wondered, *does this mean he is considering me for a job here?*

'Why do you want to leave *Indian Chronicle*?'

For the first time, Rasha lied. 'I am looking for more interesting work.'

Not one to be fooled, Surit Basu shot back, 'But you are doing enough interesting work already.' She didn't have an answer to this, so she decided to keep quiet.

Surit Basu keeps looking at your boobs when he talks. He doesn't let go of your hand after a hand shake. He always asks you out for a drink first. All the rumours that she had heard so far resonated in her head.

Rasha stole a glance at Surit Basu, who was gazing at his computer again with a distant look.

'We don't have a vacancy at the moment. But if something crops up, I will let you know. Just email me your CV.'

She was a trifle disappointed, but she didn't show it. She left.

5

AFTER HER STINT with *Kolkata Daily*, Rasha was employed as a sub-editor/reporter in *Indian Chronicle*. If it hadn't been for her boss, she would have been enjoying herself thoroughly and not looking elsewhere for job openings. In her two years with, the newspaper she had accumulated an impressive set of bylines covering crime, politics and entertainment. Although she had joined the newspaper as an entertainment journalist, soon the resident editor of *Indian Chronicle* noticed her go-getter attitude.

One day, he called her to his room. 'Elections are coming up. Would you want to do an article on all the women candidates?' he asked her.

Rasha was all too happy to grab the opportunity. She went to each and every candidate's home and did in-depth interviews with them. The facts she came back with were rather shocking. There were five lady candidates fighting the elections from different parties that year. One of them was the wife of a local councillor, one's brother was a politician and also a local goon, one was the daughter of a minister, one was a lawyer who blatantly told her that it was okay to rig on her part if the other parties did the same and another was a sex worker. Rasha only truly believed the intentions of the sex worker. She was the only one who knew the problems that women like her were facing and ardently wanted to bring change. The rest of them sounded like puppets tied to their secure lives and giving lip service to rehearsed scripts.

The story that came out the next day was sensational and stirred a hornet's nest. The resident editor applauded her, but her own boss, the head of the entertainment section—the features editor—fumed. He absolutely hated the attention Rasha got in office and did not leave any stone unturned to make her life difficult. Standing at five foot, with sinister eyes staring from behind gold-rimmed glasses, her boss gave her the creeps from day one. When Rasha had applied for the job, it was the resident editor who had conducted her interview and she had not met her would-be boss. So on her first day in *Indian Chronicle,* no matter how much she tried to convince herself in a positive way that looks could be deceptive, her sixth sense told her it was not going to be all hunky dory. Soon, Rasha realized she was not wrong in her initial judgement. Her boss was indeed a creep. Anything that happened at work which wasn't to his liking—and that could be anything from Rasha coming in late, Rasha doing more crime stories than entertainment or Rasha making friends with the guys in the office—he needed to discuss it after work. Rasha would very reluctantly follow him to a restaurant on Park Street where he would order beer. Then he would start with how he thought Rasha was talented but her career would go nowhere if she continued to disregard him.

'I have all the experience to guide you,' he would say after gulping down half a bottle of beer in a jiffy. 'But you are so stupid not to listen to me.'

The words were loaded, but Rasha ignored them. He would then inevitably veer the conversation to her personal life.

At one such we-need-to-talk session, her boss crossed the line. 'You did not tell me whether you have a boyfriend or not?' he asked Rasha.

'Aren't you getting late? Your wife must be waiting for you.'

'Why are you avoiding my question?'

'I am not avoiding. I just like to keep my personal and professional lives separate.'

'Huh! A few days into the profession and you already have a

personal and a professional life?' he smirked. 'Now you will say you are a virgin and you have never been with a man.'

Rasha could feel the blood rushing to her cheeks. In her mind, she had already slapped her boss but her face looked calm, almost serene. She had actually practised this expression to perfection at home. She sometimes wondered how the girl, who was feared by the boys in school and college, was sitting there, sipping beer and tolerating her boss asking her if she was a virgin. But life as a professional was so much different from life as a college girl. She had realized that very early in her career. Tact and not brashness helped you survive. And, at that moment, she was trying very, very hard to be tactful.

'I thought that in our culture, women have sex only with their husbands,' she finally answered.

He looked so astonished that Rasha wasn't sure if she had spoken English or Hebrew.

She hoped this would shut him up. 'I am in a hurry to go home. If we are done with our meeting, can I leave?'

'See, how rude you are. I have not finished my drink and you want to leave,' said her boss.

Rasha had almost got up, but very reluctantly slouched back into her chair.

'Your wife is very pretty. How did the two of you meet?' Rasha tried hard to change the direction of the conversation. She wasn't sure if it was for real or had she imagined that her boss's expression had become a little softer.

'I know she is very beautiful. It was an arranged marriage. What kind of marriage do you want?'

Rasha felt annoyed that the conversation veered back to her.

'I haven't decided since I am not ready to get married yet.'

'You should get married. It's nice to be married. You have a companion to share your life with.'

She started laughing.

'Why are you laughing?'

'Well, I just thought isn't that what you should be doing at the moment—sharing an evening with your companion instead of spending time here?'

He laughed. 'Doesn't this mean that I like spending time with you? I know you like being with me too, but you just won't admit it.'

Rasha rolled up her eyes. She had no clue where he had got this idea from. She tried very hard to think if she had done anything to give him such an idea. After a couple of seconds, she came to the conclusion she hadn't.

She took a sip of her beer and thought, *mom will again think I was out with my friends; and if I tell her I was drinking with my boss so late, she would throw a fit. There's no mouthwash in my bag. I will have to buy one while going home if I have to avoid another situation.*

'It's seriously getting late,' she said with finality.

'I will drop you home. Don't worry.'

He finished the second bottle. 'Rasha, why do you spend so much time in the resident editor's room?'

'I discuss stories with him.'

'But I will be doing your appraisal for the promotion and increment.'

Rasha thought she saw a twinkle in his serpent-like eyes.

'And I think you should be doing more stories on entertainment, the beat for which you have been hired and not waste your time doing other things.'

That precise moment, Rasha knew that so far as covering crime and politics went, her fate was sealed. Her boss had in effect given her a veiled threat and if she really wanted to have a career in *Indian Chronicle* and some peace at work, she had to keep his words in mind.

Finally, after finishing three bottles of beer, her boss got up on his wobbly feet. 'I will drop you,' he said.

'No, I will take a cab.'

In his semi-drunken state, he never realized that the pitch of his voice had become really high, so when he said 'I am telling you I will drop you. You are being adamant again,' everyone at the restaurant turned around. Rasha decided it was best not to say a word more and followed him to his red Maruti 800. The drive to her home took fifteen minutes. The entire evening was spoiled anyway, so she decided she would tolerate him for the duration of their journey. He precariously perched himself on the driving seat and put the key in the ignition. Rasha took a quick glance to see if his short feet were reaching the brakes and she took a deep breath as the car rolled into the traffic.

'You know, Rasha, you look really nice in skirts. I don't know why you sometimes wear those awful salwar kurtas. And stop wearing that white clip. You have been wearing it constantly for the last fifteen days. If you don't have any other clip, tell me, I will buy some for you,' her boss said. Rasha was used to her boss commenting on her clothes, but this clip bit surprised her. Her hands unconsciously touched the hair clip that kept her curled ponytail firmly in place. She had actually forgotten which clip she was wearing that day. Rasha was trying hard to hold back her irritation. She just hoped that the fifteen minutes would pass soon.

'Why do you look so tense?' he asked.

'My mom will be worried.'

'Tell her you and I had gone on an assignment. I am sure she will not tell you anything if she comes to know that you were with your boss.' And he laughed.

To Rasha's ears, it sounded like the cackle of a demon preparing to slaughter its prey.

Rasha's mom was standing in the balcony. Rasha knew she was watching her every move like a hawk. She had forgotten her mouthwash and knew drinking alone with her boss was a bigger crime than drinking with friends. So, she instantly started framing a story inside her head that would answer the barrage of questions that were coming her way.

The door of her apartment was ajar.

'Rasha, it's 11.30 p.m. Do you not look at the watch? Wasn't that your boss's car?'

'Yes, Ma, there was a party I had to attend. Then he dropped me.'

'Everyday you leave in the morning and come home late. Your lifestyle has completely changed since you joined work. Now will you have dinner or have you eaten at the party? I have been waiting to have dinner with you.'

The evening conversation with her boss had left Rasha with no appetite, but she did not want to disappoint her mom and decided to say yes to dinner, although she dreaded yet another conversation at the dinner table. She headed straight for the bathroom, stuffed her mouth with a big blob of toothpaste, took a bath, applied deodorant and hoped she had got rid of the beer stench before she joined her mother. Her dad and Rania were already in bed, and by the time her mom served dinner, she was thankfully more interested to talk about her school friend, who had come home that day and didn't grill Rasha about the party. Her mom talked animatedly about her childhood and Rasha ruminated over dal, fried potatoes and hilsa fish curry about her course of action in office from the next day. She decided it was best to turn her whole attention to entertainment. That way, she would be able to keep her boss happy and even do away with the out-of-office meetings with him. Hard news had to be traded for peace at the moment, she realized.

~

Rasha reached office early. If there was one thing that she really loathed at work, it was coming in early. All reporters came in at noon, but her boss preferred to come in at 9.00 a.m. himself and insisted that others came in latest by 10.00 a.m. Rasha argued with him a number of times that unlike others in the department, she stayed back late most days, but her boss wouldn't agree.

'If you are working late for other departments, that's your problem. I want you in at 10.00 a.m.,' he shot back.

Her boss had a little black book where he jotted down the names of people who came in late each day, something actually unheard of in a newspaper office. Rasha knew that she was a regular entry in that black book, but she didn't care as long as she had the stories flowing in. But this morning, she wanted to be sensible, she wanted to be on time.

She reached office at 9.30 a.m. only to find her boss already at his desk.

She wondered, *how does he manage to get up so early after being so drunk?*

Rasha took out her tattered phone book and dialled the number of Kumarjit. He was the reigning king of Tollywood and she hoped he would be able to give her some interesting news. A lady picked up the phone and said he was not at home. Rasha hung up, but the voice seemed familiar to her, so she called up again. The same lady picked up.

'May I know who am I talking to?' Rasha asked.

There was silence on the other end for five long seconds, then the lady hesitantly answered, 'Tista Banerjee.'

Tista was a top actress of Tollywood and Rasha was the one to take her first interview when she joined films two years back. Rasha often called her late in the night and the actress chatted with her for hours, sharing industry gossip and generally talking about herself and her struggles. Sometimes Tista even called her up if she needed to pass on some news about herself. Rasha wouldn't say Tista was a friend, but she was someone Rasha knew really well and she was aware that Tista was having an affair with Kumarjit, Tollywood's number-one actor. Rasha wondered what she was doing in his house picking up his calls.

'Oh! Hi, Tista! This is Rasha Roy.'

'Do I know you?'

'Rasha from *Indian Chronicle*.'

'Sorry, I meet so many people, I forget all the time.'

'No problem, I understand. But can you tell me which new films have you signed?'

'I am not signing any new films. I am finishing the ones that I had signed.'

'Why?'

'You can say I am just bored. I don't want to continue in the film industry. I have to go now. Bye.'

Rasha knew there was definitely more to the story than Tista revealed. She instantly called up a film director, who was close to Kumarjit.

'What is Tista doing at Kumarjit's house and why is she wrapping up her films?' she asked him.

He said a bit reluctantly. 'Rasha, you have always helped me, so I will try to tell you as much as I know, but you have to promise that you'll keep me out of this.'

'You know if I give my word, I stick to it. Now spill the beans.'

'Her parents were against her relationship with Kumarjit, so they kicked her out of the house. Kumarjit brought her home. They are getting married next week. Kumarjit doesn't want her to work post-marriage which is why she is finishing her pending films.'

Rasha thought she had struck gold. Tista, Tollywood's number-one heroine, a national award winner with a few hits in Bollywood too, quitting films was a big news in itself. Add to that the reason for it. Rasha was getting excited.

She pushed further. 'Do you know where they are getting married and what's on the menu?'

'They are getting married in a small ceremony at Kumarjit's house. I don't know anything else.'

'Can you please find out for me? I will be grateful to you forever.'

'Okay, let me try. Give me some time.'

'It has to be today, because I am filing the story now.'

∾

She went up to her boss's desk. 'Tista Banerjee is quitting films and getting married to Kumarjit.'

'Really? That's big news. Who told you?' he peered from behind his gold-rimmed glasses.

Rasha gave him a smug look. 'I have my sources. It's breaking news. Do you want to run it tomorrow? Then I will file it now.'

'Yes, we will run it tomorrow.'

When Rasha joined *Indian Cronicle* and came up with a story, her boss always asked her umpteen questions to make sure she had got the news right. But two years later, he had learnt that if Rasha had a story, he could run it without asking too many questions because she always got it right. Praise, however, seldom emerged from his lips. To notch up appraisal points from his bosses in Delhi, he would sometimes say good things about his department when they were down for their quarterly visits, otherwise it was always: 'It's your job to excel.' Rasha even imagined a hiss accompanying his favourite sentence. Somehow, her boss always reminded her of Kaa, the treacherous python in Rudyard Kipling's *Jungle Book*.

'Great story, eh!' said her colleague sitting at the adjacent desk.

Rasha smiled. 'Have you noticed my hair clip?' she asked her colleague.

She pushed Rasha's head to one side to see the clip. 'Is it new?'

'No, I have been wearing it for the last few months. You have never noticed it?'

'No, sorry I didn't. Anything special about it?'

'No, nothing.'

Rasha quickly started typing her story. She had an appointment for an interview with a Bengali model, who was going to participate in the Miss India contest from Kolkata. Rasha kept thinking how to make the interview interesting while she wrote the headline of her current story:

Headline: **Kumarjit-Tista to marry secretly**

Introduction: **Actress to quit films post-wedding**

She called her source again.

'The guest list will comprise Kumarjit's brother and sister-in-law, three directors and two actors. I will also be there, but please don't mention that. No one is coming from Tista's side. They have tandoori chicken on the menu and it will just be registration and garland exchange. She has already bought an orange Benarasi saree and a top designer has made a kantha-stitched tassar kurta for him that he will wear along with a black silk dhoti with a gold border. That's all I know.'

'Thanks a ton. You will also have to do me another favour. Get me a wedding picture. Even if you click it on your mobile, it will do. If you can click them munching tandoori chicken then nothing like it!'

'Rasha aren't you taking things a bit too far?' The director sounded flustered.

'If you can't get the tandoori chicken in the frame, it's still fine. A wedding picture will do.' Rasha hung up. A puckish grin sat on her face. She felt better.

~

Her appointment with the Miss India-hopeful was at noon. The Kumarjit-Tista article was done by 11.00 a.m. As a sub-editor/reporter, she also had to make pages, something that her colleagues in other department never had to do. Reporters only brought in the news and people at the desk edited the copies and made the pages on the computer. People working in features had to do both, but the common perception in the office was that being in features meant lighter work. Rasha found this baffling, but she reasoned that entertainment, though supremely important in the modern world, would never be taken as seriously as hard news and hence would always be perceived as less work.

She subbed a few copies and left the office. The lady's house was not too far from her office on Park Street, so she walked the distance with the photographer. She enjoyed the company of this particular photographer, who often regaled her with hilarious stories of his five-year-old son. He knew all about the altercations she had with her boss and Rasha usually told him about her boss's antics. But today, she decided not to tell him about the previous night's incident. She felt bashful about repeating the conversation. Her boss hated her proximity to this photographer and had asked her about him a number of times.

Still deep in conversation, they reached the apartment. The lady was waiting for them in a maroon polo neck T-shirt and skin-tight jeans that set off her peach-coloured skin and light eyes. She was looking beautiful, but Rasha and the photographer exchanged glances that said the dress wasn't working.

Rasha was thinking about how she would tell her that she needed to show more skin, when the photographer said, 'Can you please wear something that would show your neck, shoulders and arms? We have to get a sexy picture.'

Rasha didn't know how she would have reacted if someone had told her the same, but the lady looked unfazed. She nodded and vanished into the bedroom. She came back wearing a pink tank top that exposed her cleavage and showed off her midriff. She pulled her hair to one side exposing her neck. The photographer was happy with the sexy photograph, but Rasha was not too happy with her interview. To every question, the lady tried to be politically correct and ended up giving the most staid answers. Rasha probed her to extract at least a catchy headline, but nothing worked. She thought that the lady was perfectly prepared for the Miss India Contest where rehearsed answers worked best. But she was definitely an interviewer's nightmare. Rasha actually had to stifle a yawn after fifteen minutes. In her mind, she had already relegated the would-be beauty queen to the second or third page and had given the interview not more than three hundred words.

6

THE RESIDENT EDITOR'S secretary summoned Rasha as soon as she was back in the office after her stint with the wannabe Miss India.

'We are two reporters down today. One is unwell, one is on leave. Others are all out in the field. Can you do a quick job for us?' asked the resident editor. Any other time, Rasha would have said yes without a second thought, but after last night's meeting with her boss, she decided to be a bit more careful.

'Can you please have a talk with my boss to find out if he can spare me? I can do the story, but I think you should first talk to him,' she said cautiously.

The resident editor gave her a questioning look, 'Any problem?'

Rasha dodged the question. 'It's best if you talk to him.'

The resident editor was everybody's boss at the Kolkata edition of the *Indian Chronicle* and if he asked her boss, the latter wouldn't have been able to say no.

'Okay, I will talk to him. But first let me tell you what the story is about. A tiger has mauled a girl at the circus. The circus authorities are hushing it up, but we have inside information that the incident happened in the morning during rehearsals and they have still not taken the girl to the hospital. Your job will be to get all the details.'

Rasha nodded and left the room. Although she was excited about the assignment, she knew it was not going to be an easy one. How would she gain access to the living quarters of the circus staff, she had no idea. Surely, they would be more wary of strangers after the incident, she thought.

Minutes later, her boss came to her desk. 'Boss wants you to do a story because they are short of reporters. You can go, but don't waste too much time there. I want you to come back before the pages go to print.'

'It's 3.00 p.m. now and we will go to print at 6.00 p.m. Will I be able to come back on time?'

'You have to. You are also needed at the desk.'

Rasha sighed.

Forty minutes later, she was at the circus gate with the photographer, buying tickets. He had purposely brought a small camera with him that could fit into a handbag. Rasha and the photographer, at the moment, looked like two lovers out to have a good time. But she still had no inkling how she would get her story. They had bought tickets to the first row, so they could observe better. The show started with the clowns doing their act. Rasha thought the circus looked a lot more shabby compared to what it was during her childhood. The clothes the clowns wore looked so unwashed, the girls pranced around in cheap satin garments, with cheap make-up on and the monkeys in the first act looked completely malnourished. She was quite sure it was hunger that had turned the tiger so violent. Few minutes into the show, Rasha and the photographer left their seats. She was glad she was wearing a simple kurta that day with very little make-up and had even lazily put on her spectacles in the morning instead of her lenses. She hoped her get-up made her less conspicuous.

Just outside the tent, she spotted a young girl in costume. 'Do you know the girl who has been mauled by the tiger?' Rasha asked.

The girl was around fifteen years old and gave her a quizzical look. 'I am her distant relative. I live in Kolkata. Her family asked me to come and see her. I know her as...' Rasha searched for a name, '...Rumi. But what do you call her here?'

'We call her Mini didi.' The girl started crying.

'Can you take me to her?'

'She will die very soon,' she said, wiping the tears from her eyes.

Rasha and the photographer followed the girl down a tented alley. 'You know we don't want too many people to know that we are her relatives. Can you take us through a path where there are not too many people?' Rasha said. The girl nodded. She took them behind the tents where the make-shift latrines were located. The stench was unbearable and became worse when they passed an area that housed the animals. She could hear the roaring of a tiger even though she didn't see any cages.

Rasha asked, 'How did this happen?'

'Mini didi was practising with the trainer in the morning today. She was riding on the tiger's back, an act she has been doing for the last two years. Suddenly, the tiger attacked the trainer. He escaped by jumping off the rink, but the tiger turned his attention to Mini didi. She was not that fast and it caught up with her.' Her eyes clouded with tears again.

'Are you very close to Mini?' Rasha asked gently.

'She is the one who has been with me since my parents left me at the circus when I was nine years old. I sleep with her, eat with her and she is my only family.'

'What is your job at the circus?'

'Earlier I used to do trapeze. Then I fell down and broke both my legs. I work at the kitchen now.'

'But there is always a safety net during trapeze shows. How did you break your legs?' said Rasha noticing the girl's limp.

'There was a hole in the net and I fell through it,' said the girl, matter-of-factly.

She halted abruptly in front of a tent. 'This is Mini didi's tent. I am not going in as I can't see her like this,' she said.

Even though Rasha knew that the victim of a tiger attack would not be a pleasant sight, she was not quite prepared for what she saw. The girl's body was bandaged in old sarees. Raw flesh was visible on the arms and legs. There was a gaping wound in her throat, although her face was in a relatively better shape except for a deep gash that ran through her left cheek. She was lying on a khatiya, a basic kind of bed which has a wooden frame and the base is made of criss-crossing coarse ropes attached to the frame. She was writhing in pain and it was clear that the coarse ropes were making her even more uncomfortable. Blood was dripping into puddles on all sides on the ground that was wet because it had rained the night before. Rasha and the photographer managed to huddle inside the dingy tent. He took some snaps, but Rasha knew that the photos would never be carried because they were too ghastly for the morning paper. Maybe a mug shot of the face would be carried, but nothing beyond that. Rasha felt like holding the girl's hand and telling her that everything would be alright, but in her heart, like the girl who had led her there, she knew Mini was slowly drifting towards her death.

'Can you talk?' she asked Mini.

She said a faint yes.

'Why are you not in the hospital?'

'They said they will take me when the shows are over tonight.'

'Did the police come?'

'I don't know. No one met me.'

'Did the tiger ever attack you before?'

'Thrice. This was the worst.'

'Why did you continue in the job despite the attacks?'

'I have seven younger brothers and sisters and they are dependent on me.'

She was out of breath. Rasha felt awful to ask this girl, so much in pain, so many questions, but she had to do her job.

'Was something wrong with the tiger? Why did it attack you so often?'

Now Mini's voice came in almost a whisper. 'It was a man-eater.'

'How do you know?' Rasha quickly asked because she had a feeling Mini would not be able to talk for much longer.

'It has killed two people before.'

'Who are you? What are you doing here?' a man shouted from behind them.

Rasha almost jumped out of her skin. A stout, menacing-looking man had entered the tent.

'I am a reporter. Can I talk to the owner of the circus?' Rasha said boldly.

The man was slightly taken aback by her boldness, but the menacing expression quickly returned to his face.

'Who brought you here?' he asked.

'No one. We came on our own. Now will you call the owner?'

'Wait here,' he said and left. Minutes later, a very thin man with a mean mouth and long hair, accompanied by two even more menacing-looking men, came running to the tent.

'Are you the circus owner?' Rasha asked him.

'No, I am the manager.'

'I have lots of questions for you. But first tell me why this girl is not in the hospital.'

'That's none of your business and you know we can get you arrested for trespassing,' said the man.

The three men were now standing dangerously close to Rasha and the photographer. Rasha could feel her heart pounding, but on the surface, she tried hard to keep her composure. 'I am from the *Indian Chronicle* newspaper. Getting me arrested for trespassing might not be that easy,' she said.

The manager laughed, a dry, mean laugh. 'Madam, you don't know what I can do. You are in my area and you might just vanish. No one will find you. The lions and tigers are always hungry anyway.'

Rasha felt a chill go down her spine and she was still groping for an answer when the photographer said, 'Our car is waiting outside and we have taped everything with a hidden camera which has been directly transmitted to the office.'

Rasha thought it was a brilliant lie and hoped the manager and his henchmen would be ignorant enough to believe that newspaper reporters actually walked around with TV cameras and transmitters in their cars.

'Our editor will just call the police if we are late,' she hastily said.

The manager thought for two seconds. 'We will not do anything to you if you leave right now.'

'But you will have to take the girl to the hospital...'

She received a sharp rap on the shoulder from the photographer. 'Let's leave!' he said.

He almost dragged her by the arm. They followed the same route that they had taken to come in. The men followed them. They went inside the huge tent of the circus where the show was still on. Rasha felt safer in the midst of so many people, but the men were still on their heels. They walked out of the main gate and hopped into their car.

'Drive fast,' said the photographer.

෴

It was 6.30 p.m. Rasha had managed to do exactly what her boss had asked her not to do—she had failed to return to office on time. The face of the girl lying in a mangle of flesh-and-blood suddenly interrupted her thoughts. She felt very guilty for not being able to do anything to help the girl. All she had was a story that would make front page news and that would be discussed for a few days in print and on television. Some human- and animal-rights activists would voice their anger after that and then it would eventually be forgotten.

Rasha told her boss what had happened. 'Okay, no problem, I understand,' was all he said.

She felt this reaction was even more dangerous because this was definitely not what he felt inside. He must have already thought of ways to make Rasha suffer for the next one week. This could range from junking all her stories for the entire week, to telling her juniors to rewrite her copies because they were suddenly not good enough, to taking her out for meetings to that restaurant on Park Street to discuss work. But at this moment, Rasha was too distressed to think about her boss because Mini wouldn't leave her thoughts.

She briefed the resident editor about the story. 'Can you please tell someone from the police to go there and take the girl to the hospital?' she asked him.

The resident editor looked at her with kind eyes. 'I will do that, Rasha.'

Rasha sat down to write her story.

Headline: **Circus girl mauled by tiger**

Introduction: **Man-eater has killed before**

When Rasha finished her story, it was 9.30 p.m. She felt ravenous because all she had eaten since morning was a chicken sandwich, but the thought of food gave her nausea. She noticed her boss was still in the office, which was a rarity.

He called her to his desk. 'A DJ has come down from Mumbai to play at Iconic. I want you to do an interview with him. You can catch him at the nightclub at midnight.'

He knew Rasha had had a packed and tiring day, but still wanted her to do an interview of a not-so-famous DJ at a nightclub post midnight. This was his way of getting back at her.

'Can I do the interview over phone or email?'

He instantly shot back. 'No.'

'Okay, I will go, but I hope you are signing a car for me from the office because it will be really late.'

'You are always out partying with your friends at the disco. Tell one of them to go with you. Why do you need a car?'

'It's one of my friend's birthday today. They will all be at his party. And, anyway, I can't expect my friends to be at my beck and call at the middle of the night when I am going for an assignment. I should be going in the office car, shouldn't I?'

Her boss glared at her. 'You take a cab. The photographer will be with you. Tell him to drop you off first.'

Rasha tried hard not to let her anger show. But she was determined not to take things lying down.

'I will go if I get an office car, otherwise not,' she said stubbornly.

'You are going and you are not getting the office car. I am not going to tolerate insubordination.'

He left the office. Rasha sat there thinking what to do. She went to the photographer's room to find out who had been assigned to go to the nightclub. She told the chief photographer that she had been asked to go without a car.

'Rasha, one of our photographers didn't get a cab from Iconic last week. He walked home at 2.00 a.m. I would not want you and my photographer in a similar situation. I can't imagine you stranded without transport so late in the night,' said the chief photographer.

Rasha made her decision. She was not going. Her boss couldn't coerce her to attend unimportant events late in the night because he had a score to settle with her.

She called up the owner of Iconic.

'Hi, Mr Mukesh, how are you? Can I talk to DJ Joe over the phone for five minutes?'

'He is at dinner with me. If you call me in five minutes, I will hand over the phone to him,' he said.

Rasha thanked him and hung up. She called him again in five minutes. DJ Joe came on the line. He had a pleasant voice and an easy-going tone. He was definitely more interesting to talk to than the Miss-India wannabe Rasha had met earlier in the day. By the time she finished her interview, it was 11.00 p.m. She took the office car to drop her home. Once again, Mini sneaked into her thoughts.

～

The glum look on her boss's face told her to gear up for some tough times ahead. He didn't even say a good morning when she walked into his office and came straight to the point.

'You didn't go last night.'

'No, I didn't but the interview is done.'

'I asked you to go and you didn't. I have taken it up with the higher authorities.'

Rasha presumed it was the resident editor he was talking about. She just gave him a blank look and sat down to key in her interviews. In five minutes, the resident editor called her to his room.

'Rasha, I know something is up. Why is your boss so angry with you? He told me you refused to go to an assignment because you had to attend a friend's birthday party,' said the resident editor.

Rasha had not only missed the party, she had even forgotten to wish her friend because she was so busy all day. She told the resident editor everything that had happened the day before. He listened attentively. 'You should have asked me. My driver is always waiting downstairs. He could have dropped you?'

'Is that a solution to the problem? If he asks me to go for late-night assignments everyday without a car, will your driver drop me and pick me up?' Rasha asked indignantly.

'Calm down. Everything will be fine.'

But Rasha was quite sure nothing would be fine and she would have to find a solution herself.

The resident editor then changed the topic. 'Rasha, you did a very good job with the circus story. By the time, the police reached there the girl had died, but they have arrested a few people.'

Rasha felt like someone had struck her heart with a hammer and the pain spread through the arteries to every inch of her body. She had known all along that Mini wouldn't live, but she found it hard to deal with the reality of her death. She rushed to the washroom. Rasha thought she and Mini were similar in so many ways. She had put up with the repeated attacks of a tiger to keep her job to feed her family. She was being mentally mauled everyday by her boss and was putting up with it because she had her ambitions to keep up with. Rasha thought if she didn't want to die like Mini, she had to find an escape and that would be finding another job.

Next day, she called up Surit Basu, the editor of *Our Times*.

∽

After the interview at his office, Surit Basu had made it clear that there were no vacancies at that moment. Since there was no possibility of a job shift for her, she decided not to give in to her boss' demands. She did more showbiz stories, but did not completely give up on hard news. And she was determined that she was not going to go out with him for their 'meetings' anymore. She was ready to face the consequences head-on whatever they might be. So, every time her boss asked her out, she would say she had a doc's appointment or she had an upset stomach and needed to go home.

At the morning meeting one day, her boss told her, 'I was wondering how you manage to go on assignments on a perpetually upset stomach?'

He was hoping to embarrass her in front of the team so that she would stop fibbing about her health.

She smiled slyly. 'That's not a problem. Wherever I go, there is always a five-star hotel in the vicinity. And you have to agree it's always a pleasure to use their aroma-oil scented, glistening tiled, white-towelled washrooms.'

'Okay, okay, I get it. Guys, now tell me what story you have today...'

Rasha held on tightly to her smug expression. She was happy to have finally taken the bull by its horns.

~

A month later, Rasha's boss called her to his desk. His expression was grim. Instead of peering from behind his glasses, he was looking down.

'The increments and promotions are due. I am afraid you are not getting any promotion although others are. You are not ready for a promotion. You need to work on a lot of things before you can get one. Barnali is getting a promotion. I am telling you about her because I don't want you to find this out from someone else,' he said.

Rasha and Barnali were of the same age and they had joined *Indian Cronicle* on the same day.

'Barnali is working at the desk and there if you are good at subbing and making pages you are good enough. But in features, you have to be an all-rounder which you have not yet become. But if you are a good girl for the next one year, you will definitely get a promotion,' he smiled. The smirk never left his face.

Rasha didn't say a word.

'I don't think with your capabilities you can land a job anywhere else at the moment. You need to work hard and prove yourself.'

She just kept looking at him uninterestedly and that seemed to annoy him. She had wanted to slap him so many times and today she was ready with the biggest slap that would hit him where it hurt the most.

Rasha handed him a piece of paper. It read:

Dear Ms Rasha Roy,
We are glad to offer you the post of senior sub-editor/ reporter in *Our Times*. As discussed with you, your joining date will be 1.3.2005.

Thanks,
J. Kamaraju
VP, *Our Times*

Now it was her turn to speak.

'You might not think I am ready yet, but then a newspaper with three times more circulation than yours thinks I am.' She tried hard to imitate his smirk.

Rasha had waited for this moment for two long years. So many times in bed at night she had thought of ways of getting back at her boss. She had plotted and re-plotted in her mind. But she felt she just did not have it in her to deal with her crooked boss in a crooked way. She was too straightforward for her own liking. Then she would go off to sleep thinking, *my time will come one day.* Finally, her time had come. And she just wanted to enjoy every bit of it like one enjoyed vintage wine—pouring it in a glass and letting it stand for some time for the different flavours to mix, then deeply inhaling the aroma and finally taking a sip and swirling it in the mouth for the taste to seep in.

She loved sitting there, watching her boss's expression going from surprise to anger, although he tried hard to cloak it all.

He made one last attempt to make things difficult for her.

'I don't know if we can release you that quickly. I have to check your contract.'

Saying this, he went to the resident editor's room. He came out fifteen minutes later and told her his boss was calling her.

Rasha, until then, had not thought of how the resident editor would react to her leaving *Indian Cronicle,* because she was so engrossed with her own boss. Now she felt a bit ashamed of facing him. This man had given her a lot of opportunities that people as young as her didn't usually get. Rasha didn't know how to say goodbye to him. She sat in front of him sheepishly. He looked as kind as ever.

'So you are joining *Our Times*. Good!'

Rasha looked up.

'According to your contract, you are supposed to serve a three-month notice period, but I guess you are joining them in a month. Your boss doesn't want to let you go before three months, but I have checked with the HR and you still have two months of paid leave that can be adjusted, something I have not told your boss.'

He smiled. 'You will be able to join *Our Times* on time.'

Rasha said a feeble thank you. Then the resident editor dropped a bombshell. 'I am sharing a secret with you that no one here knows. I am leaving too. I am moving to Delhi as the editor of one of the biggest magazines. I will give you the details later, but right now keep your mouth shut.'

Rasha finally breathed freely.

'I know you were having trouble with your boss, so I think it's a good idea to move on. But I am not sure if you are landing from the frying pan into the fire. I don't know Surit Basu personally, but I have heard a lot of things about him. But good luck. Life is a journey and you have to undertake it.'

The resident editor's last words kept ringing in Rasha's ears—from the frying pan into the fire. But at that point, she preferred trying out the fire because the frying pan had left her scarred, de-motivated and exhausted. She did not mind exploring new possibilities even if it meant dealing with yet another letch of a boss. But she reasoned that the supposed fire she was jumping into had already given her a career leap at least. From a sub-editor, she had become a senior sub-editor/reporter.

∾

Surit Basu had called her a week before. 'There's a vacancy in *Our Times*. One of our reporters is going to the UK to study. Can you come and see me?'

Rasha went to meet him the same day and he sent her to the VP and the HR head for further interviews. After the interviews, she went back to Surit Basu's room.

'Sir, I am currently a sub-editor. Will it be possible to give me the post of a senior sub-editor?' she requested.

'Let me see,' Surit Basu said.

Rasha was elated when she was handed the offer letter. She had not only got a better position, but also a better salary to go with it.

Her *Indian Chronicle* boss threw a goodbye party for her at Someplace Else at The Park. From the day Rasha put in her resignation, he was a changed man. For the one month she was there, he did not tell her to go out with him, was pretty chirpy in office, smiled more than ever but remained disinterested in her work. Rasha felt that he was trying hard to show that her leaving the newspaper did not make any difference to him. At the party, he sat next to Rasha the entire evening, and talked to everyone else but her. Finally, he asked her to dance with him.

'I tripped on the stairs last evening. I have a bad sprain,' she promptly said.

Instead of asking someone else to dance, he sat down and never looked at Rasha again. When the bill came, Rasha took a peek at it and saw a whopping amount of Rs 15,000. He paid. Rasha wondered why he had bothered to spend so much money on her. She came to the conclusion that he had a point to prove both to her and to his boss. He wished to tell her that he didn't care if she left and wanted to show the resident editor that he had given her a nice and expensive farewell and was after all a good boss. Politically correct outside, a creep inside—Rasha believed he had all that it took to make it to the top. One Rasha gone would surely not make any difference to him. He would promptly find another one for his after-office chats.

7

RASHA WORE A churidar kurta in light pink, with small green and blue flowers printed on it. Her lovely lips were lined with a dark pink liner and she filled it up with her favourite pink shade L'Oréal 211. To complete the look, she wore a pair of smart white strappy sandals and carried a leather bag. She left her hair open and shoved her sunglasses on top of her head like a hair band as she entered the office. It was her first day at work at *Our Times.*

There were nine people working in the features department and all looked up as she entered. She had met some of them earlier at different assignments and some were completely new faces. She smiled at them and headed to Surit Basu's room.

'Welcome! Make yourself comfortable. Like the rest of the team, you can call me Surit da.'

Then he pointed to the desk just outside his room, 'That's where you will sit.'

Rasha could hear the alarm bells ringing in her head. *This is not a good sign. Why does he want me to sit right outside his room, where he can see me all the time?* she wondered.

'So, do you have a story ready for today?' he asked.

'A small-time actress has pressed rape charges against actor Sunil Bhattacharya. There is an arrest warrant against him, but he has been absconding since last night. The girl alleged that he has been raping her for some time,' said Rasha.

Surit da shrugged. 'This story has come out in a single column in the *Paribartan* today. All other newspapers will carry it tomorrow. What extra information can you provide?' Rasha was tongue tied.

She didn't have anything extra to offer and could feel her confidence already taking a beating on her first day in her new job.

'We can do an interview with the girl,' she said.

'The girl will be talking to every newspaper because she wants publicity. I know Sunil Bhattacharya is absconding, but if we can get an interview with him, then we have a story there. Can you get him?'

Rasha gulped. *How the hell will I get hold of an actor who is on the run?* she thought.

'Do you know Sunil well?' asked Surit da.

'Yes I know him well, but now the situation is different. He will surely have his phone switched off and will not be at home.'

'Trace him. Prove to me how good a reporter you are.'

~

Rasha sat at her new desk. The space delegated to the department was small and the computers were huddled together. Her colleague sitting next to her would be able to latch on to all her phone conversations and see every word she typed on the computer. But she saw she had a phone on her desk and an internet connection at her workstation, luxuries that were not granted to her in *Indian Chronicle*.

Rasha called up Sunil Bhattacharya's number, but as she had presumed, it was switched off. Then she called up a few of her sources, who might have had a clue as to what had happened, but no one could say where Sunil was at the moment. All she learnt was that Sunil had met this girl on the sets of a film where she was doing a small role. They were sometimes seen together at parties but, Sunil never introduced her as his girlfriend. Some said he had apparently promised to marry her. But the girl lodged a police complaint saying he had raped her. However, she was willing to withdraw the case if he married her. Rasha even went to the studios to look for a lead. She got all kinds of versions of the entire incident, but no leads to Sunil Bhattacharya's whereabouts. When she went back to the office, Surit da didn't ask her anything, but she told him how she had all the facts and could file a good story with it. She hoped he would agree.

'You have time till tomorrow. I want Sunil,' he said.

Then he asked Rasha to drop in at the launch party of a film that evening.

When Rasha went to the party, she saw that Surit da was already there with a drop-dead gorgeous lady. She was fair with hypnotic jade eyes. Her long brown hair cascaded down her shoulders and her beauty was magnified by the large red bindi on her forehead. She wore a classy silk saree and looked absolutely ravishing. Rasha felt a bit self conscious next to her in her simple pink salwar kurta.

Surit da introduced Rasha to the lady. 'Meet Gia Sarkar. She is a Bengali from Delhi.'

'Glad to meet you,' Rasha said.

Rasha was still uncomfortable with him because she had so far failed to deliver her first story at *Our Times*. She preferred to move away from him and Gia and instead talk to some of the actors, directors, producers and other media people at the party. She was hoping to find a story that would cover up for her inability to find Sunil. She was engaged in small talk with an actress when she spotted a guy who used to manage PR for Sunil Bhattacharya. She had known him for some time. He was not a very likeable person and could be extremely pushy at times. Once, when she had gone to cover an outdoor shooting, the PR guy had asked her to sit with him and a bunch of other men—some of whom were from other media houses and some were film crew—in order to hear ghost stories late in the night. Rasha was the only woman from the media on the sets and she was extremely uncomfortable with the proposition. She said she was tired and retired to her room. After that, whenever they met, she put on her no-nonsense persona. Although he was helpful when it came to work, Rasha chose to stay away from him at social dos.

That day, however, Rasha stopped short of rushing to him. 'I called you in the morning and your phone was switched off. I am sure you are the only one who knows where Sunil is. You just get him to talk to me for five minutes. That will do.'

'Let me finish my drink. You are around, right?'

Rasha's heart was racing when the guy came to her half an hour later. 'Sunil is on the line, can you talk now?' Rasha took his mobile phone and swiftly moved to the room next to the banquet and shut the door. She did not want anyone else from the media to see her, lest they get a hint of what was happening.

'Hi Sunil, I am sorry about what happened. I have joined *Our Times* and we want to publish your version of the story. Can I ask you some questions?' she said.

Rasha sat in the room for the next half an hour and jotted down every word that Sunil said. He agreed he was seeing the girl, but marriage was not on the cards and he had no idea where rape came in because everything was consensual. He told her their relationship had hit rock bottom because she was an alcoholic and had a corrupt police officer for a boyfriend, who, he felt, gave her the idea to frame him. 'Had I raped her, why would she want to drop the charges if I married her?' said Sunil.

After she hung up, Rasha heaved a sigh of relief. When she entered the banquet, she saw the PR guy there and thanked him profusely.

'This interview will help Sunil too. He is in a big mess,' he said honestly.

Most people at the party looked sloshed. But the dance floor was alive. Rasha took a glass of orange juice because she was thirsty. And, anyway, she had decided never to tell her new boss that she liked drinking beer too. She was determined not to repeat the mistakes she had made in her previous job. There would be no meetings over beer in her new job, she was sure about that. She could not spot Surit da and Gia anywhere and presumed that they had left.

Her eyes went to the spread at the buffet table and the hunger pangs that she had lost since morning suddenly returned with a vengeance. In Kolkata, be it a press conference, a film launch, or a fashion show or even a shraddh ceremony, it has to end with good food. A party bereft of a scrumptious spread would not only create an atmosphere of incompleteness at the event, but would often transcend to the reports published in the newspaper the next day. Rasha picked up a plate from the table and helped herself to warm nans, delicious chicken butter masala and delectable malai prawns. She let out a sigh of relief. She had finally managed a headline that would most likely impress her boss—her first day at *Our Times* wasn't so bad after all.

~

Rasha woke up early the next day, something she rarely did. She could hear the chirping of the birds in her ultra-urban locality, she could hear the leaves rustling in the wind and she wasn't at all annoyed by the neighbours squabbling in the apartment next door. She shared a cup of coffee with her mom and told her what had happened the night before.

'God is always with people who make an effort,' her mom smiled. Rasha had been so engrossed with herself for the past few months that she had not had a proper conversation with her mother. She decided to make up for it.

'Do you want to have your favourite Tutti Frutti ice cream and fish and chips at Kwality restaurant today? We can all go together.'

Her mom smiled again. 'First you come home on time, then

we can decide...oh! Rasha, I forgot to tell you. There's this new girl in the serial *Tapur Tupur Brishti*; you can interview her. She is not only pretty, she is doing a good job with acting too.'

Rasha hugged her mom. 'Thanks, Ma. I desperately needed someone like that. *Our Times* has a new face on TV column every week, so you saved me the hunt. But do keep a lookout for new talented faces. Will you? You are really good at star-spotting. Remember you were the one who told me about Tista after she debuted in a serial and I interviewed her. Now she is the biggest star in Tollywood.'

A sense of pride washed over her mother's face. She knew Rasha appreciated her efforts to help her out. As a token of her appreciation, a few months back, Rasha had taken her mother to a musical show put up by some of the younger actors and musicians in Tollywood. When she introduced her to them, they all said, 'Oh, mashima, thanks for coming,' and touched her feet. A veteran actress even insisted that mashima had dinner before she left. She personally escorted mashima to the buffet table and handed her the napkin and plate. Mashima revelled in the spotlight.

Later in the cab, a visibly dazed mashima could only manage a sentence. 'I can't believe all those stars touched my feet.' Rasha knew that was too big a moment for her star-struck mom and she just let her enjoy it. She did not have the heart to tell her that this respect wouldn't possibly have come her way had her daughter not been an entertainment reporter in a widely circulated daily.

∼

Rasha left for work happy in the thought that she would step into a new office with a new story. She walked through the gates of *Our Times* and headed straight for Surit da's room.

'Where did you vanish last evening?' he asked.

'Actually I was in the other room talking to Sunil Bhattacharya.'

'Really! I am impressed. How did you find him?'

Somehow Rasha didn't feel comfortable telling Surit da what she always told others—'I have my sources'. She felt that he knew the trade far better than her, so it would be best to tell him the truth. She did so.

'Good job. Now write the story,' said Surit da.

'By the way, you don't have a mobile phone, Rasha?'

'No. I have never felt the need for one.'

'You are probably not too keen on staying in touch with your boyfriend all day, but I am very keen on staying in touch with my reporters. I hope you are getting one today and make sure to keep it on twenty-four hours.'

Rasha blushed. She knew there was no argument there.

When she was walking out of the door, Surit da said, 'By the way, Rasha, I want you to give me six exclusive stories in the next six days.'

Rasha keyed in:

Headline: **'If I am a rapist, why does she want to marry me?'**

Introduction: **In an EXCLUSIVE interview to Rasha Roy, actor Sunil Bhattacharya defends himself**

Getting six exclusive stories was hard work, but Rasha managed to do it. She felt drained, but she was happy. Surit da showered her with appreciation for each story she covered and that motivated her to do even better in the next one.

'I want you to make twenty phone calls everyday to your contacts. Attend parties as often as possible, because that is where networking happens,' Surit da had told her on the first day.

Rasha followed his instructions diligently, read all the newspapers, made all the phone calls and came up with good stories. She liked Surit da's enthusiasm at the morning meetings. He encouraged everyone in the team, added his own ideas to the stories and kept the department in high spirits. But he was a hard taskmaster. He did not take no for an answer, pushed everyone extremely hard and only settled for the best.

In the ten-member features team in *Our Times*, there were four boys and six girls, including Rasha. From day one, she noticed that all the girls shared an excellent rapport with Surit da. They joked with him, pulled his leg and most of the team joined him for lunch in the office cafeteria. Rasha was wary the first day Surit da asked her to join him for lunch, but when she realized everyone else would be there as well, she loosened up. At lunch, they talked about everything but work. They discussed films and gossiped about other journalists and actors. Surit da often zeroed in on someone and very good-naturedly went on pulling the person's leg during the entire lunch session. Rasha found the atmosphere invigorating. Her own interaction with Surit da was thus far limited to stories and lunch sessions. The other girls were friendlier with him, but even though Rasha liked her boss immensely, she consciously kept her distance.

In the days that followed, Rasha realized Surit da was nothing short of a genius at his work. The way he conceptualized and often rewrote stories, headlines and introductions, proved he was a man of good taste. She thought she had much to learn from this man. Although he was extremely strict about deadlines and stories, he was rather lenient about the time people walked into office.

'I am here by 10.00 a.m., but everyone else starts walking in at noon. Isn't it supposed to be the other way round?' he often joked. He was cool about casual leaves too. If one told him truthfully that one could not come to office because of a hangover, he was fine even with that. In her third week at *Our Times*, Rasha was sent off to cover the International Actors' Convention in Delhi.

'I am invited there, but I want you to go,' Surit da told her.

'Umm…are you sure?' asked Rasha.

'Aren't you the one covering entertainment? Stop asking silly questions.'

That year, Rasha was made the coordinating editor of the year-end supplement. She worked round the clock organizing photo shoots, getting copies ready and working with the design team. Rasha got a very good raise by the end of the year and by the end of the second year, she had been promoted to the position chief sub-editor/reporter. Her relationship with Surit da had become much more informal. In her two years at *Our Times*, Rasha had never noticed Surit da looking at her breasts and he had never asked her out alone. By then, Rasha was sure that the stories about his ways with women were cooked up. She wondered where those came from.

Gia was a constant presence in his life. She accompanied him to each and every party and often visited him in office. Rasha found out that Gia had come for internship as a Page 3 journalist in *Our Times* and that's when sparks flew. Gia was doing her PhD from Delhi University and her research paper was on Page 3 journalism in India. She was in her early thirties and Surit da was completely into her. Although he seldom talked about her, during a party organized at his home, it was clear she was in charge because she had arranged the house, the food, the drinks and the music. Everyone had a ball at the party and a very emotional Surit da kissed her in front of everybody. Everyone cheered. He looked like a man who was happy in his personal life and seemed to be rocking in his professional life too. Not a single person in that room that night had any inkling of the ominous turn of events that would take place in the days that followed.

Interlude

• • •

Rasha went through the email that said that the HR head wanted to take her exit interview and also talk about the final financial settlement. The email had an attached questionnaire that she was supposed to fill up and carry with her to the interview. Rasha's years in the professional world had taught her one thing—that all exit interviews were actually a sham. She felt if the company really cared for her opinion, they would have asked her when she was working there and not when she was leaving.

In any case, Rasha felt that exit interviews were a meaningless exercise besides being a vicious tool to settle scores, something she absolutely despised. And her thoughts were ratified by what the publishing director told her the next moment after having led her into a glass room.

'If you have anything to say against Sabrina, then you can go ahead at the exit interview,' she said.

The publishing director was a British woman, who was just thirty, but looked forty. Without having any idea of the Indian film industry, she would sometimes meddle with the stories that would go in the Bollywood magazine. She once even ordered superstar Rajnikanth to be thrown out of the special issue named India's Top 50 Stars just because he did not look glamorous to her. But that did not stop her from throwing her weight around and sensationalizing cover lines at the last moment that made Rasha cringe for fear of libel.

'Why should I say anything against Sabrina?' snapped Rasha.

The publishing director was taken aback by her curt reply. She hated Sabrina and she wanted to cash in on Rasha's resignation.

'I thought things were not fine between you and her,' she still pushed.

'If you think so, then you should take it up. You are the publishing director after all,' said Rasha derisively.

The publishing director was intelligent enough to understand the conversation was not going anywhere, so she said, 'Good luck,' and shook hands with Rasha.

Rasha cleared her desk and put all her belongings inside a cardboard box. There were a few magazines and books, some diaries, writing pads and a few pens. A perfume she always kept handy at her desk, a pair of lipsticks and lip glosses. That was about it. She felt like a refugee dislodged from her own land and walking around with her belongings, not knowing what the future had in store for her. She looked at her mobile phone, sitting silently on the desk. It had virtually stopped making any noise from the day she had put in her resignation. She did not know when it would buzz with life again.

She sat down to fill up the questionnaire.

What is your main reason for leaving?

Did anything trigger your decision to leave?

What was most satisfying about your job?

What would you change about your job?

Did your job duties turn out to be as you expected?

Did you receive enough training to do your job effectively?

Did you receive adequate support to do your job?

Did you receive sufficient feedback about your performance between merit reviews?

Were you satisfied with this company's merit review process?

Did this company help you to fulfill your career goals?

What would you improve to make our workplace better?

Were you happy with your pay, benefits and other incentives?

What was the quality of the supervision you received?

What could your immediate supervisor do to improve his or her management style?

Based on your experience with us, what do you think it takes to succeed in this company?

At the end of the questionnaire, Rasha wrote a two-word answer: NO COMMENTS!

Be it Dubai or Kolkata, the truth will stay with me. *Rasha sighed.*

Part 3
Lightning Strikes

• • •

8

RASHA LOOKED AT the message from Surit da once again. I have put in my resignation. I have left the office and please don't call me right now. I have to gather my thoughts.

She tried hard to decipher the mystery hidden in it. She went up to the crime reporter, who was very close to Surit da, and asked if he knew anything about the reason behind Surit da's sudden resignation. From the expression on his face, Rasha could make out that he did not want to be a part of any discussion on the matter.

'Rasha, I don't know anything, and my advice to you is don't ask around. You have an edition to release, think about that first,' he said. Till then, Rasha had not thought about the edition. An hour was left before it was to go to press and Surit da was the one who checked each and every line written in the newspaper before he signed off the pages. Who was going to do that now? She went to the HR manager and asked her what had happened and who would release the pages.

The manager shrugged. 'Nothing! Your job is to release the pages, just do that. I will ask the news editor to help you out with it.'

'Why did Surit da put in his resignation?' Rasha asked, rather stupidly as she realized later.

The manager looked at her with cold eyes. 'Your boss is not working in this organization anymore. That is all you need to know.' Rasha was surprised by her reaction, but left it at that.

With the help of the news editor, the edition came out smoothly. The confusion on the faces of her colleagues had transformed into despair. But strangely, no one discussed the happenings of the day much. Once the pages went to bed, they all left immediately without exchanging a single word.

After a shower and coffee and some refreshing egg rolls that her mom had made that day, Rasha lay on her bed with a book. She had kept her mobile phone on silent. News about Surit Basu's resignation had spread like wildfire and she was getting ten calls a minute which she didn't want to take since she had no answers to the questions asked. Her mind was buzzing like a bee that had lost its way. She closed the book and tried to piece together the puzzle that was troubling her.

~

The hunky-dory ambience of *Our Times* had changed suddenly in the last few months because Surit da was a changed man. He was extremely irritable and got angry very easily. This often resulted in huge showdowns with people both inside and outside the department. Rasha had a column in the newspaper where she was critical of the film industry. In the column, she sometimes lambasted the producers, directors, actors and sometimes praised them. She sometimes wrote their names and sometimes left it open to guesswork. The column became fodder for drawing-room, make-up room and shooting-floor conversations. It often happened that Rasha would be stepping into a party or event and she would immediately have a curious few asking her who she was talking about in the previous week's column. She'd had the odd angry actor who accused her of having the cake at the film press conference and then being critical of the film or an actress accusing her of having a soft spot for her boyfriend. 'You wrote since I am not getting roles I am staying in the news through my star boyfriend. You are crazy for him yourself, I know that,' one screamed hysterically into the phone at 7.00 a.m.

While Rasha dealt with the reactions, Surit da was on the other hand happy that the column kept people talking about the newspaper. He even told Rasha, 'We will put in a photograph of yours with this column.'

But the very next week, when she went to discuss the subject for that week's column, he told her he would scrap it. 'I am dropping the column. I think it has run its course and is no longer interesting.' Rasha was dumbstruck. She enjoyed writing the column and it gave her a strange sense of power that she thoroughly relished. She wanted to argue with her boss and save her column, but Surit da was already typing on the keyboard making it clear that he was closed to further discussion.

A couple of days later, her landline rang at 6.00 a.m. and Surit da barked into the phone, 'I want you to keep your mobile on 24x7 so that I don't have to call you on your landline.'

'What happened?' asked Rasha, groggy and tense.

'Why weren't you there at the party last night?'

'I told you I had a very bad toothache. I sent somebody else. The party was covered.'

'Oh! I forgot about that.' He hung up.

Rasha found this erratic Surit da a complete departure from the so-much-in-control boss she had known thus far. While on the one hand she liked her boss, she also found this transformation hard to handle. Sometimes he forgot to shave, sometimes he ended up spending his entire time in the smoking area and a deep crevice became a permanent feature between his brows. He looked infuriated and restless all the time and didn't take much interest in the activities of his department. He stopped joining the team for lunch and had it alone in his room. He got drunk on weekends and most often didn't turn up in office on Mondays. Then everything would have to be done over the phone—the story list narrated, followed by the headlines and introductions, then the changes written and rewritten—it became a nightmare of a process.

Finally, Surit da went a step too far. It was a party to which Rasha was also invited and Surit da had told her that he would be going, so he would pick her up. But Rasha couldn't make it at the last moment because her uncle had been hospitalized and she had to rush.

That night, she got a call from a friend from another newspaper. 'Your boss badly abused an intern from a magazine today. It was verbal, but very nasty.'

'An intern? Why?'

'This guy was talking to a lady called Gia. Do you know her? Your boss suddenly started abusing him with the choicest expletives. He was stark drunk. Some people tried to take him aside, but he would not budge. He threatened to beat that guy up. He had to be escorted out of the building by security. It was a big mess.'

Rasha thought instantly, *then, is something wrong with his relationship with Gia? Is that the reason for his weird behaviour?* She was determined to find out.

The next morning, the furrow between his brows looked deeper and he was clearly brooding. Rasha was careful enough not to talk about the events of the night before early in the day. She intended to do that later on.

'Can we go for coffee today in the evening?' asked Rasha. It was a rare occasion when he joined the rest for lunch.

'I like to ask girls out on a date. I don't like girls asking me out,' said Surit da seriously. 'Okay, we will go to Barista on Park Street today.'

Surit da had a very dry sense of humour and Rasha was relieved to see it was still intact. She had earlier gone out with him a couple of times and talking to him was an exhilarating experience. He was a bottomless well of knowledge and experience and she absorbed every word like a sponge with every sip of her favourite latte. He never asked Rasha about her personal life although she had told him about Arun. Surit da had met Arun at a couple of parties and he had later told her that he liked him.

Rasha sat beside him in his Honda City. Park Street was just minutes away from their Chowringhee office and they reached Barista in two minutes. She ordered a brownie and coffee and Surit da went for Darjeeling tea. He absolutely hated coffee. They talked about this and that and then Rasha came to the point a wee-bit tactfully.

'You are my boss and I don't know if I should be asking you this. But you are a very different person since the last few months. I heard what happened last night. If you permit me, can I ask you if everything is alright between you and Gia?'

Surit da took a long sip from his tea and a drag from the cigarette that made Rasha unsure of her next words.

'Nothing is right,' he finally said. He put one arm on the backrest of his chair and sighed deeply.

'I met Gia for the first time when she came to interview me for her research on Page 3 journalism. You can say for me it was love at first sight and I wanted to see her every day, every minute. So I suggested she intern with us to get a hands-on idea about Page 3 journalism. She agreed. Then I asked her out for dinner. She agreed. A week later, I proposed marriage. She agreed. Her mother had passed away a few years back and she did not get along with her father, who had married again and moved to the US. So there was nobody I needed to meet to ask for her hand in marriage. But she wanted to marry only after she had finished her PhD. I did not want to be an impediment to her studies, so I agreed.'

Surit da paused to take a sip from his cup. Rasha held her breath because she could not understand where this was leading to.

'Then six months ago, my driver told me that Gia was going to a particular five-star hotel very frequently. I just casually told her that she had been spotted at the hotel by some people I know and she went ballistic. She accused me of not trusting her.'

He paused again. 'That's when I approached a friend of mine, who runs a private detective agency, to run a check on her.'

Rasha gave Surit da an exasperated look. 'How can you unleash detectives on the person you love?'

'Love is not that simple, Rasha. At your age, it might be, but not at mine,' he said.

'And what did the detective find out?' asked Rasha with reluctant interest.

'He found out lots and everything was discouraging. Gia was having an affair with the owner of the hotel that she was frequenting. Before me, there had been two other men, both rich Marwari businessmen. She had told me she had just landed from Delhi, but my friend found out that she had been living in Kolkata for five years. She first lived in an apartment on Camac Street funded by her first boyfriend, then in an apartment in the posh Tivoli Court funded by her second. Then she became the owner of an apartment in Jodhpur Park that was bought by me.'

Rasha's mouth was agape as she looked at Surit da. 'Sorry to say this, but she sounds like a con woman.'

'Sounds? She is one, and big time. Dating Marwari businessmen gave her money, but not a high-flying lifestyle where she would be attending parties and meeting stars at high-class dos every day. I guess she zeroed in on me because I held the ticket to all that.'

Surit da leaned back again as if he was drained of all strength. 'It was too late before I realized,' he said.

'Why? What happened?'

'My parents had a house in North Kolkata which I had sold and put that entire cash into that apartment in Jodhpur Park. In a moment of insanity, I bought the apartment in her name since she was staying there and I planned to move in there from my company accommodation after we got married.'

Rasha felt that for once, the crisp copy writer was taking too long to narrate a story. She was bursting at the seams with curiosity.

'What happened to the apartment?' she said.

'She sold it.'

'What?'

'And she didn't tell me. I only found that out later. She had been telling me that she needed to go to Mumbai to research for her thesis. The day my friend unearthed everything about Gia, she was travelling to Mumbai. I thought I would check things with her when she came back. But something inside me told me to check things out at the Jodhpur Park apartment first. To my immense distress, I saw a family moving into my apartment with truckloads of stuff. When I asked them what was going on, I was told by a gentleman that he had bought the apartment from Gia Sarkar a month back for forty lakhs.'

'She had pocketed the money?'

'Of course.'

There was a formidable stillness at the table for some time till Surit da spoke again. 'She never came back from Mumbai and I did not make an attempt to contact her because no matter how much I love her, my ego is finding it hard to accept the reality that I have been conned.'

No wonder he has been so irritable, Rasha thought. 'Forgive me for saying this, but how could you be so stup...err...naïve?' said Rasha, mustering a lot of courage.

'Weren't you talking about love a few minutes ago? Love does strange things to you. I think I am still in love with Gia. I am like a teenager madly missing his first love. I hate her for what she has done to me, but I still love her.'

His eyes had a searching look and his childlike face looked vulnerable. The crease in his forehead had been ironed out by sadness.

'And what about yesterday?' asked Rasha.

He snapped out of his thoughts. 'When I walked into the party, I was surprised out of my wits to see her. I had no clue she had returned. The sight of her made my blood boil. On top of that, she was flirting shamelessly with this young man. I just don't know what happened to me. I just couldn't take it.'

'Will this go down well with the management—the editor of a newspaper openly abusing the intern of another newspaper?'

'I called up his editor in the morning today and apologized.' He became thoughtful. 'This is not going to happen again. I won't let Gia bother me anymore.'

Rasha was not too convinced. Gia had already been playing with his fertile brains for the last few months. At work, Rasha could still see flashes of his genius, but he clearly was not his usual self. And if Gia continued to reign in his mind like that, he was heading for more trouble, she was pretty sure.

'I think you are wasting your time on her. You are such a brilliant journalist and a good man, you have better things ahead of you.' Rasha felt she sounded like an older sister consoling her younger brother who was crying over lost love.

He nodded. 'I don't know. If she had just said goodbye to me, that would have been one thing, but selling off my apartment and pocketing the money...' He didn't finish the sentence and Rasha didn't want to egg him on.

~

Surit da, nevertheless, did try to mend his ways in the coming weeks. For starters, he was still full of out-of-the-box ideas that made the content of the newspaper vibrant. Rasha told him that she wanted to do an article on domestic violence on women since new statistics showed that Bengal had a very high rate of violence.

'Do it. But next week do a story about violence on men.'

'Come on, the story won't stand. Men don't have to face violence at the hands of women,' Rasha said.

'I am telling you. You will find loads of information,' he winked.

Rasha hadn't known that her expression had given away her thoughts.

'No. Gia didn't beat me up,' Surit da said.

He started laughing. The name of his ex-girlfriend did not create the creases on his forehead anymore. Surit da had finally come to terms with the reality that he had been conned by the woman he loved and had trusted the most.

Rasha called up a few lawyers for her story on violence against men and stumbled upon astonishing facts. Most of the lawyers were fighting divorce cases for men, whose wives had either beaten them up in a drunken state or had been beating them regularly in fits of rage. Some women were having multiple affairs while some had taken control of their assets and thrown the men out of their own homes.

'You, at least, figure in the last category,' Rasha stated with a smile.

'I am plotting my revenge. I will tell you when I am done.' He returned the smile. Rasha was happy to see him in a better mood which meant less work-related stress for her and the entire department. She hoped that if this mood continued, she might even be able to resurrect her column in the coming weeks.

'Behave as if she never existed and move on,' said Rasha in her elder-sister tone.

'Could you have done that?' he asked.

'Oh, yes, I have done that so many times. I was dating this guy, who is now a famous designer. Please don't ask me the name. We were about to go out on a date when he asked me to wait at the bus stop while he urgently went looking for a washroom in a restaurant. I stood at that bus stop for two hours, but he never came back. Then I went home. After that, he stopped taking my phone calls and we never met. Since we had seen each other for only two months, I shrugged it off and moved on. Then there was another guy whom I really liked and he also gave me signs that he liked me. We went on a number of dates before he broke the news that he had decided to get married to a childhood friend in Australia because he would get an Australian passport and—here's the punch line—he said he loved me. I was pretty upset after that and even took to boozing and partying wildly out of sheer sadness. But in two weeks, I straightened myself out thinking that he was having a ball in Australia with his new wife and new fortune while I was ruining myself. Stupid me! I forgot him that day. Then my longest affair ended when my boyfriend started seeing a sixteen-year-old PYT. That left my ego really bruised and battered. But I have never sought revenge. I feel I would be giving them too much importance if I did.'

Surit da listened to Rasha's long sermon without batting an eyelid; and Rasha, who usually clammed up about her personal life, was pretty astonished with herself for sharing her life's details with her boss.

His expression remained stoic. 'But none of them have left with all your money. It's hard. Rasha, believe me, it's very hard. This makes you vengeful. I am only human.'

∾

Gia probably got unnerved by what her brief appearance did to her ex-fiancé, so she decided to swiftly leave the city (where to, Surit da had no idea). She stayed the furthest distance away from Kolkata. Rasha was thankful that all his anger had been directed at the boy that day. Had Surit da reacted to Gia directly, it would have given birth to a scandal that could not have been buried so easily. Meanwhile, Surit da had gone back to being boisterous, ultra-smart and the genius that he was. Rasha thought the storm had passed.

But now, she was faced with another predicament. Tongues wagged every time she accompanied Surit da to a party. People knew he was back to being single and they supposed it was only natural that he had started dating his young and attractive subordinate on the rebound. But she couldn't care less. She was sure that like it happened at the end of most Hindi films, where the jilted protagonist meets another girl, Surit da, too, would find his girl. And she was certain it would not be her.

However, months passed but Rasha's dream girl for Surit da remained elusive. He went out with starlets, sometimes met old colleagues his age and even bonded with people on networking sites. About some dates, he told Rasha and about some, he didn't.

'I went out with Malavika last evening,' he said.

'Shit...no way,' said Rasha, puckering her nose.

'Why, what's wrong with her?'

'Gosh! Have you taken a look at her feet? She has the dirtiest feet imaginable and unwaxed legs. She had come for a shoot like that when she knew she would have to wear a short dress. We actually sent her to the salon next door to get her legs fixed and *Our Times* had to pick up the bill!'

'Really! You never told me this.'

'We don't tell the editor every "dirty detail",' she said wickedly.

'Anyway, she is too young for me. She was really keen to go to my apartment after dinner. She had no brains for conversation, wanted me to put her on the front page of the newspaper and she even hinted she was willing to take her clothes off to be out there. She really scared me when she kept telling me she wanted to see my home. She was wearing a saree so I couldn't see her feet,' he said.

'All covered up? Beware!'

9

THEN SURIT DA fell seriously ill. He was down with malignant malaria and couldn't get out of bed. Since he was alone at home, people from his team took turns to visit him in the morning and at night. Rasha couldn't manage to go and see him because in his absence, one had to be more alert with the edition. She managed to visit him only on her off day.

Surit da looked extremely weak. He was propped up on the bed by a couple of pillows, there were dark circles under his eyes and he was unshaven. The red on his cheeks looked lighter. Ugly crow's feet had started making their appearance in the corners of his eyes and his usually taut skin looked dry and tired. Rasha wondered if it was malaria that had left its mark on him or was it the trauma of losing his lakhs to the love of his life?

Rasha sat down on a chair next to his bed. 'I have been dying to tell you something,' he said eagerly.

'What?'

'You will be surprised to know what happened. Sumana had come to see me a couple of days ago. At around 9.30 p.m. Alone!' he said.

Sumana Das worked in *Our Times* under Surit da. She was a twenty-three-year-old pretty girl with a petite frame. She was fairly okay at her job, but Rasha found her pesky and lazy. She took leave at the drop of a hat and kicked up a huge fuss if she was told anything about her constant absence. She expected somebody to always hold the fort for her as the numbers on her leave chart multiplied. She and Rasha did not get along at all and there had been some ugly showdowns in office where Surit da had had to intervene. She had made it clear to Rasha several times that she believed the reason Rasha was going up the ladder of success was because she was sleeping with the boss. Rasha had just laughed at her allegation and chosen not to defend herself. Surit da knew about these allegations too.

'She came with chocolates and flowers. I thought that was very sweet. She even made coffee for me,' said Surit da

Rasha just raised an eyebrow but didn't interrupt him.

'Then like an idiot, I told her I had a headache. I don't know what she thought. She just went to the bathroom, came out in the nude and offered me a teat massage with her breasts. I just did not know how to handle it. For once, I really wanted to crawl into the bed with her because I haven't had sex in a long time.'

Rasha was listening to him with rapt attention although the last bit made her a bit uncomfortable.

'Then I thought that if I had a daughter, she would have been her age. I begged her to put her clothes back on. She refused and continued to obstinately sit on my bed. Then to my horror, she started massaging me. My head suddenly started reeling violently. I guess I passed out. When I woke up, she was gone.'

A week after that incident, Sumana put in her resignation saying she wanted to stay at home and look after her ailing mom. Only Rasha and Surit da knew the real reason. But Surit da was relieved she was gone. 'I couldn't have handled her at work anymore,' he told Rasha.

Rasha realized that underneath that quick-witted extrovert, was a man who was actually shy and immersed in middle-class Bengali values. *Otherwise, looking at a beautiful naked woman, offering a massage in an empty apartment, which man would have thought about his daughter?* she thought.

~

A few days later was Surit da's birthday and the entire department, who by then knew about his break-up with Gia (but not about the con job, of course), decided to cheer him up by organizing a surprise party for him. The party was being organized at the cosy restaurant Tangerine and the theme was black and blue. One of the guys was given the responsibility of dressing up Surit da in black and blue and leading him to the venue. Other responsibilities were divided among the team. While some organized the menu, some others took care of the decorations. Rasha was supposed to get the cake. She picked it up on her way home from Cakes on Ekdalia Road. She stopped by at Pantaloons on Gariahat to pick up some clothes in black and blue.

She was caught completely off the guard the moment she walked into Pantaloons. Surit da was rummaging through the racks. Rasha tried hard to lose herself in the stack of clothes all around, but he saw her.

He didn't ask her why she was there. 'I just thought I will gift myself something since no one wished me on my birthday. Can you help me choose some clothes?'

'Oh sorry! Happy Birthday,' Rasha said half-heartedly.

She turned her attention to an aquamarine silk shirt with an embroidered collar.

'That's too bright for me,' he said.

'No, it isn't. Buy it. And make sure you get a nice pair of black trousers with it.'

'No, no, too bright.'

Rasha was getting late. She would have to pick up the cake and dress up for the party too. A light bulb flickered in her mind.

'I saw Amitabh Bachchan wearing the same colour at a press conference on TV recently,' she lied.

Surit da was such a die-hard fan of the superstar that if you told him Amitabh lived on raw vegetables he would have even been willing to try that. He kept looking at the shirt for a few seconds trying to visualize Amitabh in it. 'Okay, I will take it,' he finally said, satisfied with his visualization.

'I have to go, I am getting late. I have to go somewhere with my mom today,' she lied again.

Rasha quickly picked up a cobalt blue top with net collars. She thought it would complement the black bias skirt she intended to wear in the evening.

Once out of Pantaloons, she called her colleague. 'Surit da has just now bought a blue shirt and black trouser, so make sure he wears it tonight.' They both laughed and she hung up. She hurriedly did her make-up and added a dash of blue eye shadow. She sprayed some Dior gifted to her by her NRI uncle and told her mom, 'It's Surit da's birthday today. I will be late.'

Her mom had by now got fairly used to her getting home late from work. And when she went out partying with friends, Arun was with her most of the time, so that helped her avert the uncomfortable questions at home. Rasha found it sickening that the presence of a man—one particular man—made such a difference to her parents' perception of her nocturnal escapades. She detested this attitude, but since this arrangement meant less stress for her parents and herself, she went with it, however much grudgingly.

Surit da was surprised and happy when he entered the quaint restaurant located on the second floor of an old building behind St Xavier's College, off Park Street. He got very emotional when he cut the cake that read: 'We love you'. He took swigs from his favourite Chivas Regal and watched the team dance. Some tried to pull him to the floor, especially created for the party, but he refused to oblige blaming his two left feet. Everyone had a whale of a time and devoured the crispy chicken, momos, American chopsuey, fried rice, chilli chicken and manchurian fish that was on the menu. It ended with the Tangerine speciality, brownies and ice cream that some even mixed with whisky. They partied till 3.00 a.m.

The next day, all came in to work late, including Surit da, and discussed the activities of the night before and pulled each other's legs. Like true Bengalis, the fabulous food at Tangerine was the focal point of their conversation. A fabulous mimic, Rasha acted out what her intoxicated colleagues had done the night before. Everybody roared with laughter. Rasha didn't even spare Surit da. He took it in good spirit.

For Rasha, the rest of the day was spent chasing the elusive Raj Puri and when she went to the office the next day armed with her story, she saw her boss engrossed in mobile phones.

THE TREMOR CAUSED by Surit da's resignation was felt all around. Rasha, who had so far felt so smugly settled and appreciated at her workplace, was completely shaken and lost. She selfishly thought that the promotion which was due a few months later would probably not happen because of Surit da's exit. She would have to prove herself all over again to whoever came in his place. Like the rest of the team, she too felt frustrated and cheated. There was mayhem at work. Some seniors in the department thought that they would be the natural choice after Surit da's exit. To Rasha's immense irritation, they started behaving like the boss from the moment he was gone.

The pandemonium continued a day after Surit da's resignation, but Rasha thought that it was better to go about her routine than to get involved in the cold undercurrents cutting through at her workplace. She left office along with the crime reporter to find out about the rape and murder of a fifteen-year-old girl in a slum in Narkeldanga.

'You called Surit da, didn't you?' her crime reporter colleague asked her. Rasha didn't deny it.

'Has it ever occurred to you that your mobile phone might be tapped?' Rasha almost toppled from her cab seat.

'Why would anyone tap my phone for calling up Surit da?'

'You are too naïve to understand how things work. As a friend, I am telling you there is more to this than you think.'

'Then tell me.'

He kept quiet, irritating Rasha to the core.

'You won't tell me anything, but you come up with this outrageous warning. I just don't like this,' she said.

'I have spoken to him a couple of times since yesterday. Then Sumana called me up today and quoted from my conversations with him,' he said.

'What?'

'Yes. I have a hunch she is involved in some way with whatever is happening. She absolutely hates him.'

Rasha didn't tell him anything about what had happened between Sumana and Surit da. Instead, she asked, 'Why?'

'Do you remember Surit da did not allow her leave to go on a trip with her boyfriend and her group of friends because we were closing the Puja issue and supplements?'

'Yes, I do.'

'She couldn't go. But her boyfriend went and shared a room with her best friend. When he came back, he dropped her like a hot potato. She always blamed Surit da for her break-up.'

'That's childish!'

'You mean to say you thought she was very mature?' he said incredulously.

'True. Not really.'

'If you promise me that you will keep your mouth shut, I will tell you one thing more.'

'You know me.'

His voice dropped almost to a whisper. 'She is seeing Ansh Ramchandani.'

'The stinking-rich producer/industrialist? How come no one knows about it?'

'He is very secretive. You should be knowing that.'

~

Everyone knew about this upcoming businessman, Ansh

Ramchandani, who was pumping money into hotels and Bengali films, but avoided newspaper reporters and photographers like the plague. The only time Rasha had seen him was when an actress friend took her to his annual party held at his palatial villa in Goa as her personal guest. Rasha had to promise that she would not write a word about what she saw there. 'Just remember one thing, if you write anything, my career will be finished,' she had pleaded making Rasha more curious. But she indeed wasn't ready for anything like what she saw.

She, along with most of the other invitees from the film industry, assembled at the airport to be flown first class to Goa. Ansh had just started his aviation company and Rasha presumed he wanted to flaunt his new fleet, if not to the media, to the film fraternity for sure. Halfway into the flight, the guests were drunk on their Chivas and Black Dogs. They seemed to be impressed even before touchdown.

Rasha meanwhile enjoyed her window seat next to her actress-friend Chandrima.

'Have you told Ansh I am coming?'

'I had to because everyone here knows you. He wanted you to sign something called an anonymity contract so that you do not write or talk about this party. I told him you are not going as a journalist, you are going as my friend. So please, please don't put me in a spot.'

'You don't have to plead and worry like this. You know me,' said Rasha.

Chandrima relaxed. She gestured to one of the hostesses.

'Can I have a champagne?'

'Which one, ma'am?'

'Rasha, what about you?'

'Orange juice.' Rasha was happy that she had managed to stick to her orange juice resolution through her entire time in *Our Times*.

'Moet and Chandon for me, please, and orange juice for the lady here.'

Chandrima took off her sunglasses and rested her head on the soft backrest and closed her eyes. The skin below her eyes was dark and puffy. She wasn't wearing any concealer or heavy make-up, so all the dark spots and lines were visible. Rasha thought of her flawless face on screen and her face now. Her coloured hair looked awfully dry and was devoid of any kind of shine. Patches of the scalp were visible here and there. Inadvertently, Rasha ran her hand through her own thick curly hair and thought of the fabulous work the make-up artists do on the stars. But Chandrima was a brilliant actress, she was a box-office favourite at one time and she was also one of the few in the Bengali film industry without any pretensions.

'Tired?' she asked Chandrima.

'Yes. Very.'

'I know films are tough.'

'More than that, surviving in the Bengali film industry is tough. Here I am sipping Moet on a first-class flight to a lavish party, but did you know that today I had to pay from my pocket because I wanted to use the air-conditioned dressing room? The producer would not spare those few extra hundreds to give that basic comfort to the heroine. As such, the studio floors are non-Ac and awfully hot. I need to be a bit comfortable in the dressing room at least. This is what I have been doing since they started these air-conditioned rooms in Indrapuri Studios—paying from my pocket for cool air. Horrible!'

Rasha felt thankful that she could sit in an air-conditioned office all day.

'Add to that the bathrooms. At least the ones in my AC room are better. You will cry if you see the other ones,' the actress said angrily.

'I hope Ansh starts his studio soon. At least we will have a better place then.'

'Ansh is starting a studio?' asked Rasha cautiously.

'Off the record, yes. He's got the land already.'

'Will you be angry if I tell you something?'

The actress now looked alarmed.

'Can I do a story about this thing that producers are not giving you basic facilities like AC rooms and clean bathrooms?'

Chandrima flashed a relieved smile.

'You can. Quote me on this. Send your photographer and we will do a shoot too.'

'You will pose in the bathroom?' Rasha asked.

'No, dumbo! Inside the make-up room and you will write I am paying for it. I have bought a mini-dress from Bangkok. I will wear it at the shoot.'

Both realized the ridiculousness of the discussion and laughed. But both knew the photo shoot and story could become the talk of the industry and town as well.

They disembarked the airplane at the Goa international airport. The airhostesses, in their red-and-green midriff-revealing lehengas, stood by the exit. Rasha was reassured to know that it was a uniform for special occasions like this one, and they usually wore suits. At least twenty men in spotless white chauffeur uniforms were waiting for the group. Groups of two people were allotted a Tata Indica each. Chandrima and Rasha hopped into theirs and headed for the hotel. It was 4.00 a.m. when they checked into their separate rooms. The five-star property had a view to die for, the reception staff informed them.

'We are the only hotel right on the beach apart from the Taj Aguada. Just go to the balcony in the morning.' They weren't wrong, she realized.

She saw the sunrise from the balcony and only then crashed on the comfortable bed. The Goan sea from Rasha's balcony looked so peaceful and beautiful.

At breakfast, Rasha realized that the rest of the group was not staying at the hotel. Chandrima shed light on her bewilderment.

'The rest are staying in the guest house on Ansh's villa premises. He told me to check in here with you. I think he wants to keep the journalist at arm's length.' She laughed.

Rasha felt angry at this treatment.

'This is just not done. What does he think of me? I am sorry you have to stay here because of me.'

'I am not complaining,' said Chandrima, digging into a slice of pineapple.

While her plate was piled with fruits, muesli and yoghurt, Rasha's only had sausages, salami, a plump omelette stuffed with cheese and mushrooms along with a selection of chocolate muffins and vanilla mousse.

'This hotel is nice enough. And, any day, I would prefer your company to the mindless bitching that must be going on at the moment at the breakfast table in the guest house.' She finished the fruits and sipped pomegranate juice.

Rasha smiled gratefully. Chandrima's words made her feel a bit better but the ill-at-ease feeling refused to leave Rasha. Her thoughts were broken.

'Are you, by any chance, actress Chandrima?' asked an enthusiastic young girl, whom Rasha had earlier seen staring at them. She looked confused yet excited. Rasha knew exactly what she was thinking. It was actually hard to recognize Chandrima without make-up.

'I am not too sure but I think so,' replied Chandrima.

While the girl was still detangling her answer, Chandrima walked into the lift with Rasha. They both were in splits. Rasha suddenly realized why she liked Chandrima so much. They both had the same sense of humour.

~

Once Rasha reached Ansh's villa for the party, the ill-at-ease feeling came back with a weird intensity.

The drive on the empty road up the hill and the approaching dusk gave Rasha a spooky feeling. Her black gown, golden danglers and curls, still fuming from the blow-dry, did little to get her into the party mood. She was feeling so insulted by Ansh's attempt to segregate her that she wasn't sure if she really wanted to experience his party. The car stopped at the giant gates. The driver punched in a number and the gates opened. The car went further uphill. She could see the lighthouse of the seventeenth century Fort Aguada at a distance. The car came to a halt.

Three buggys were stationed at a small building that looked like a hotel lobby.

'Is it so big that you need a buggy?' she asked.

'It is bigger than you imagine.'

The buggy took them to a roundabout with a lit-up sculpture of a woman. On either side were vast manicured lawns. And a helipad too.

'There, there is Ansh. Some celebrity must be arriving in a helicopter,' said Chandrima.

Rasha craned her neck as the chopper landed and out emerged the wife of the biggest star of Bollywood.

Awe was replacing Rasha's anger now.

'Should we expect a lot of Bollywood stars at the party?' she asked.

The star wife was now sitting beside Ansh in another buggy.

'Not a lot, but a few I am sure. Ansh resurrected her hubby's career with which Bengali film I am sure I won't have to tell you...' Chandrima said, gesturing at the star wife.

'I get it. The star got a national award too,' said Rasha absent-mindedly because she could see a palace, yes, actually a palace, looming in the distance.

'Oh my God! That's his holiday home!' she exclaimed.

'And look to your left. Those are the guesthouses.'

Rasha saw a number of Tollywood stars getting into the buggy stationed at the guesthouse stairs. The balconies of the guest house were built in a Chinese pagoda style. Ansh's house on the other hand looked like a replica of the City Palace of Jaipur with red walls and Rajasthani architecture. Rasha found this a bit jarring in a place like Goa where she had expected a laid-back villa strewn with sun loungers—definitely not a Rajasthani palace on one side and a Chinese Pagoda on another!

As they entered the gates of the palace, they were served welcome drinks by four beautiful women in red sarees and flowing hair. After dropping his guest at the guesthouse, Ansh had now taken his position behind the pretty women to welcome all his guests personally. He was in his late thirties, wore a white Armani suit and looked pleasant and well-groomed.

When Chandrima introduced Rasha to him, he was cordial.

'Enjoy the party. When is your flight tomorrow?' He didn't look in the eye when he spoke.

'Afternoon,' replied Rasha. She was now sure he was keen on packing her off on the plane than having her snooping around his property.

While expensive wine flowed endlessly and at least twenty-five dishes were served from starters to the desert, Rasha didn't have anything much to do except sit at a table, munch and chat with the other guests. A few songs from a well-known Bollywood singer was a welcome relief, but that was it.

'There is money flowing in this party, but it's boring,' stated Rasha.

'His exciting parties are for the closer bunch,' enlightened Chandrima.

'Have you been to any?'

'No. But I heard recently he threw a pool party in a five-star hotel in Kolkata where he handed out bikinis to the guests. He didn't invite me. I am sure he didn't think my body bikini-worthy.'

Chandrima had a straight face. Rasha didn't know if she should laugh or sympathize.

Chandrima laughed. 'I don't care as long as he gives me a lead in his films.'

Rasha saw Ansh mingling with the guests, many of whom were foreigners, but she had lost all interest in him by then. So she didn't make an effort to hatch a conversation. At the end of the party, Ansh bade everyone goodbye personally. And Rasha thought when it came to her, he dropped the 'see you again' deliberately.

At the airport next day, when Rasha was reflecting on whether the trip was worth it, she pacified herself by enlisting that through the trip she got to know Chandrima better, got a few stories from her and from the other stars too and piled up on gossip for the next one year.

Ansh can go to hell, was her parting thought from Goa.

෴

Now this same Ansh, who hated journalists and who could have any model or actress entwined around his little finger all the time, was actually having a relationship with Sumana. Of all people Sumana! It sounded bizarre to Rasha.

'How did she manage to land such a good catch? Miss Lazybones will live her life like a queen.'

'Now you are being childish. I don't know why every woman thinks all affairs end in marriages,' the crime reporter said with disgust.

'Then?'

'Ansh is a spoilt brat who is doing really well for himself, but he is a kinky kid.'

'Kinky?'

'He is into the threesome-foursome scene. You can say he is also the torch-bearer of the underground rave scene in Kolkata. He has his bevy of high-society call girls to keep people-who-matter happy. He is hugely into the pornography scene too.'

She did know about Ansh's wild parties but pornography…

'In what way is he into pornography?'

'Apparently, most of his moolah comes from producing porn. He shifts some of it to legitimate Bengali films and serials.'

'How come his name never came up when we did that story on a porn racket a few weeks ago?' asked Rasha.

'I guess people are really afraid to take his name in the media because he is really vindictive. But apparently what you wrote in the story led the police to him when they cracked down. He landed in deep trouble with the authorities and he is really angry with *Our Times*.'

'How do you know all this?'

'I have my sources,' the crime reporter said proudly.

'Yeah, stupid of me to ask.'

She now looked concerned. 'But isn't Sumana playing with fire if she is dating a man like that?'

'She is. But if she is zipping around town in a Honda Accord these days, do you think she cares?'

'And you are saying Sumana might have a hand in Surit da's sudden resignation…'

Suddenly, the crime reporter clamped up and became reluctant to talk about it anymore. 'It's just a theory. I don't have any proof. When I have some, I will tell you.' And he didn't say a word more.

On their way back, the crime reporter uttered just one more

sentence on the matter.

'Rasha, all I want to say is Ansh is very angry with you and Surit da for that story...if I were you I would be more careful.'

'Really?' said Rasha defiantly. 'Are you trying to scare me?'

He gestured with his hands and shrugged. 'Up to you how you want to perceive it.'

THE CAB THAT Rasha and the crime reporter had hailed was speeding through the Sealdah flyover. As she looked out, she saw the cars and buses spilling over to the tram line as a tram desperately tried to nose its way through. The buses, in their bid to go faster than each other, were raging past the bus stop or ramming on the brakes at the last moment to avoid hitting each other. In the midst of it all, jay walkers were zigzagging across the streets. The chaos on the flyover was akin to Rasha's thoughts, the only difference being that the jaywalkers knew where they were going, but her thoughts didn't. She finally decided she had to meet Surit da to ease the turmoil in her head.

That evening she planned to call up Surit da and drop in at his place. She was tired of fielding questions wherever she went. Surit Basu was not the kind of editor who sat in office editing the newspaper and remaining faceless. He was out and about and everyone knew him. Hence his sudden exit was bound to become the biggest topic of discussion at every press conference, the toxic zone where all journos gossiped mercilessly. She needed to know the truth so that she could formulate her lie.

It was 8.00 p.m. and she was about to turn off her computer. She had called Surit da a few times on his mobile phone to ask him if she could drop in that evening. The phone went on ringing and he never called back, which was very unlike him. Rasha expected a call any moment. Instead she received a message from him:

I have decided to leave town today. I cannot leave a forwarding address.

This incensed Rasha. She could feel blood rushing to her cheeks and ears and she could feel her head throbbing.

How could Surit da do this? He, of course, knew some answers which he could have shared with me, was her furious thought.

Rasha decided that was it. She would not bother about him anymore. He had taken his decision and she had taken hers. It didn't really matter to her anymore why he put in his resignation, as long as she had her own job intact.

Let him run away from his life, how does it matter to me? He was just a boss, thought Rasha crossly.

She craved for a drink to calm herself. Kolkata was not a place where a woman could walk into a bar alone and ask for a drink. Earlier, even two girls together, without being accompanied by a man, were refused alcohol at restaurants. Now even if two girls were served, a single woman wasn't. Rasha knew a few lounges where she would be happily served by the bartenders, because she knew them well, but she could not imagine dealing with the stares of the men or the passes they would make at her as if she was waiting to be picked up. She wanted peace and quiet and that wouldn't come with a hundred ogling men breathing down her neck.

Arun had already left for Dubai, otherwise he could have taken her out. She called up Zohaib Khan, her best friend.

'I am in the mood for beer. Will you join me?' she said.

'I would have loved to, but no one is at home and I am babysitting Rehanna. Why don't you come over?' he said.

Rehanna was Zohaib's five-year-old niece who was extremely fond of Rasha. She thought she could do with some innocence therapy by spending time with a child. She readily agreed.

'Okay, I am coming. Do you have beer at home?'

'Sorry, I don't. And I cannot leave Rehanna alone at home. Can you get it on your way here?'

'Trust you to be so hopeless!' Rasha said good-naturedly.

She went to a liquor store on Russell Street. It was never too crowded and she felt utterly comfortable purchasing beer there. Otherwise, women buying liquor at a store attracted stares. Rasha had got used to that though. She took a cab and headed for Zohaib's house that was just two blocks from her own.

~

Zohaib and Rasha were childhood friends. They had grown up together playing cricket on the streets of Gariahat, cycling together on a bandh day when the city would be deserted, and discussing their crushes and their questions about sex sitting by the water tank on Rasha's terrace. Zohaib's parents were extremely liberal. They had no qualms about Zohaib drinking at home, sometimes even with his father, unlike Rasha's parents, who could not imagine their daughter opening a bottle at home, although she had often done that secretly in her room when her girlfriends would be sleeping over.

Rasha was clutching the newspaper-wrapped beer cans in her hand, thinking of a relaxing evening with Zohaib, when her sharp eyes rested on a black Santro. The car had been maintaining its pace behind the cab right from her office. She looked through the rear-view mirror and saw two tough looking men sitting in the front. As the cab pulled up in front of Zohaib's house, the Santro pulled up behind it. She got out and stood on the footpath for some time. When the cab left, the Santro also followed it and pulled out of the lane, although she could see both men glancing at her when they drove past. When she was sure that the Santro was nowhere in sight, she got inside Zohaib's apartment building. He opened the door and hugged Rasha. Rehanna also came running and hugged her.

'I have this strange feeling that I was being tailed,' said Rasha, as she closed the door behind her.

'What have you been up to recently?' Zohaib asked.

Rasha caressed her lips with her fingers as she searched for an answer.

'I would say, don't bother. Could be bored guys looking for excitement by following a beautiful girl,' he said.

Zohaib was speaking from experience. During her teenage years, guys did follow her around. There was a boy who would follow her to school in his car every day. Zohaib had to go over to his house and give him some soft threats to ensure he didn't do it again. Zohaib was six-feet tall and regular workout at the gym had given him a body that could scare off any man and set any woman dreaming. He was solid yet lithe. He was fair and preferred to wear his hair in a crew cut that ended in a tapering line at his nape. He had a Bengali Muslim father and an extremely pretty Kashmiri mother. Rasha was never aware of his good looks till all her girlfriends started falling for him.

Zohaib was a model, who nursed dreams of making it big in Bollywood. Rasha and Zohaib were what one would call bumchums. Although they made a really good-looking pair when they walked together, never in their life did they feel any kind of attraction for each other beyond pure friendship.

'So what made the very busy Rasha Roy remember Zohaib today?' he said, opening a can of beer.

'I wanted to drink.'

'And you didn't want good company?'

'No, I just wanted to drink. If I had wanted good company, I would have gone somewhere else.'

Zohaib smiled. That's how Rasha always spoke to him and he was used to it. She sat with her legs folded on the carpet of their sitting room and helped Rehanna with a painting project. She felt like telling Zohaib about what had been happening at work.

But decided not to talk or think about her ex-boss anymore. She concentrated on the can of Heineken in her hand. After finishing two cans, Rasha felt a little relaxed. It was 11.00 p.m. Zohaib had fed Rehanna and she was cosily tucked in bed.

'Do you want to watch a movie?' he asked.

'No. Can't you talk?'

'I can. What do you want to listen to?'

'Gossip!'

Zohaib was one of Rasha's best sources in the modelling industry and he had given her some of her scoops, but right now she was just in the mood for some plain chit-chat.

'Okay, here is the latest. So far, you had heard of gay choreographers and designers asking men to sleep with them. Recently, a gay police officer asked one of my colleagues to sleep with him. A model from Delhi was caught at the Hong Kong airport carrying drugs. He had apparently named my colleague as the person who had put it in his bag. The police officer said that he would bury the case if he slept with him.'

'Did he?' asked Rasha eagerly.

'Oh, yes, he did. He was so scared of going to jail that sleeping with a man was a much better option. But the problem is that the police officer is now taking him to hotels two-three times a week. The man is a sadist and his fantasy consists of slicing up skin with a razor.'

'Oh my god! What will your friend do?'

'There is no other way but to escape to Mumbai. He can't go to higher authorities because he was the one who had actually put the coke in the model's bag. It's another thing that the model had asked for it and had forgotten about it later on.'

'That would make a brilliant story,' she said, and then immediately changed her mind.

'You carry on. I don't want to think about stories today.'

While talking to her, Zohaib had taken out a pack of cigarettes from a drawer and offered one to Rasha. She took a long drag from it.

'Aren't any of our friends going to the disco tonight? It's Saturday.'

'Yes, I got a few calls but since I am with Rehanna, I said no.'

'When are your brother and sis-in-law coming back?'

'They have gone to a party. They should be here by midnight.'

'Then let's go after they are here. I need to dance.'

Rasha had informed her mom that she was at Zohaib's place, but if she had added that she was heading to the disco with Zohaib, with Arun out of town, she was sure her mom would have said, 'Which man would accept his fiancée partying at the disco at midnight with another man?' Arun though had no qualms about it because he perfectly understood the relationship between Rasha and Zohaib, she could not risk it with her mother.

Rasha had gone to work in her short kurta and churidar that day. She would have preferred to wear something western but she felt too lazy to go home and change, and also face the interrogation. She just darkened her make-up. She added some more kajal, used a dark-brown lipstick and smudged a pink lipstick on her cheeks to give the impression of a blush. She was happy with the results when she looked at herself in Zohaib's bedroom mirror.

Rasha decided to call her mom and inform her that she and Zohaib were going to Tantra. Although her mom had never been to Tantra, the nightclub at Park Hotel, the very mention of the word 'Tantra' always did something to her.

'Again? And Arun is not in town...' she said.

'All our other friends are there. All the other girls, I mean,' said Rasha.

'I don't know what kind of friends you have who stay awake all night when they should be in bed.'

Rasha ignored that while her mother continued. 'Your father will be very angry that you have decided to go to the disco again. But he will be fine if you come back within an hour.'

Her mom told her she was allowed an hour at the disco like she was telling a child she could play at the park for an hour.

Rasha choked on her beer and quickly started looking for a solution. 'No, all the girls are staying over at Piyali's place. I will join them too.'

Her mother sighed. 'That means you are not coming home.'

'I will be back very early, maybe at 6.00 a.m. Will that do?'

'What can I say...'

'If I come in the morning, people will think I was at work all night...'

This line always had an effect of a soothing balm on her agitated mom.

Rasha often wondered how many working women in their late twenties had to actually give an explanation every time they went to a nightclub. She consoled herself thinking it had to be many. Bengali culture was truly dichotomous.

∾

She sat behind Zohaib on his bike. The roads were quite empty except for the taxis parked in a queue at the Gariahat junction. Some private cars were on the road and a few men were standing here and there chatting. A lone traffic policeman manned the booth at the Gariahat junction. As they turned left from the junction, Rasha's heart skipped a beat. She thought she saw the same black Santro parked on the left. She had noted the number in her head. The Santro had started crawling slowly behind the bike, but the speed-freak Zohaib was already miles ahead. So, she could not see the number. The next time she looked back, she could not spot the car.

On Saturday night, Park Street looked very different from the rest of the city. Although the restaurants lining either side of the road had rung the closing bell, the street was still bustling with people. Families with the satisfaction of a hearty meal written on their faces, men in business suits in a semi-drunken state and men with other people's wives or call-girls, thronged the sidewalks. But the serpentine queue of cars at the entrance to Park Hotel made it clear that the whole of Kolkata had come down to party there. Thankfully, they managed to zigzag through the bevy of posh cars on Zohaib's bike and found a parking space in the basement.

The entrance to the disco, manned by a mountain of a bouncer and a petite-yet-firm looking girl, looked chaotic. Groups of single men stood in anticipation of spotting some single women, who wouldn't mind walking through the doors of the disco with them. There were plenty of girls in the tiniest of skirts, who looked less than eighteen, hanging on the arms of thirty-something men, who wore their branded shirts and perfumes with elan. Everyone seemed to be talking at once. Their voices, mixed with the booming music blasting from the speakers inside, created a cacophony that enlivened Rasha's beaten spirit.

She often covered events at the hotels, so most of the staff knew her. She skipped the queue and dragged Zohaib to the front. She just brought her face to the girl's vision, who smiled and then nodded. Once inside the club, Rasha and Zohaib walked in to the greetings of their friends, who were comfortably seated on huge bean bags on the raised platform on the left. Rasha was already feeling better. DJ Aqeel had come down from Mumbai and was spinning heady beats on the turntable. He stood on the second-storey bridge that was meant to connect the strictly members-only lounge to the area that could be frequented by anybody—it was actually the bridge that was meant (or not meant) to connect the haves and the have-nots.

Rasha sat on a stool at the huge bar that was positioned in the middle of the disco and ordered a beer. While waiting for her drink, her eyes went to a sofa that stood in a dim corner right next to the bar. She saw the wife of a famous musician lip-locking with a man much younger to her. She didn't, in any way, want to be seen by the lady and get into an awkward situation. She had come to have fun and dreaded what would happen if the lady saw her. She would keep calling her asking her not to publish anything, not realizing that Rasha didn't intend to anyway. Rasha quickly got up and slid into the darkness behind a pillar. A third can of beer was all she needed to hit the floor and dance away the sudden changes in her workplace that she found hard to keep pace with. She convinced herself that the departure of an old boss and the arrival of a new one did not make any difference to her life. One had to be professional. But deep inside, she knew that there was one thing she would always miss—appreciation. Something Surit da was always generous with.

12

PIYALI GANGULY HANDED Rasha her fourth can of beer. 'I hope you will not be angry,' said Piyali.

Rasha was back from the dance floor and was grateful someone had vacated her favourite corner at the bar in Tantra.

'Is he here?' she asked.

'Yes.'

'How many cans did he buy?'

'He bought ten for ten of us,' giggled Piyali.

'You know this is not funny anymore,' said Rasha.

'He is loaded. He is not losing anything by buying all of us beer. And he is not asking you anything in return,' said Piyali.

'I am a bit worried. I spotted him near my office...' Rasha couldn't finish the sentence.

'Hi! Rasha,' said the man in question as he placed his legs on the bar stool *a la* Clint Eastwood. Piyali pulled back the high stool for him, winked at Rasha and left like the madam of a brothel does after striking a good deal between one of her girls and a client.

Rasha felt like throwing up the beer which she wished she hadn't already sipped and hitting her friend hard on the head with the beer can. Desi Clint Eastwood Vineet Agarwal, complete with the cowboy hat, was in his late twenties. He was balding viciously, but still preferred to keep his hair long enough so that it curled outwards at the nape. Just below the cowboy hat, he wore dark aviators but the only blemish on the nearly perfect get-up was the protruding paunch that threatened to tear out of his tight black Ed Hardy T-shirt. With Vineet, it had all started as a joke, but Rasha right now felt it was heading towards a possible disaster. Vineet had got friendly with their group at the nightclub and told her friends that he really liked Rasha. Her friends decided to take him for a ride and said they would introduce him to her if he bought them drinks. That he readily did.

When Rasha came to know about this, she was annoyed. But her friends shut her up by saying, 'We are getting free drinks yaar. He is a harmless chap, so be cool.'

Then the months passed and Vineet continued to buy the gang drinks and Rasha even devoured a few gallons herself. But she felt the sting of their joke when she spotted him in the vicinity of her office twice, in the last one week. He had purposely dodged her and looked away. She had thought she would tell her friends that this episode had to end, but before she could do that, here he was buying them drinks again and sitting next to her. Rasha had told Zohaib her fears that Vineet might be turning into a stalker. Sensing her discomfort, Zohaib pulled up another bar stool next to Rasha. Their eyes crossed and Zohaib knew Rasha was getting ready to grill Vineet.

'I saw you at Chowringhee last week. What were you doing there?'

'I live there. Actually, we have recently moved into an apartment there,' said Vineet sheepishly.

'What's your address?'

'I know your office is next to my apartment building.'

Oh my god! thought Rasha, *I just hope he does not turn up at my office, I just hope he doesn't end up waiting for me every day after work, I just hope…* Every stalker story she had read in the newspapers started invading her mind.

Zohaib was listening to the conversation with rapt attention.

'Why did you behave like you didn't know me when you saw me that day?' she charged him.

Now Vineet looked truly distressed. 'I can't talk to you near my house. I have a request, Rasha, you also should never talk to me. Please, please. If my father sees us talking, he would kill me. I belong to a very conservative family. We are not supposed to talk to girls, especially outside our community.'

He didn't look at Rasha, he kept looking at the beer can on the bar.

Before Rasha could ask him any further questions, the music suddenly became louder and the DJ announced that the greatest entertainment was about to begin.

Two Russian girls—with legs that refused to end and clothes that could pass off as beachwear—dashed down the rectangular bar top gyrating to the rhythm of the music. Rasha was too late to react to the girl coming her way. She managed to withdraw her fingers in the nick of time from under the six-inch golden heels that threatened to crush her bones. The girl probably realized what she was about to do, so to make amends she stopped. Rasha looked up at her infinite legs. Along with those blood-red lips, a crevice of a cleavage was smiling down at her. She leaned down sending the crowd around her into a tizzy and extended her long fingers to first touch the tip of Rasha's nose and then in the most erotic manner her lips. She mouthed the word 'sorry' and moved on.

Vineet had fished out his mobile and was making the most of the moment with his camera. Rasha wondered what his father would have said if he had seen him now. In fact, by now, she could feel the lecherous looks all the men around her were giving the Russian dancer. They all drew closer to the bar, hoping she would do the same to them, but Ghontachenko—that was her name, Rasha came to know later—was sensible enough not to create a mob frenzy and give the bouncers a hard time.

Rasha was still recuperating from Ghontachenko's amorous pet and Vineet's confession when Piyali plonked herself on the stool that Vineet had vacated.

'Don't look so flabbergasted, babe,' said Piyali. 'I went to an all-girls party at a nightclub last week. A stripper had been flown in from Mumbai. He poured chocolate sauce on himself and chose me to lick it off him on the bar top.'

'What? Did you do it?' asked Rasha impishly.

'Nah!' said Piyali flicking the ash from her cigarette into the ash tray. 'No way! Although he had a body like John Abraham, but I am sure he gets licked by a hundred women on a regular basis. I can't be one of them.'

Rasha looked happy with the answer.

'But did anyone else do?'

'Yeah, yeah! Lots of aunties were too keen. One heavyset was chosen. I tell you, Rasha, it looked so gross.'

'My Russian babe was heaven compared to your chocolate boy,' Rasha laughed.

'Trust me, girl, she was. Come, let's dance again,' said Piyali.

∾

Rasha was dancing with a group of four girls while the men in her group, including Zohaib, sat on the bean bags, their feet magnetized to the floor. She could feel she was drenched to her innerwear, but she didn't feel like letting the night go. Zohaib came and stood next to the floor calling Rasha over to him. She reluctantly went, thinking he was planning to leave for home.

In his efforts to be heard above the music, he shouted into Rasha's ears. 'Nisha wants me to call her now. I am going to look for a phone booth.'

Rasha pointed at his mobile phone. 'No balance,' he said. Rasha had some on her own, but no international call facility on it.

'I will go with you,' said Rasha. Zohaib nodded.

Nisha was Zohaib's girlfriend, who was studying in London

School of Fashion. Zohaib had met her at a fashion show for upcoming designers where he modelled her clothes. They had been in a relationship for six months now.

Rasha and Zohaib walked out of the hotel into the silent night. Park Street had finally gone off to sleep except for a few cab drivers who stood in front of the hotel hoping to find a good catch.

'Do you think Vineet was telling the truth?' Rasha asked Zohaib.

'I cross-checked with his friends when you were dancing. He has an autocrat of a father and he is perpetually scared that he would curtail his allowance if he gets to know about his way of life. So, I think you don't have any reason to worry. He was telling the truth.'

'Then why is he following us now and ducking behind a pillar at the moment?' said Rasha.

'What? That's a bit absurd,' said Zohaib instinctively looking back.

'You are right. I saw the cowboy hat.'

The fear of being stalked came back to Rasha, but she wasn't too worried since Zohaib was with her now.

'Anyway, tell me where will you find a phone booth open now?' she asked.

'There's a betel shop around the corner. The man has a landline that I can use.' The betel shop also doubled up as a one-stop shop for cigarettes, foreign chocolates, potato chips and an astonishing variety of condoms. Rasha stood at a distance, refusing to listen to Zohaib's conversation, although he insisted that she could.

'I am not going to have phone sex,' he laughed.

As she sat on the steps of a closed shop, she saw Vineet dart into a narrow dark lane between two residential buildings, still trying to be invisible.

She lit a cigarette and inhaled deeply. Then she froze. She saw the black Santro creeping in her direction. Despite her slightly tipsy state, she was sure it was the same number plate. Then she recognized the two men sitting in front.

Rasha threw away the cigarette, jumped on her feet and told Zohaib, 'Let's go.'

He was talking on the phone, but he could sense the urgency in Rasha's voice. So, he instantly hung up and started walking with her.

'We have to get into the hotel quickly,' she said.

She looked over her shoulder. The men had got out of the car and were walking towards them. 'Run!' Rasha shouted.

But she was too late. The next moment, she felt a cold metal touching her back through her sweat-soaked kurta. A voice said, 'Get into the car.'

Rasha looked to her left to see a tall, well-built man in a black T-shirt with an ugly scar that ran from the corner of his one eye, through the lips to the end of the chin. The deep wound, sewn up unevenly, had healed a long time ago, but had left an ominous mark on the face that made Rasha's blood curdle in fear. She thought of screaming and running, but the man was now holding her arm tightly and the other man held another gun behind Zohaib's back. Zohaib looked at Rasha with eyes wide open. The gun pressed harder on her back. She and Zohaib were pushed into the car and it got rolling.

The car left Park Street, took the Eastern Metropolitan (EM) bypass and then took a right turn into Salt Lake.

'Where are we going? What's happening?' asked Zohaib. Rasha just looked at him with fear-filled eyes. She couldn't speak.

'Where are they taking us? I can see this is Sector 5, the IT hub of Salt Lake.'

While one man drove, the other man with the scar on his face had his pistol trained on Rasha and Zohaib. He tightened his grip as soon Zohaib spoke. The car stopped. He brought out two handkerchiefs, rolled them and came to the rear of the car to blindfold Rasha and Zohaib. The other man, who was driving the car, now took his turn with the gun. They drove for a short distance, then the car stopped again and Rasha and Zohaib were pushed out of the vehicle. The silence all around was so deathly that the din of the crickets hammered on Rasha's ears like a thousand drums. The high that Rasha was revelling in an hour back had now given her a throbbing headache.

They were pushed inside, through what Rasha presumed to be a gate, and then she walked up a couple of stairs and went through another door. The man took off their blindfolds. The room was well lit and well decorated with large sofas, heavy maroon curtains and an expensive Kashmiri carpet. The wall-to-wall cabinet had a huge TV with a 60-inch screen and the shelves were stacked with VHSs and DVDs. Seeing the room, Rasha felt slightly better. She was half expecting to rot in a dingy dark room where rats would be walking over her like it happened to journalists in Hollywood movies.

'What has Vineet got us into,' thought Rasha. She realized soon enough how wrong she was.

∾

'Why have you brought us here?' asked Rasha mustering courage.

'You will soon know,' said the scarred man.

She thought of her mom, and then thought what a sensible idea it was to have told her she wouldn't be home that night. Or was it?

A short man in a red T-shirt and black trousers came to the room. Rasha and Zohaib were seated on a sofa and the man pulled up a chair in front of them. Then he looked at them with a half smirk.

He looked at Rasha. 'Do you want to vanish like Surit Basu?'

'What happened to him?' Rasha asked, feeling the panic-stricken droplets gathering on her forehead.

'Nothing. He's fine. But if you care for your mother, father, sister, then you will keep your pokey nose in place.'

He pulled on a pleasurable expression on his face. 'We have some lovely plans for you. You will really enjoy it.'

'Who are you working for?' she asked.

'See, you have started asking questions. Boss was right. You are one stubborn girl.'

'Who is your boss?'

'Do you want us to tie you up?'

They took away her bag and their mobile phones.

'How long do you plan to keep us here?' she asked.

'Boss will decide.'

The man in the red shirt left the room and closed the door. All this while, the two men who had brought them there, were standing next to the door. Their pistols had been put away though. Rasha's nimble mind had never before betrayed her so badly. She could not think of a single way of getting out of her high-security, plush prison. She looked at Zohaib, who looked strangely relaxed. A faint smile appeared in the corner of his lips. She raised her eyebrows, but he did not respond. She looked at her watch. It was 4.30 a.m.

'We are all set. Let's go,' said the man with the scar.

'Where?' asked Rasha. He didn't reply.

They stepped out of the drawing room into a hall and then were made to walk up the stairs that had an elegantly designed wooden banister. Rasha and Zohaib stepped into a large bedroom with a bed in the middle and four movie cameras standing mutely on four sides of the bed. Rasha couldn't believe her eyes. A few weeks back, she had interviewed a small-time actor who had been asked to go to a house for audition. They offered him huge money if he took part in a porn film, but when he refused, they locked him up in the bathroom. He managed to escape through the bathroom window. The man had described a similar set-up to her. And he told her it was a house near Salt Lake.

So did her kidnapping have something to do with the porn racket? she thought. She remembered the crime reporter's words earlier in the day. The droplets on her forehead felt cold and clammy.

Her thoughts were interrupted when the man in the red T-shirt came into the room and caught Zohaib completely unaware. He jabbed him in the arm with a syringe. Zohaib turned around and instinctively hit the man hard on the nose. He fell to the ground bleeding, but the other two men instantly caught hold of him and tied him to a chair. Rasha looked around the room and saw a camera tripod. She picked it up and whacked the scarred man on the back of his head just when he was finishing tying up Zohaib. The man hurtled backwards but he regained balance quickly and stood up. He pinned down Rasha to the bed with overwhelming strength and the other man tied her hands tightly to the wrought-iron bedstead. Rasha pulled her hands, but the rope only scraped her soft skin. She rested her head backwards in exhaustion. She couldn't think clearly. Zohaib was sitting on a chair opposite her with his hands tied behind him.

Finally, the man in the red T-shirt spoke. 'The injection will help him grow up,' he said, chuckling and pointing between Zohaib's legs. Blood had clotted where Zohaib had hit him. He was nursing his nose with a handkerchief.

'This is going to be a fun video, a journalist being raped by her friend. It will fetch a good price,' the man said.

Now Rasha was left in no doubt that she was in the same place from where the actor had escaped. She could feel horror crippling her entire body. Even nightmares were not made of what she had landed herself in. *Is this Ansh Ramchandani's way of venting his anger?*

She looked at Zohaib. His eyes lacked clarity and he looked a bit dizzy. Rasha had heard of performance enhancement injections used in blue films, but she was not sure if that was what Zohaib had been administered. But the more she looked at him, the more she felt he was losing his senses.

Harsh lights were switched on in the room and the three men set the cameras rolling. They unfastened Zohaib and brought him to the bed. He looked drugged. They instructed him to take off Rasha's kurta. She didn't scream, she didn't cry, she just stayed still. Zohaib also didn't move. The men prodded Zohaib with a whip. He crawled towards Rasha on the bed. Then he unsteadily straightened his body on his knees and took off his T-shirt but he tried to tell her something with his eyes. He dropped on all fours again and was on top of her. Rasha closed her eyes.

Somebody was banging on the door and the sound was deafening. 'Open the door!' the voice said. Zohaib instantly broke out into a drugged smile. The man standing on the other side of the door with four machine-gun wielding men was Saleem bhai.

The three men, who so far looked pleased with themselves, now looked terror-stricken.

'It worked,' Zohaib said.

'What worked?' she asked.

'Later!' whispered Zohaib. He tried to untie Rasha and one of Saleem bhai's guys came to help him out.

Saleem bhai looked at the man in the red T-shirt and said, 'Do you know this man here is my brother? I am shocked at your audacity.'

'How would we know he is your brother, Bhai?'

Bhai came towards Zohaib and gave him a big hug. 'I will fetch you from hell if you are in trouble.'

Bhai, who was in his late forties, was trendily dressed in a pair of ragged jeans and a casual red-and-navy-blue check shirt in a fashionable short length. He was not too tall with a slim and toned body, and his hair had a mohawk cut, coloured golden brown at the tips. A thick gold chain dangled around his neck and he wore a diamond stud in one ear. He had mean jaws, alert eyes and a sharp nose. In all, he looked more like the college punk than the underworld don that he was.

∾

Rasha had met Saleem bhai only once before. It was at a nightclub. He had ensured that the DJ emptied the dance floor for him and his flock of PYTs for half an hour. Rasha had found that an unnecessary show of power. Zohaib had introduced her to him then. The next moment, they came to know that Saleem bhai was footing the bill for their entire gang of friends for the rest of the night. The fact that she was downing beer on gangster money did make her uncomfortable, but she guzzled nevertheless. Days later, she came to know that Saleem bhai had been accused of murdering his wife and her boyfriend and was in jail.

'Can you do a story on all the social work he does? He supports the education of children in three slums in Kolkata. It might help him get bail,' Zohaib had asked her.

'No way! His case is very messy and I will land in trouble if I try to push his brand of philanthropism into my newspaper.'

Now she felt a bit ashamed that of all the people in the world, Saleem bhai had come to save her. Then she consoled herself by thinking: *He has actually come for Zohaib. I am just a latch-on.*

Saleem bhai turned to the man in the red T-shirt again, 'If you trouble them again, I will have all of your heads for dinner.'

The man nodded feebly. 'How were we supposed to know he is your brother?' he asked again.

Saleem Bhai now barked. 'Next time, do your research before taking on a job.'

He led Rasha and Zohaib out of the room, into the hall, out of the main gate and to freedom.

Rasha got into his Mercedes E-Class without a word. There were two Scorpios and one Tata Sumo packed with men, parked outside. Saleem bhai had come prepared for battle, Rasha could see that. She caught a glimpse of the first rays of the rising sun and looked at her watch. It was 6.00 a.m. She had been worrying stiff about her parents, but she was glad she would be able to just cut the deadline.

'Thank you, Saleem bhai,' she said.

He just waved his hand dismissively. 'Anything for Zohaib,' he said.

Rasha found Saleem bhai's cavalier attitude hard to swallow. Zohaib understood that and smiled at Rasha, trying to say, 'No offence.'

2

Zohaib had a very special relationship with Saleem bhai because of what happened on a particular winter night. Zohaib was returning from a fashion show at the Taj Bengal hotel on his motorcycle. It was really cold and late in the night. He took the deserted road next to the National Library, hoping to shorten his journey to his home in Gariahat. He saw a man standing with a bicycle waving at him frantically. Initially, he decided not to stop because that was a patch where robberies were rampant, but then he changed his mind. The man on the cycle was pointing to a man lying on the side of the road inside a bush.

'He is still alive. He wants to say something,' he told Zohaib.

Zohaib went near the body and saw the man's throat had been slit and he was lying in a pool of blood. He was trying to say something, but the words were not audible. All Zohaib heard was, 'I am Saleem.' Then he passed out.

Zohaib had rushed to the police station nearby and had seen to it that Saleem bhai was immediately hospitalized. After that, he had to face police interrogation for months because of Saleem bhai's underworld status. Finally, the police were convinced that he was just a passer-by and had no connection with the underworld.

Saleem bhai had survived and pledged his lifelong friendship to Zohaib for saving his life. Although bhai never told the police about the person who had left him in that state, he went for his own brand of revenge which landed him in jail later. The perpetrator was his wife's boyfriend, who was also a member of his gang. He had gone out for a drink with him. He mixed something in his drink, slit his throat and left him to die. Saleem bhai killed his wife and the man in a similar way.

Rasha shuddered when she thought about that. The man was ardent in loving and hating—he was as volatile as a Molotov cocktail. Rasha was glad that she was at the receiving end of neither of his emotions. But she was still baffled how he had got a whiff of what was going on in that house.

'Bhai, do you know who these guys are working for?' asked Zohaib.

'They are into the pornography business. But I am surprised why they decided to take the risk of abducting a journalist and her friend for one of their dirty films. It remains a mystery. I will dig into it later,' he said.

Despite the earlier snub from him, Rasha hauled up her body from the comfort of the black leather reclined Merc seat. 'How did you know we were there?' she asked.

'Ask your friend' was his nonchalant reply.

Rasha looked at Zohaib. 'Saleem bhai was the last person I had spoken to last night on my mobile. When these people came and pushed us into the car, I just pressed the redial key. Bhai listened to our entire conversation. You remember the scarred man was getting angry because I was constantly talking about the location…'

Zohaib stopped mid-sentence and turned to their saviour. 'But how did you know the exact location?' he asked.

'I didn't. I checked with my contacts for operators in Salt Lake and around. I came to know about two. I checked out on this one. If I hadn't found you here, I would have checked the other one.'

Zohaib had always been intelligent, but his presence of mind was what Rasha lauded at the moment. The car pulled up in front of Rasha's apartment building. Her heart was now thumping more than it had thumped when she was being abducted by menacing armed men and was on the verge of becoming a porn star. She hoped her parents and Rania would still be asleep. She took the elevator to their apartment and put the key in the latch. Often her parents sat on the couch in the drawing room waiting for her when she returned late, but thankfully, now it was empty and looked cosy and warm in the morning light.

Rasha peeped into all three bedrooms and saw to her satisfaction that her family hadn't woken up from their Sunday morning slumber. She tiptoed into the bathroom, brushed her teeth and washed her face. As she looked in the mirror, she saw the tired face of a girl who was tottering on the brink. Rasha was not religious and hardly went to the temple, but she believed in a supreme power as the creator of the universe, the power that had come to her rescue that day.

She suddenly felt desperate for her forty winks. She crept into the bed next to the soft body of her mother. She stirred. 'What's the time?'

'Early enough to sleep more,' replied Rasha, as she put her hand around her mother's waist. She had never felt so safe in her life. She slept like a baby.

An hour into her sleep, she woke up with a start.

Interlude

• • •

A sliver of sunlight made its way into the room through the curtains. The walls were white and Rasha was tied to a white bed. Zohaib was standing next to the bed, then she saw Arun next to him, then Saleem bhai's face came within her vision and then her father's face. As soon as she saw her father, she started screaming.

Rasha woke up. Since that incident, the white room came to her dreams often. Rasha lay in bed waiting for her heartbeat to normalize. She did not get out of the bed. There was no immediate necessity to wake up on time. Joblessness did have its virtues. She wouldn't have to report to work at 9.00 a.m. sharp. She ruminated over her past—a morning ritual she had been indulging in since she quit Silver Screen two months back.

Arun walked in with two cups of tea and Rasha's favourite choco caramel McVitie's Digestive biscuits. She rolled over as he placed the tray next to her on the bed and kissed her on the lips. Arun always made tea in the morning and they chatted over the hot brew talking about Kolkata, work, their travel plans and the plans for the weekend.

'I have to be in office early today. What do you plan to do?' asked Arun.

'Laze, surf, cook, clean,' said Rasha.

'Take it easy. If I had been you, I would have enjoyed the break. You are ending up dumping too much housework on yourself,' he said.

Rasha smiled. 'Why don't you pick up some clothes for me from Dubai Mall?' he said.

That was Arun's way of trying to push Rasha out of the house because he knew she was used to anything but life at home.

Finally, when she managed to pull herself out of her comfortable bed, she threw on a pair of jeans and T-shirt and stepped on the pedal of their BMW. Driving emptied her mind off all negative thoughts. She felt relaxed, almost tranquil.

Instead of going to Dubai Mall, she took a detour and hit the Jumeirah Road. It was unusually cloudy and there was forecast of rain. She parked her car next to a public beach on Jumeirah and walked barefoot on the sand. As the emerald waves caressed her feet and the sun played hide and seek atop the Burj Al Arab, Rasha felt despondent about the lack of dynamics in her own life.

Only one question troubled her—Was it worth leaving Kolkata?

Part 4
A New Turn

• • •

13

THE SCRUB IN Arun's hand was furiously making circles on the dishes in the kitchen sink. Rasha was standing at the kitchen door, dressed in a white sleeveless shirt and jeans. She had her snickers on. She was ready to walk out of the door.

'Come on, Arun, we are getting late. Everyone must be waiting for us at the picnic.' Her voice gave away her impatience.

'Just one plate left,' Arun held up the bubble-bathed plate. 'You know I cannot leave the house with dirty dishes stacked in the sink.' In the one month that Rasha had been in Dubai, she had realized that sharing the same roof with Arun was a totally different ballgame compared to sharing pizzas and momos on a date with him.

There was a totally different side to him that Rasha never imagined existed. The boy, who regularly walked into college in uncombed hair and muddy shoes, was a stickler for cleanliness at home. He would toss and turn in bed if the dishes were left in the sink overnight. He took great care to make the bed in the morning, and once he was done, it was hard to spot a single crinkle on the bed linen. His wardrobe was colour coordinated with the dark coloured clothes on one side, lighter ones on the other and he had different racks for summer, winter and evening wear. He liked the towels in the bathroom neatly arranged, the placement mats on the table in the right position, the sauces in the refrigerator to follow an alphabetical order and the kitchen, generally, spic and span. Thankfully, he did not expect Rasha to do all the cleaning; he did everything himself and seemed to enjoy it. He always hummed a happy tune whenever he did housework. After he came back home from work, he spent at least half an hour dusting the entire house. He claimed that that helped him to de-stress as did ironing clothes, which he did at least three times a week.

He told Rasha that in his growing-up years, he was expected to keep the house in order before his working parents came home. At that time, it was his job to organize a team of three servants, but now that he was on his own, he wanted that same order. So, he did it himself.

Rasha, on the other hand, was used to dumping her worn clothes on a chair in her bedroom from where her mom took over. Her mom put away her clothes for washing and ironing, organized her wardrobe and even her room. After she cleaned up her study table, Rasha would complain that she can't find her books and notes. When the maid didn't turn up, it was Rania who helped her mom with the housework, Rasha was never expected to do it. So, once on her own in Dubai, Rasha struggled to keep her wardrobe tidy. Because of Arun's cleanliness mania, she felt a bit ashamed to leave her clothes lying around; so she dumped them in the wardrobe, but soon they threatened to tumble out the moment the doors were opened. Finally, Rasha was forced to arrange her wardrobe on a regular basis. She managed to cope with it too. But there were times she would get irritated with Arun.

For instance, right now she just saw it pointless doing the dishes and getting late in the process. According to her, this was something that could be easily done later.

Arun dried his hands in the red-and-white checkered kitchen towel and lovingly put it back on the hook. He opened the shoe cabinet and brought out his shoes. Rasha looked at her watch.

While tying the shoe laces, something caught his eye.

'There is dust on the TV screen,' he said.

'I will knock your head off with the duster if you bring it out now,' Rasha threatened.

'Okay, okay. I am leaving.' Arun gave in.

'Really, Arun, I don't understand how you came to college looking like that when you keep your home so clean.'

'What do you mean by looking like that?'

He tickled her waist.

She wiggled. 'You never combed your hair, I am sure.'

'Wrong. I always did. Then I messed it up by running my fingers through it to give me that unkempt look.'

He ran his fingers through his hair. 'I am doing it right now. Don't I look good?'

'Anyway you noticed my hairstyle, didn't you? So, my unkempt look was after all attractive.'

Rasha gave him a disgusted look. Then grabbed him by his nape and pulled him close to her. She kissed him.

'Well, on second thoughts, you do look good,' she said.

They got out of the lift and got into the car.

'Rasha, I really don't know, why you always choose the lift to show your affection.'

'I really don't know, but the lift does something to me.' She giggled.

∾

There were at least eight families at the picnic, but Rasha knew only two well enough. The rest she had met for the first time that day, although Arun knew all of them. Some of them were Arun's colleagues and some were friends of friends, who belonged to the common group.

She looked at Arun. He was in his beach shorts and T-shirt, helping the men at the barbeque oven. Their kiss in the lift came back to her. She felt a tingle on her skin. She compared the Arun in khaddar kurtas to this Arun in beach shorts and branded shoes and laughed to herself. Dubai had done him good. He had more time on his hands to hit the gym and also to swim. He looked fitter than ever before. And to Rasha's delight, he had started taking an interest in his own wardrobe too.

Rasha felt relaxed. Something she hadn't felt in a long, long time. The ambience helped too. Mamzar Park, where the picnic was being held, was a beautiful park with a beach, something that she had never seen before. Rasha stood in front of a small red building with a clearing in front that had a barbeque oven in one corner and a long white table with two benches lined next to it. The building was actually a stand-alone air-conditioned room designed like a Swiss chalet with a sliding roof. It had been hired for the day for the picnic. Inside, it had a settee, some chairs, a small dining table, a kitchen area and a small washroom with a shower and a washbasin. The building was located inside Mamzar Park that had lush green trees, manicured lawns and virgin sands that slithered into the blue sea.

She took a place on a white bench in front of an inward creek that ran around the chalet. The high waves lashing on the rocks sprayed her face with salt water. She watched the jet skis gliding on the waves as the tall buildings of the emirate of Sharjah kept a close watch on the park from the other side. She thought a setting could not have been more blissful.

Rasha was madly in love with the sea. From Kolkata, she had been to the favourite resort of Bengalis—Puri in Orissa, at least six times; and Shankarpur and Mandarmani, the ones closer to home, were her weekend retreats. She had been to Goa, to Vishakapatnam, to Chennai's Marine beach and to Pondicherry, just to experience the sea. Now the sea had come to her. It took just a drive of fifteen minutes from her home to reach the beach and thirty minutes to reach Mamzar Park.

From where she sat, Rasha had a clear view of the beach too.

She watched children making sand castles and a group of girls in abaya and sheyla bathing in the sea, completely at ease next to the bikini-clad European women swimming close by. A couple of Indian women were splashing around with a few children. They were in swimming costumes that ended in frock-like frills. An elderly lady in a saree, presumably South Indian because she had a garland in her hair, was giving a bath to a toddler. The beach wasn't too crowded. Some young men were engrossed in beach basketball and Rasha shamelessly marvelled at their six packs. Another couple sat under a thatched umbrella, the man giving a rigorous suntan massage to the woman. Everyone was lost in their own little world.

Rasha was lost in hers too. A number of thoughts clouded her mind, but she tried hard to push them all aside. She had told Arun about her abduction, but chose to leave out all the gory details of that night—especially the part about her and Zohaib being almost forced into a porn video. She just couldn't bring herself to telling him anything. She wasn't comfortable. As such, after hearing what had happened Arun had wanted to take the next flight out to Kolkata. It had taken a lot of convincing on her part to keep him in Dubai.

Rasha looked at Arun lovingly. He was putting the marinated chicken in the barbeque skewers and saying something that was not audible to Rasha over the sound of the waves, but she could see that everyone around him was bursting into peals of laughter with every word he uttered. Arun's subtle sense of humour came from his intelligence. There were times people did not get his punchlines, but when they did, they laughed till their insides ached.

Arun felt Rasha's eyes on him and waved at her. He thought she looked picture perfect sitting on that bench, her curly hair making waves in the wind. She hadn't applied any make-up on her supple skin and he felt she always looked her best that way. He was happy about her decision to join him in Dubai. Although what led to the decision was unpleasant and Arun could sense her frustration of leaving a career behind that had been painstakingly built on sheer hard work. But he had missed her immensely in the last six months—missed her wise words, her laughter, her touch—so he was glad she was right there in front of him now, to admire and love.

Arun called out to Rasha, 'The sausages are getting cold. Come quickly.'

She walked across the green grass and stood next to him. He fondly put his arms around her shoulders.

'I was just telling them about my house-hunting experience here,' said Arun.

'Oh! Gosh. That is indeed a story,' said Rasha.

Arun continued the monologue. 'After walking around Karama for eight hours in the blazing sun, I hadn't found a single accommodation. My last hope was an advertisement in the newspaper and that's where I was headed to. The ad was for a studio apartment. I saw myself standing in front of a dilapidated building and knocked on the door of an apartment. A man opened the door and showed me around. The studio looked worn but spacious with a separate kitchen and balcony. I thought it would do for the moment. The man was subletting it and asked for two months rent that was quite a steep sum of Dhs 8000 (approx Rs. 90,000). As I was dishing out the amount, another man peeped in through the door. When he was told that I had already taken it, his eyes penetrated into me like a sharp dagger. I perfectly understood his feelings. He had probably walked the area longer than me.'

Arun stuffed his mouth with a slice of barbecued pomfret as everyone listened in rapt attention. 'I moved from my company accommodation of a five-star hotel to this studio. Three days later, when I went to the grocery next door, the man behind the counter informed me that the house would be pulled down next month and a new one would be built in its place. I went and checked the small print on the notice board that was almost impossible to pick out amidst the many other notices that were put up there. The man was absolutely right. So, I went back to house hunting again.'

Arun took a sip from a can of Pepsi and continued. 'I found my current apartment quickly enough, but the biggest obstacle was retrieving the one month's rent from that man who had rented me the apartment. I confronted him with the truth. He refused to relent and instead said it would be pulled down only the following year. I said I didn't want to stay on and wanted a month's rent returned. He refused to relent. I started badgering him with phone calls saying I didn't have any money because I was new in Dubai and would starve if he didn't return my money. Finally, he softened and agreed to meet me at a dosa joint.'

'What happened then?' someone asked from the group.

'I went to meet him in an unshaven state, trying my best to look tired and emaciated. Then he asked me if I had lunch. I lied to him that I was only on water since morning. He ordered a thali for me and one for himself. I found it hard to go through the contents of the thali because chilli chicken and fried rice from my office cafeteria were already swimming inside my stomach. He returned my money, but I forgot my sunglasses on the table when I left. Next day, he called me to say he had it and he could come to my new place to return it. When I opened the door, you should have seen his face. One look at my apartment and he instantly knew I was fibbing all the time.'

To this, everyone laughed, including Rasha.

'But it didn't end there. He looked around my empty apartment like a real estate agent and said, "Why does a single man need such a big apartment? You should sublet the sitting room and stay in the bedroom. There are two bathrooms anyway. I can get you some tenants, just give me a good commission."'

~

Rasha knew Arun's initial months in Dubai were a struggle. It was especially hard for him since unlike Rasha, whose background was strictly middle class because her father had retired from his teaching job in a college a long time back and never went for private tuitions after that and her mother was a housewife, Arun had grown up in the lap of luxury. His parents were well-known doctors in Kolkata and they were the owners of a four-storey house with a huge lawn in a posh area of Alipore.

Rasha, however, knew nothing of his financial status till he took her to meet his parents. Rasha realized that Arun actually had a floor to himself, complete with a table tennis board and a gym. No one could have imagined that the same Arun, who always took a public bus to college, wore the same three kurtas day-in and day-out, actually went back home to tone up in his own gym.

When she stepped in through their front door for the first time, Rasha was pretty shocked at the opulence that his Alipore home stood for.

'You never told me that you have so much money?' she said.

'What would you have done then?' asked Arun.

'Not agreed to marry you probably,' she teased him.

'That's the reason I didn't tell you,' he laughed.

'These are the results of my parents' hard work and not mine. When my own hard work pays off, I will tell you.'

During his first few months in Dubai, Arun survived on instant noodles for dinner and slept with the rats playing hide-and-seek below his bed in his run-down studio. He would dream of his comfortable bed in his huge bedroom in Kolkata and think of all the lip-smacking dishes their cook of twenty-five years, Kashi da, made. He dreamt of playing with his dog, Snowy, every morning in his garden and dreamt of his gym where he worked out every evening with his father, engaging in man-to-man talks with him. One night, he woke up with excruciating pain. A rat had ventured into his bed and bitten his left toe. He had to rush to the hospital to get rabies shots.

He enjoyed his work though, in a top-notch real estate firm, and became friendly with his colleagues. All his colleagues had struggled to get a foothold in the Dubai sand, so they were all compassionate towards his initial experiences. 'These days will pass,' they assured him.

Arun soon found out that they were right. The days passed really quick. After the first hurdle of finding a nice home, the next one was getting a driving license. Although he often drove in Kolkata, he failed the first five driving tests in Dubai and passed only at the sixth attempt. Every time it would be some small mistake like not looking into the rear-view mirror well enough while changing a lane, taking too long at a roundabout or speeding too much after the traffic signal turned green. After every failure, he would have to return to his driving school for some more classes and he felt like he was becoming less of a man when he had to face his instructor. His ego had never been bruised so badly.

When he was waiting to be called for his sixth test, a man came and sat next to him with a wide grin. 'I passed today,' he told Arun.

'First try?' Arun asked.

'Are you crazy? Eleventh.'

This man's words had the effect of Asterix's magic potion on Arun's taut nerves. That day, he drove with all his heart. When the examiner told him, 'You pass!' he couldn't believe his ears. He almost collapsed with relief.

The next day, he bought a second-hand BMW, on distress sale, from a Lebanese expatriate leaving town. The deal he got was awesome. He paid with some cash from his pocket and for the rest he took a bank loan. Arun had arrived in Dubai only four months ago, but he had already earned enough to have a home in a good locality, buy a BMW and he had managed to save some money too. Arun was happy with his small achievements in this new country. And he was happy to be inching closer to his real dream. He wanted to build a home for destitute children in Kolkata. Starting from his first pay, he had been putting away money every month to realize his dream.

Arun had landed in Dubai at a time when the success of this emirate in the UAE had reached its zenith. The real estate business was flourishing incredibly, making the players in the field millionaires overnight. The construction cranes in the horizon outnumbered the stars in the sky. Every day, almost eight hundred people were making Dubai their home, filling in the employment gaps in industries such as hospitality, medical, aviation, PR and, of course, construction. This pushed the rents sky-high, but people didn't mind shelling out hideous amounts because they all wanted to realize their dreams. And they all believed Dubai was the rocket that would take them to the moon they were aiming for.

∾

The full moon was coming out of the sea. Its reflection created a silver line in the water and an ethereal ambience. Rasha and Arun sat on the beach at Mamzar Park with their fingers intertwined. The food at the picnic had turned out to be hedonistic. Rasha had cooked malai prawns. The other dishes included mutton curry, pulao, paneer butter masala and kheer. These had all been brought by Arun's friends' wives along with the marinated chicken and fish.

Rasha always had a penchant for cooking, if not housework. But apart from an occasional sweet-and-sour chicken or some momos that happened over a gap of six months, Rasha hardly got the time to cook in Kolkata. In Dubai, she seemed to have regained her culinary skills. She promptly borrowed cook books from her new haunt, the amazingly stocked local library, Book World. Rasha's repertoire stretched from Bengali dishes to pasta and desserts and Arun actually ended up chucking the rest of the instant noodles packets into the dustbin because he couldn't stand their sight anymore.

Rasha thoroughly enjoyed the company of Arun's friends at the picnic. They were all Bengalis settled in Dubai for a long time. They discussed with Rasha the new restaurants that had come up in Kolkata, the new malls, the new Bengali films and the new actresses in Bengali serials. The ladies were more devout followers of the soaps than any Kolkata housewife could be, but unlike most Kolkata housewives, they bought diamonds at the drop of a hat, holidayed in exotic locales in Europe and Africa and were the owners of luxury apartments in swanky properties in Kolkata. The apartments had been under lock and key, but they hoped to live there when they returned home eventually. And no, they didn't know when exactly they would return.

～

Social life could be quite hectic in Dubai, Rasha realized. Almost every weekend there were inivitations to parties, picnics, dinners or even after-dinner nightouts. Rasha enjoyed these outings, but she longed for a stay-at-home weekend with Arun, lazing on their couch and watching movies back-to-back.

But that had to wait. They were expected to attend the birthday party of Ankita Bagchi, wife of Hiran Bagchi, a recent acquaintance of Arun, to be held on a boat at the Dubai Creek. The boat that Hiran Bagchi had hired was a typical Arabic dhow, a two-storey marvel with the lower deck being an air-conditioned dining room while the upper deck was an open space set with tables, candles and snacks.

Dubai looked lovely in the evening breeze. All the buildings on either side of the creek were lit up beautifully; and the water of the creek, which reflected on the glass façade of some of the buildings, created an unearthly charm. The reflection on the convex sail-shaped façade of the Emirates Bank building was particularly mesmerizing.

The majestic white yachts docked on either side of the creek added to the dazzle on the water. There were some more dhows decked in strings of bright yellow lights, plying across the evening waters. Most of the dhows had the usual mix of tourists and residents. But none of the boats had as much din as theirs. The DJ was playing music in full blast and the entire party had shifted from the upper deck to the lower deck. Rasha quickly found her footing on the dance floor and let her hair down. Arun joined her and soon heads started turning in their direction. They did make a great dancing couple.

Birthday girl Ankita Bagchi was not a part of this happy commotion. She sat on the now-empty upper deck, nursing her glass of wine. It was her forty-fifth birthday, but thanks to regular yoga and a strict diet, she looked much younger and hardly the mother of a fourteen-year-old. She wore a silk saree that her husband had especially bought for her from the famous Nallis located in Dubai's Meena Bazar. She absent-mindedly fiddled the 22-carat solitaire on her shapely fingers, as she mulled over a life gone by.

From the time she had set her eyes on Rasha, she had felt a restlessness she had not experienced for a long time. She had been resigned to her plush-yet-mundane life in a swanky villa at the man-made palm-shaped island better known as Palm Jumeirah. Every morning, she welcomed the sea at her doorstep as she prepared tea sitting on the porch overlooking their private beach. Her husband jet-setted round the world in his high-profile job as the CEO of a very successful business firm, while she stayed home bringing up her daughter and often socialized with Dubai's swish set. But she missed the madness of the newsroom, memories of which Rasha had immediately brought back the moment she walked into her life. Ankita felt Rasha was everything that she was fifteen years ago. As the editor of the women's magazine *Winds of Change,* life for Ankita was a constant source of excitement. The magazine had humble beginnings in Kolkata with focus on beauty and fashion. But when Ankita had stepped in as the editor, she brought relevant issues to the fore, tackling topics like eve-teasing, domestic violence and rape. It carried information that would empower all women with basic facts about monetary investment, handling a teenage daughter, or dealing with in-laws in an extended family. The magazine started selling like hot cakes and Ankita single-handedly scripted a success story that very few women could ever dream of.

From the dizzying heights of a dream career, Ankita was brought down to reality with a thud when she was faced with a difficult pregnancy that relegated her to bed for months. Post-childbirth, the lady who spent more than half her day at work, was suddenly intent on reaching home early. The management of her company was anything but supportive of her efforts to balance motherhood and a demanding work schedule. They started dropping hints that either Ankita put in as much time in the magazine as she did before or quit.

To her chagrin and her husband's immense relief, she finally decided to take a break. But the break extended to thirteen years and Ankita had almost forgotten about her triumphant stint as the editor of a magazine when Rasha suddenly surfaced and tore open the raw flesh below an old wound that she had tried hard to bury under the rubble of her career aspirations. Ankita had never met Rasha before, but she had always admired her byline in *Our Times,* the newspaper she regularly read on the internet and subscribed to every time she went to Kolkata. She secretly admired the girl's penchant for hard-hitting articles. But when she met the same girl in flesh and blood, she hated her. Ankita was pretty surprised with her own emotional yo-yo.

~

Dancing was over and the dinner gong was sounded. Ankita's eyes searched for Rasha as she took the stairs to the lower deck. Rasha was in a sleeveless, red salwar kurta with muted gold sequins. She wore flat gold chappals. She didn't have any jewellery on and her eyes and lips were the only places with a hint of make-up. Next to her, Ankita felt like a Christmas tree. She had got her make-up and hair done professionally, was wrapped from head to toe in diamonds, including a diamond hair pin.

Is it her youth and beauty that I am jealous of? Ankita thought. She instantly ticked off the possibility.

Rasha was sitting at one of the tables, close to Arun. Two ladies were sitting opposite them and as Ankita approached them, she overheard them asking, 'Rasha, have you met Shah Rukh Khan?'

She nodded in the affirmative, but didn't speak since her hands were working adroitly on a piece of tandoori chicken.

Ankita stood in front of her quietly. 'And Salman and Aamir?' asked another lady.

'I have met almost all of them for interviews,' was Rasha's nonchalant reply.

When she said this, Ankita looked for a trace of arrogance, but she saw that Rasha was more interested in the chicken than in the conversation. The lady's husband was standing next to them now.

'And which one was your most dangerous assignment?' he asked.

'It was a story that landed me in the most dangerous situation,' Rasha said.

That was when Ankita managed to pinpoint the precise reason for her hatred for this girl. Rasha was still a journalist with a bag full of current news, while she felt like a forgotten fossil.

'Tell us about the story,' the man said.

Now, Rasha was not sure if she wanted to talk about that fateful night when she was abducted.

14

~

SURIT BASU TRIED hard to listen to the voices outside. But all he could make out was some muffled sounds. He was lying on a bed. He didn't bother to raise an alarm because nobody would be able to hear him anyway. The wall and the ceiling of the room were heavily padded to make it soundproof and then covered with luscious white silk.

The bed he was lying on was a comfortable one, covered with expensive linen. There were no windows in the room and two film cameras stood on stands at the foot of the bed. An elegant stand lamp on the side of the bed was the only source of light, although he could see two lights used on film sets standing in the shadows. The room gave him a sense of deja vu, but he could not think of where he had seen it. Or had he read about it? He was unsure.

His mouth had gone dry and he could not remember how long he had been lying there. After the muffled sounds stopped, the silence felt more deathly than the hopelessness of his situation. So much had happened in his life in the last two days that his mind was a swirl of thoughts. He had been happily looking at mobile phones when the HR head had called him to her room.

'Sumana had mentioned in her exit interview that you were sexually harassing her, but we did not pay any heed to it because she was leaving the organization. We thought she was just trying to malign you,' she said.

'You are right. She was trying to malign me. I am not that kind of a man. You should know.' He smiled smugly at the HR head.

'But we are not that sure anymore. She has sent us a video

that will force us to set up a committee to investigate the whole matter according to the Supreme Court's directive on dealing with sexual harassment at the workplace,' she said.

'What video? What the hell are you talking about?'

She turned her laptop towards him and tapped on the play button. Surit had never been more shocked in his life. His expression went from disgust to shame to fear and finally embarrassment because the lady HR head also had her eyes on the screen and was scrutinizing every twitch of his face from the corner of her eyes.

He realized that when he was down with malaria, Sumana had come to see him with a hidden camera. She had not only recorded the first bit where she was sitting next to him in the nude, but there was a lot more to the video. She had positioned herself with her back to the camera and ensured that Surit's unconscious face was not visible.

He was enraged. 'She drugged me. She had come to see me because I was ill and she must have drugged me with the coffee she made for me.'

'Can you prove it?' she asked.

Surit bit his lips. No he couldn't. He sat there silently.

'This is a serious matter and if this is what you have been doing, we cannot let you function as the editor. I would suggest you take leave for sometime till the investigation is complete,' she said.

Surit's face flushed with anger. 'You don't believe me, right? And you plan to humiliate me by forcing me to take leave and then slam this bullshit enquiry on me.'

She kept quiet.

'Have you forgotten *Our Times* is the best newspaper today just because of me?'

She looked at him with a cool-as-cucumber expression. 'Surit, we value your contribution. But this is a very serious allegation backed by evidence. We have to look into it. If this video goes to other media houses, they will be after us. You calm down. We will surely get to the bottom of this.'

Surit had stood up, but sat down again. 'How will the newspaper come out if I go on leave for an indefinite period?' he said with concern.

She put her elbows on the table and cupped her face with both her hands and then smiled a smile that most HR heads practice in their bathroom mirrors.

'In your entire career, have you ever seen a newspaper failing to meet the deadline because of the absence of a member of the team—be it the editor or the peon who distributes tea?'

Surit could feel the aching veins in his temples. *How dare she talk to me like that?* he thought.

'Fine. I am putting in my resignation right now. I am not going to take this f*****g shit,' he said.

He had half expected her to coax him to calm down again, but all she did was give him a blank A4 and her Cross pen. He wrote his resignation and walked out of the office.

'You had misbehaved with an intern of a newspaper at a party recently. Hadn't you?' The HR head said as he was about to shut the door behind him.

He turned around with eyes that could char her.

'I suppose I don't owe you an explanation since I don't belong to this organization anymore.'

Once in his car, he typed the message to his team: 'I have put in my resignation. I have left the office and please don't call me right now. I have to gather my thoughts.'

∾

He had spent a long time sitting on a bench overlooking the Ganges. The sun was setting, bathing the river and the surroundings in a lovely yellow hue. Surit looked at the Howrah Bridge and the oar boats passing below it—the backdrop of so many Bengali and Hindi films. The serenity of the view calmed him a bit as he thought of his parents, who used to bring him to the strand on Sundays and bought him ice cream from the roadside vendors. They gave him ten paisa to shoot balloons with air guns.

Now the ice cream vendors and the air gun man sat with a bored expression as most of the people disembarking from the cars went inside Scoop to savour ice cream and pizza and the view of the Ganges along with Bollywood beats blaring from the overhead speakers. Seeing couples walking hand in hand, he missed Gia. He felt his life had collapsed like a pack of cards and the two things he lived and was prepared to die for—his workplace and his girlfriend—had decided to turn their back on him.

He thought of Sumana. He could never imagine such malevolence was lurking inside that young girl with limited acumen and fluttering eyelids.

I should have done her that day. Then, at least, there would have been some satisfaction, his irate mind thought.

Surit knew Sumana was angry with him due to the leave issue. She had sulked for days squarely blaming him for the break-up with her boyfriend. She had even gone to his room one day when the department was empty and with tear-filled eyes accused him.

'If you had let me go on this holiday, my best friend wouldn't have bagged my boyfriend. I just hate you,' she had said. He was dumbstruck at her emotional outburst, but preferred not to say anything and hoped she would get over it.

She seemed to have bounced back and was faring quite well at work.

The human mind is a bottomless pit, Surit told himself, *and I have found that out the very hard way.*

He left the strand for home. He could not imagine telling

Rasha what had happened because he thought she would finally be sure that she had the most stupid man as her boss. His ego stopped him vehemently.

He called Sumana instead. 'Hi Surit da. How are you?' she giggled.

'I am very well. Thank you for making me the hero of a porn film. But can you please tell me what made you do that?'

She giggled again. 'Actually, my boyfriend is very angry with you.'

'Really? I thought you had broken up with him?'

'No. No. This is a new one.'

'And what did I do to anger him?'

'Arrey, Surit da, that story you did with that bitch, Rasha. It has landed him in a lot of trouble. So he just wanted me to fix you. I did that. I hear you have left your job. Is it true?'

'Yes, Sumana, how can the hero of such a great film continue as the editor, a job meant for lesser mortals.'

Sumana giggled. Surit wasn't sure if she understood his sarcasm. 'But tell me, which story are you talking about?' he asked.

'That porn racket story.'

'What does it have to do with him?'

'It shut down his business and the authorities gave him a lot of trouble.'

'Your boyfriend is a porn star?' he asked.

Sumana sounded dead serious. 'No. No. His company shoots those films and sells them abroad.'

Surit felt that somebody had taken a bag of ice and slammed it on his spine. The name, he needed the name.

He tried hard to stick to the same tone. 'And, dear, what is your boyfriend's name?'

The two second of silence on the other end felt like an hour. 'Ansh will kill me if I tell you.' She hung up.

Surit Basu called his detective friend next. 'In half an hour's time, can you give me details of a guy named Ansh who is big time into the porn racket in Kolkata?'

'Are you talking about Ansh Ramchandani?'

A bell tinkled in Surit's head. 'I am not sure. But isn't Ansh Ramchandani the nouveau rich hotelier and producer? What connection can he have to a porn racket?'

'I know for sure he is into the high-society call-girl racket and I have heard that people pay through their noses to be a part of his wild parties. I will check out the porn bit.'

The detective called back in ten minutes. 'My source says that he is definitely into the porn racket. But he is lying low at the moment because of some article that came out in your newspaper. Apparently, he had to shell out millions to politicians to keep the police from arresting him. Why, what happened? Can I help you in any way?'

'I will tell you if I need help.'

The next day, Surit made an appointment with the police commissioner. He had met the commissioner at a couple of parties and felt that he was an honest and educated gentleman who would be able to address his woes. Surit was adamant that he would not let some stray Ansh Ramchandani and a giggle-head like Sumana trample his career. Although he had an offer in Bangkok that he planned to take up anyway because there was no question of going back to the ungrateful *Our Times*, he wouldn't leave Kolkata before settling the score.

When Surit stepped out of his house at 6.00 p.m. that day, he noticed two men, especially a man with a menacing scar, standing in front of the gate of his apartment building. His driver hadn't turned up for work that day, so Surit stepped on the sidewalk to hail a cab. Before he could understand what was happening, the man grabbed him by his shoulder and pushed him into a waiting

Santro. He didn't utter a word because he felt the nozzle of a gun pushed deep into his neck. They pushed him face down in the leg space of the back seat. Surit found it hard to breathe, but he stayed still. After a drive, he was shoved through the door of a palatial villa and locked up in a room on the first floor.

A man in a red T-shirt came to the room. 'So you were planning to meet the police commissioner?'

Surit's eyes revealed what he thought. 'We know everything. We have been keeping track of your moves and tapping every call. Sir loves to play these games. It's his hobby.'

'Sir?'

'Ansh Sir!'

'Why is he after me?'

'You are not the only one. He's finished so many people. In fact, you are just a small fry. He has fixed big police officers, politicians and businessmen,' he said proudly.

'That article you published landed him in a lot of trouble. It took him a lot of money and influence to remain in business. But he took care of everything,' he said.

'Then what's the problem?'

The man didn't answer this question.

Surit prodded further. 'What do you plan to do with me?'

'We are waiting for orders. Right now, we are going to get Rasha Roy. We were expecting her to react after we sent her a message from your mobile phone about you leaving town, but she hasn't responded yet.'

'But why her?'

'Boss wants her picked up. We don't ask questions.'

Surit wished he had not got so excited about Rasha's findings about a porn racket a few weeks back. He wished he had not gone digging for more information himself and positioned the story as an exposé and then forgotten all about it after it hit the news-stands.

The man in the red T-shirt left the room leaving Surit sitting on the bed. It was clear that this move to kidnap him was triggered by his bid to meet the police commissioner. Strangely, he felt no fear, only resignation of being sent to the gallows twice over. Stripped off forty lakhs by the woman he loved, conned into a video by a woman he had not given a second look and enticed into an exposé by a woman whom he held in very high regard. Surit laughed to himself thinking what strange roles women had come to play in his life.

I would not be surprised if a woman walks me to deliverance now. Who is it going to be? he thought.

He looked around the room for the umpteenth time. Finally, he remembered. The room fitted the description in the article written by Rasha after she interviewed the actor, who had escaped from being forced into a porn film.

And journalists think they can change the world. Stupid! For starters, nothing has changed about this room, he thought.

He could hear a faint commotion outside, but didn't bother to strain his ears. He had mentally relegated himself to his silk prison for quite a while, although he felt really hungry now. Suddenly, the door opened and four men walked in with machine guns. Rasha stepped in behind them alongside another man who wore his hair in bizarre gold spikes.

The four armed men and the gold-spiked man entered and exited with the speed of a squall and took Surit Basu with them. Only when they were in the car did Rasha ask, 'Are you okay?'

He nodded and smiled. 'How did you manage this?'

'It's a long story. I was in that room next to you last night. But we have to thank Saleem bhai for everything,' Rasha said with a tired smile.

She pointed at the man sitting in the front seat of the Scorpio. 'Pardon me. I forgot to introduce you,' she said.

Saleem bhai was much more forthcoming in accepting Surit's gratitude than he was with Rasha's the same morning. But she had to admit that Saleem bhai did go out of his way to save them. Rasha was sure that he was far superior to Ansh in the power game. Unlike Ansh, he wasn't hiding his true self under the veneer of snazzy suits and respectable status. On the contrary, he was an open book—blatant and potent.

~

On their way back from that house in Rajarhat, traffic was pretty thick on EM bypass, although it was a Sunday afternoon. The cars had halted at a traffic light. A Scorpio full of dangerous-looking men and a lone girl drew some curious glances. Otherwise everyone else—in their posh Hondas, Hyundais, Chevrolets and a few Marutis—were busy in their own air-conditioned comfort. A lone Ambassador stood at a distance as a reminder of India's attempt and success at indigenous auto manufacture.

Rasha noticed a man peering from behind the wheel of an adjacent car.

'Oh no, not now!' She looked the other way and wished her shades would protect her identity. The man was her next-door neighbour and her dad's good friend. She hoped to keep this whole incident a closely-guarded secret if she wanted to have any amount of freedom left and keep her parents' blood sugar and blood pressure levels in check. She prayed the man had not recognized her. If he went and told her dad that he had spotted his daughter with five dangerous-looking men in a Scorpio, the interrogatory missiles that would be launched by her parents would be deadlier than the actual mess she had landed herself in that night.

As such, she had rushed out of home barely an hour after she had walked in after a 'night of revelry' at Tantra. She was half asleep when the incidents of the night came back to her like a bad dream. She had seen something there and had been disturbed about it, but somehow could not recollect what it was. In her semi-somnolent state, she saw the shoes—the pointed patented leather shoes in brown. Her eyes immediately flew open and she sat upright on her bed.

The shoes she had seen outside a door when she was being taken to the first floor room by Ansh's thugs belonged to Surit da. It could not be anyone else's. It was a pair of ultra-fashionable limited edition Alexander McQueen shoes that he had got from a trip to Paris. To his immense annoyance, his style-challenged colleagues had pulled his leg about his fashion forward feet when he wore the pair to work.

Rasha was now sure that Surit da had not gone anywhere, he was being held captive in the same house. She rushed to Zohaib's house, but by then the shot he had been given hours before in captivity had started acting and he had slipped into a drugged sleep. He refused to wake up even after Rasha poured water on him. She stood there biting her lower lip. She needed a solution quickly and it had to be Saleem bhai. He knew the place and had the power to wrangle out Surit da from the clutches of his kidnappers. She took Zohaib's phone, found his number and called him.

Initially, he was reluctant to go back. 'This completely goes against my ethics,' he said.

But Rasha went on pleading shamelessly till he relented.

Rasha was asked to wait outside in the car with the driver as Saleem bhai and four of his armed men went inside the house. The sight of the house incited strange feelings of fear and anger and she found it exceedingly hard to sit in front of it, acting as if nothing had happened. Around fifteen minutes had passed when she heard faint gun shots. The house was in the middle of nowhere. It was actually off Salt Lake in a secluded section of Rajarhat. It was more in the rural periphery of Kolkata where green paddy fields stretched behind the house. She could not see a single soul around who could have heard the shots.

Then Saleem bhai came out. 'Do you want to go inside and get your boss?' he asked in a sarcastic tone.

She ignored the tone and asked what happened inside. 'I have struck a deal. One hurt, two tied up. Their boss can't blame them so they are okay with it. He is in the room on the right side of the first floor. I have got the keys. Now let's get your boss and move out.'

Surit had dozed off sitting next to Rasha in the car, but Saleem bhai's words woke him up.

'Where should we drop you?' he asked.

'Lovelock Lane, please.'

As Surit got out of the car, Saleem bhai gave him a Sig Sauer pistol.

'I don't know what all this is about. But in case there is more trouble, this will help you.'

'No. No. I don't know how to use this,' said Surit uncomfortably.

'You just have to unlock it like this and shoot,' Saleem bhai demonstrated.

'Thank you, but I will manage without it.'

'As you wish,' he shrugged.

~

Rasha's tired feet felt unsteady when she got off the Scorpio below the Gariahat flyover and walked back home. Saleem bhai hadn't, of course, offered her a gun.

It was a Sunday, but it was her working day. So she called the news editor to inform him that she was unwell and would not be at work that day.

Her mother overheard the phone conversation. 'You said you had an early morning appointment for a story. Now you call your boss and say you are not going to work. What's going on?' she asked. Rasha gritted her teeth silently and hoped her mother would not start pelting her with endless questions and would be happy with the explanation Rasha gave.

'I got the story. I will send it later. I am feeling very feverish now, so I decided not to go to work today.'

Concern creased her mother's eyebrows and her palm touched Rasha's forehead affectionately.

'It's not too hot, but you don't look well. Have a Calpol and get into bed. I think you are overworking yourself these days. I have made some bread pudding. I will get it for you.'

Caramel bread pudding and mom's soft hand stroking through her hair, lulled Rasha to sleep immediately. She slept till next morning. When she woke up, Zohaib was leafing through a magazine sitting at the foot of her bed. He had recovered from the effects of the drug, but he was hurting a wee bit.

'Rasha, I hope you know I was in my senses and was just playing along biding my time for Saleem bhai to arrive. You looked so petrified that I believe you actually thought I was going to rape you,' he blurted out.

'How long have you been sitting here to tell me this?' Rasha asked, as she pushed her pillow against the bedstead to prop herself up.

'An hour.'

Rasha slumped back. 'I wasn't sure you were in your senses. The situation was so weird that I really did not know how to react,' she said truthfully.

Zohaib laughed, trying to make the conversation light.

'I called Saleem Bhai from your mobile and...'

'Yes, he told me. He said that he hates women, but after meeting you, he has started looking at women in a different light. He feels you are selfless and daring.'

Rasha blushed, Zohaib laughed again.

'The good thing is that you can call him directly if you need him. He will help you. By the way, tell me something, how did you land in shit like this?' asked Zohaib.

Rasha told him the entire story and also her boss's bit that he had shared with her in the Scorpio.

'From what Saleem bhai tells me, Ansh would not want him as his enemy. Not many people in their senses in Kolkata would. So Ansh will end the matter here. I think the ordeal is over,' said Zohaib. Rasha hoped so.

'I got an email last night,' said Zohaib.

'What email?' Rasha looked at him with alarm.

'I have been chosen for a lead role in a Hindi film. I have to be in Mumbai by next week for the next couple of months.'

'Oh my god!' Rasha put down her cup of tea and rushed to hug Zohaib. The two started dancing.

The next day, when Rasha went to work there was an email sitting in her inbox too:

Dear Ms Rasha Roy,

It was great having you as my guest, but sadly we couldn't meet. Although I am not too fond of journalists and hate it when they write things that turn out to be an irritant in my life, it is always a pleasure to have some fun with them. But, sadly, your friend barged in and spoiled all my fun.

I am okay with it as long as you don't try to write things that bother me or your boss tries to meet the police and pour out his woes to them. I know for a fact that your father goes for his evening walks everyday at 7.00 p.m., your sister reaches her office in Dalhousie at 9.00 a.m. and she goes to her friend's place in Gol Park on Sundays. Your mother goes to a social work organisation on Elliot Road on Saturdays and Tuesdays.

Kolkata roads are too unsafe and accident-prone, so it will be sensible on your part to tell them to take care of themselves.

Hope you have a great career ahead.

Cheers,
YOU KNOW WHO

PS: I heard that you have spoken to a few college girls, who perform at my parties. If I were you, I wouldn't touch the story.

15

RASHA POURED THE tea in two cups, took out chocolate McVitie's biscuits from the pack, put it in a plate along with her homemade brownies and took the tray to their bedroom. She placed it on the bed, next to Arun, and he lazily raised his body on an elbow and reached out for the brownies. Arun loved brownies which Rasha baked every Thursday so that Arun could have them over the weekend—Friday and Saturday. In Dubai, the working week starts on Sunday.

'So what's for lunch?' he asked.

'Thai green curry and jasmine rice.'

'I can't wait to have it,' he said.

Rasha smiled a bit distractedly.

'Is everything okay in Kolkata?' asked Arun.

'Yes!'

'I would suggest you don't worry about it anymore. If you are here and Surit da is in Bangkok, Ansh will not be interested in your family.'

'I hope so too.'

Arun put his hands in Rasha's. 'I know it was hard for you to leave Kolkata.'

'It was. But I am happy here. I have you and there is a whole new world to explore.'

'But you miss the excitement. Don't you?'

'A little bit. But I gave it a lot of thought and took my decision. I could have taken up cudgels against Ansh, but I am not sure if it would have been worth it. I could have gone to the police, but he would have immediately bought out most of them. I could have told Saleem bhai, but I was scared that he would have taken some drastic measures that could have meant more trouble. As such, he has done a lot. I didn't want to bother him further. Then I found out some of Ansh's legitimate companies advertise in *Our Times*. I am sure the newspaper wouldn't have wanted to lose out on revenue by supporting me. And I would have died of guilt if anything happened to my family.'

'Your decision could not have been more sensible, Rasha,' said Arun.

He and Rasha were probably having this conversation for the tenth time since she came to Dubai, but Arun always let Rasha talk because he felt the whole issue was wedged in her heart like a shard of glass. She needed to get it out slowly without hurting herself.

'But I always feel I chickened out. I didn't have the courage to fight,' said Rasha finally.

'Was this worth it? You tell me?' asked Arun.

'Probably not,' Rasha shrugged.

'Did Surit da ever take up the matter after that day? He just booked the next flight to Bangkok and left. He also knows it is pointless.'

'Guess so!'

'I know what irks you the most. It was the promotion,' said Arun.

Rasha worked in *Our Times* for exactly a month after the incident. She ignored the subtle threats that sat in her mailbox on a bi-weekly basis and tried hard to concentrate on her stories. She turned her entire attention to entertainment and never touched hard news again.

After Surit da's exit, the company installed a new editor fairly quickly. The new editor, Viren Rao, who was her age, or probably younger, came from another newspaper. She had met him earlier at a couple of assignments and shared a cordial relationship with him. In the very first week, he made it clear that he would not be in office before 2.30 p.m. However, he expected his team to be there much earlier and start working on the day's edition. He did not hold any regular meetings, never came up with story ideas, was quick to shoot down others' ideas and changed each and every copy so drastically that at the end of the day the articles looked like they were written by the same person. Rasha was getting along fairly fine with Viren Rao, but he was a man who had no passion for work or a will to drive his team. He treated the newspaper as a six-hour job, where you filled the empty spaces on the blank sheets with a few good-sounding words and glamorous pictures. Whether those interested the reader or not was inconsequential.

When she told Arun about the situation at work, he insisted she join him. 'There are so many opportunities here. *Our Times* can't be the last stop for Rasha Roy. On the one hand, you are constantly worrying about your family, and on the other, you are not enjoying your work. What's the point?'

The day Rasha went to submit her resignation to Viren, he said, 'Rasha, I was about to call you. You have been promoted to the post of deputy editor. Congratulations!'

In the next few days, Viren poured in all the passion that he didn't put in his work, to convince Rasha to stay on. 'It's stupid to throw it all away and go to Dubai. Does journalism exist there? I really don't know. You are making a big mistake, Rasha,' he said.

But in her mind, Rasha was already sunbathing on the beach.

∾

'Your tea is getting cold, Rasha.' Arun's voice nudged Rasha out of her thoughts. She had been cuddling her cup for too long.

'Tell me what you want to do today?' he asked to make her feel better.

'I was thinking if we could go skiing at the Mall of the Emirates, it would be great. It will be so thrilling to ski down an icy slope in the middle of a mall. We can save money on Switzerland travel,' said Rasha, snapping out of her dark thoughts.

'So be it,' said Arun.

She took a sip and looked at the wall clock. 'It's noon already. It will be 1.30 p.m. in India. I have to call home,' she said.

Her parents had finished lunch and were engrossed in a Bengali serial when her mom took the call.

'What were you doing?' Rasha asked.

'Watching *Debi* on TV. What about you?' asked her mother.

'Having tea with Arun?'

'You woke up now?'

'It's Friday, Arun's holiday.'

'Do you and Arun have separate rooms?' asked mom.

Rasha knew her mom had been trying desperately to ask her this question from the time she landed in Dubai. It took her one whole month to finally pop it.

'Yes, of course.' She winked at Arun.

'He has the larger room with a big bed and I have the smaller room with a single bed.'

Arun laughed silently and just mouthed the word LIAR!

Rasha wasn't sure if she imagined it, or did her mother genuinely sound relieved, but she did come across as more cheerful when she asked how her cooking was going. Rasha told her she had learned to cook palak chicken and gave her the recipe. They talked about food for ten minutes, then her mother finally came to the question.

'When are you getting married? Your father was saying we will not live forever. And when it is fine with Arun's parents too, I think it will be a good idea to make it soon.'

'Anyway once you are married you won't have to sleep in

separate rooms.' Mom laughed nervously because she was not sure how Rasha would react to her last sentence.

Rasha thought how naïve her mother was. But she replied grimly. 'Marriage? Umm… Let me see.'

Arun was making the bed and listening to the conversation. 'But does Rasha Roy have enough money to fund her own wedding?' he asked after Rasha hung up.

She smiled. 'I have around Rs 1.5 lakh in my bank account. If we keep it simple and small, then I don't think I will have to spend all of it.'

'Now there are a couple of things more that we will have to look into. The visa that I have got for you is valid for only three months. After that, if you want me to sponsor you, you will have to be my wife. If you don't want that, then you will have to find a job so that the company sponsors you.'

'I want to be your wife. I want to be a housewife.'

'I am sure about the first, but I am not so sure of the second,' said Arun.

'Why? Will I not make a good housewife?'

'I don't have any doubts about that, but there is a possibility you will drive me up the wall when I come home. If you get bored, you will have to find a way to entertain yourself.'

'Do you get gigolos in Dubai?' Rasha asked.

'I am sure there are plenty, but since you know so many gigolos in Kolkata, having interviewed them, you can import a few if you want. I will pay for the tickets.'

Rasha laughed aloud. 'Let me see if I can find a few in Ski Dubai,' she said.

'I will keep my eyes and ears open on your behalf,' said Arun.

Rasha and Arun took a whole lot of pictures in their skiing outfits and both were as excited as children when they went up the man-made slope in ski lifts and skied down like pros.

'We are actually skiing in the middle of a desert. Have you thought about that?' Arun asked.

Rasha made a snowball and threw it at Arun. He hit back. They got into a snowball fight.

~

Afterwards, Rasha picked up a top from H&M and Arun a T-shirt at Hang Ten at the Mall of the Emirates. Happy with the discounts they got, they proceeded for dinner to the food court and settled for Arabic mixed grill kebabs, lentil soup and turkey manakish at Al Halab.

A guy waved at Arun from the next table. Arun excused himself and went to greet him. He spoke to him in hushed whispers and came back to his table with a bleak look.

'Anything wrong?' asked Rasha.

'That gentleman is from my office. He told me a guy in our office went with his live-in partner to the hospital recently because she was feeling unwell. They ran medical tests on her and found out she was pregnant. The guy landed up in custody because pregnancy out of wedlock is a punishable offence here.'

'What? You are joking!'

'No, I am not. Dubai is liberal regarding many things, but you have to abide by the law of the land—the Sharia law. Rasha, I don't want to land up in jail.'

Arun was talking seriously, but his expression made Rasha laugh.

'You are talking as if I am already pregnant.'

'No contraceptive has hundred per cent guarantee,' said Arun with authority.

'Well! You are thinking of jail...I am thinking of my mother. How will she react?'

'For starters, she might wonder how you got pregnant after sleeping in separate rooms.'

16

ARUN COULDN'T TAKE his eyes off Rasha the entire evening. Although he had to greet each and every guest with warmth, tend to the arrangements on the lawn and personally escort the elderly to greet the bride, his eyes constantly went darting back to Rasha. He had imagined how she would look in her wedding attire, but his imagination had fallen way short of reality.

Rasha was wearing the traditional red Benarasi sari, but it was not as ostentatious as a conventional saree worn by Bengali brides. It was a brick red one with zari dots on the entire fabric and the gold border was not more than two inches in width. A thin necklace encrusted with rubies in the shape of leaves, gifted by her mother-in-law, sat daintily on her shapely neck. Her blow-dried curls danced on her shoulders every time she moved her head. Sans the glittery veil, the rangoli of sandalwood on her forehead and reams of gold around her neck, she looked everything but a traditional bride. Other ladies at the wedding had definitely decked up much more than Rasha, but she still managed to look drop-dead gorgeous in her usual simplicity.

Arun had chosen a self-embossed, off-white sherwani designed by Snehashish Bhattacharya. The designer had added his trademark touch with embroidery in maroon at the elbows, on the lapel and in the back. Arun just loved himself in the mirror and thought his attire complimented Rasha's saree perfectly.

After attending umpteen Bengali weddings since childhood, he was clear about the things he did not want to do when he went to the altar himself. For starters, he was put off by the pointed headgear called topor, made of shola, or Indian cork, with two balls sticking out on either side, that every Bengali groom was expected to wear. He had always wondered why the groom was made to look so inelegant on his wedding day with the topor slammed on his head and the weird dots of sandalwood drawn on the forehead in the name of tradition. He had expressed his fears to Rasha.

'I completely agree with you. I can't imagine myself as the demure bride sitting on a throne straining under the load of a heavy saree and tons of jewellery. That's just not me. We will plan our wedding in such a way that we can also enjoy ourselves,' she said.

The planning was done meticulously by Rasha with inputs from Arun. For once in her life, her parents let her take her own decisions entirely, simply because they were overjoyed that their supremely stubborn daughter had finally decided to tie the knot and put an end to the arrangement of living in the same house with her fiancé, although all their relatives in Kolkata were told that they had so far been living in separate houses in Dubai.

All the events were held in Arun's Alipore house because they both agreed that it was unnecessary to hire a venue when there was so much space there. The couple's party was held at his house too, on Arun's floor. There were not many people to invite because most of their college and school friends had moved to other parts of India or abroad. The guest list had twenty names, mostly their ex-colleagues and cousins. One of Arun's cousins was the DJ for the night and was excellent at mixing music. Everyone danced till the wee hours and welcomed dawn at Arun's huge balcony with hot jalebis, prepared at the local sweetmeat shop at the crack of dawn.

Rasha's parents organized a separate pre-wedding party where they invited their own friends. Of course, Rasha and Rania were a part of it. Their parents' friends did not need any egging on when their mom brought out her dusty harmonium and sang energetic numbers from Rabindranath Tagore's repertoire. Everyone joined her. Then all the aunties got into the Rabindrik dance mode after downing a few pegs of whisky and vodka. Rasha thought the energy and enthusiasm at her parents' party was definitely several notches above the couple's party they had had the day before. She was happy. The wedding and reception were held on the same evening and Rasha and Arun, together, footed the entire bill. The wedding vows included signing on the dotted lines in the marriage registrar's form, followed by garland and ring exchange. After the formalities were over, the marriage registrar was served Pepsi and a plateful of sweets.

Suddenly, the reporter in Rasha took over from the bride.

'Have you ever been in a situation where you have been forced to marry someone off?' she asked.

He was about to put a sweet in his mouth, but put it back on the plate and looked around with fearful eyes.

'Why? Why do you ask this question?'

Arun gave Rasha a don't-start-here-too look. 'Never mind. I was just curious,' she said looking away.

The marriage registrar came close to Rasha and whispered into her ears.

'It happened once many years ago. Few men came to my house late in the night, blindfolded me and took me to a place where a man wanted me to register his marriage to a girl. The girl looked very scared and I was sure she had been abducted. But I was so scared, I just signed and they dropped me back home.'

Hearing the registrar's account, Rasha's mind strayed to her own abduction and the consequences. She looked at the happy faces of her parents as they spoke to the guests. Then she noticed Rania, who was sitting at a table with her boss as he ate dinner. Her hands were playing with the candle stand on the table and she was laughing. The twinkle in her eyes was brighter than the candle flame. Rasha had never seen Rania in such a bubbly mood.

Her family exhaled cheer and she felt content. But little did she know that she was in for two big surprises that very evening.

∿

Rasha and Arun had made it a strictly no-gifts wedding, so the bride didn't have to sit in one corner to accept the gifts and smile till the muscles on her cheeks ached. She was free to roam around and meet and mingle with the guests. She was just doing that and also enjoying the ambience created by the wreaths of yellow, green, red and blue lights wrapped around the trees in the garden, when her eyes went towards the entrance where her father and father-in-law were taking turns to personally welcome the guests.

She saw Surit da walking in looking as handsome as ever in a striking blue silk kurta. The colour was very similar to the blue shirt that she once virtually forced him to buy. She had sent him an e-invite to the wedding as a mere formality knowing that the editor of *Bangkok News* would not get the time to make it all the way to Kolkata for a wedding. He emailed back saying he would try. Rasha had thought he was being polite. Now she was delighted that he had made the effort to come. She quickly summoned Arun to her side and they both welcomed him. In her excitement of meeting Surit da, she had not noticed the lady standing quietly next to him in a striking gold-and-white Kanjeevaram saree. When their eyes met, Rasha tried extremely hard to hide her shock but she failed. Surit da was grinning and holding the lady's hand as if he was playing to the galleries.

'Gia and I are back together,' he said.

Rasha managed to transform the shock on her face to a welcoming expression.

'Congratulations!' said Gia.

'Thanks. Thanks for coming.'

She felt like blurting out, 'How come? How did this happen?'

but she thought it would be downright rude to ask any question there; she would corner Surit da at a later opportunity.

Rasha's ex-colleagues from *Our Times*, came running to greet Surit da as if he was a long lost friend. Rasha almost felt like telling him how he had ceased to exist for them from the moment he left the office. As she left them to greet another guest, she overheard one guy telling Surit da, 'Should I send you my CV? It will be great to work under you again.' Rasha frowned.

Saleem bhai's mohawk hair now ended in green spikes and to complement that he wore a green sherwani. Two thick gold chains dangled from his neck and his sleeves were rolled up to reveal his tan and the expensive Omega watch that he was sporting on his wrist. Rasha was conscious that he attracted stares. Then her father did the unthinkable. As she introduced Saleem bhai to him, to Rasha's immense embarrassment, he remained cold and indifferent.

'Who is this punk? Whose guest is he—yours or Arun's?' he asked as soon they were out of his earshot.

Daddy dear, your daughter is standing here in one piece because of this punk, Rasha felt like telling her father.

'He is Arun's very good friend,' she said instead. She knew her father would not ask any further questions then. He didn't.

When Rasha went back to Saleem and Arun, Surit da had joined them and Arun was introducing both of them to his parents. Arun's parents welcomed them with the same warmth that they had reserved for every guest that evening. Rasha really liked her in-laws. They were involved, but also reticent when required, were rarely flustered and had a poised calmness that Arun had so obviously inherited. They all talked for some time about Bangkok and Dubai, both places frequented by Saleem bhai. Arun then took him to the buffet counter for dinner. Rasha zeroed in on the opportunity to catch Surit da since Gia was talking to another guest.

'What are you doing with her?' she demanded.

'She sent me an email apologizing. She wrote I was the love of her life and she could not get over me. You know I couldn't either. I was dying after she left me. Now she lives with me in Bangkok.'

'Lives with you? It's gone that far…'

'Why? You don't approve?' Surit da was smiling, but he looked hurt that she didn't share his joy.

'No, no, not that I…I just… What happened to the forty lakhs?'

'She wrote to me only after depositing the entire amount in my bank account. She said that she could understand how much I loved her after what happened at the party that day. She felt that she just couldn't cheat me.'

'Good for you! Good for you!' said Rasha in a softer, but unconvinced tone.

Gia joined them and she put her arms around Surit da's waist looking at him tenderly. For once, Rasha didn't feel self-conscious seeing her gold Kanjeevaram because she herself was amply dressed.

'I can see you have not invited any of the Bengali film stars. I thought you got along with them really well,' said Surit da.

'I am not with *Our Times* anymore and I was not sure they would come.'

Surit da laughed. 'You have become a cynic already.'

'No, I invited only two people from the film fraternity. Actor Pranjal Ganguly, who took the trouble to come to my house to say goodbye to me on the day I was leaving for Dubai with a ceramic mug which had "Gonna miss you" written on it, and character-actor B.D. Dasgupta. He was nice enough to call me for dinner to Dalhousie Club and gave me a pen saying, "This is to say you should never stop writing, wherever you are". But they have left. You are late, Surit da.' Actress Chandrima would have probably been on Rasha's guest list too had she not stopped taking Rasha's calls after the abduction episode. It was clear to Rasha that she wanted to keep her distance, so she kept her's too.

'So you invited people who care about Rasha Roy, not the journalist Rasha Roy.'

'Yeah, people like you maybe…' Rasha smiled.

~

Since the venue of the reception was Arun's house, there was no deadline to pack up as it usually happens with hired venues. Family and friends sat in circles and chatted till late. The younger crowd preferred to indulge in ice cream eating competitions. Kenny G. and Yanni took over from Pandit Hariprasad Chaurasia and Pandit Ravi Shankar for the background score of the wedding.

Rasha and Arun sat next to each other enjoying their simple wedding menu of chicken biriyani, fish kebab, mutton rezala and paneer butter masala, finishing with ice cream.

Looking at her crammed plate, Rasha felt like a glutton.

But what the hell, it's my own wedding. I have to remember every single taste for eternity, she thought, and stuffed her mouth with mutton rezala. She looked at Arun. He had placed three napkins covering the entire front part of his off-white kurta.

'Not taking chances with my wedding kurta. Don't want any stains on it,' he explained.

Surit da and Gia were sitting at the same table opposite the bride and the groom. Rasha kept looking at Gia from the corner of her eye, trying to figure out if she was conning Surit da again. Then she gave up as her attention went to a man from the courier service. He had come to deliver a huge bouquet of expensive— probably imported—flowers and a gift-wrapped box. She opened the card tucked inside the box. It read:

Dear Rasha,

Congratulations on your wedding. Thanks for being a good girl.

My best wishes to both of you.

Cheers,
YOU KNOW WHO

The biriyani that had gone on a downward journey just then, suddenly threatened to come up the same way. Rasha pushed it down again with a gulp and passed the card to Arun, who in turn gave it to Surit da. All three of them knew who had sent it.

'What's inside the box?' asked Arun.

'I don't know if I should open it,' Rasha said looking at the huge square box in a glittery silver wrapper.

'Don't be silly,' said Arun, touching Rasha's hand reassuringly.

'It's not a bomb, that's for sure,' said Surit da.

She unwrapped it. It was a box of expensive chocolates. Rasha felt nauseated again at the sight of it.

The tense expression on Rasha's face made Surit da laugh.

'I would not be surprised if it's laced with a potent aphrodisiac,' he said.

She gestured to a guy from the catering company who was serving them ice cream. 'Are you married?' she asked him.

'Yes, Madam.'

'This is for your wife.' The man took the box and beamed at Rasha.

Ansh Ramchandani's gate crashing letter and gift made her miss her best friend Zohaib all the more. He could not make it to the wedding because a watertight shooting schedule kept him back in Mumbai, although he promised he would spend time with them in Dubai during his schedule there, which would be within a month.

Rasha looked forward to his visit at her new home. She cleared her thoughts as she finished the last of her third ice cream cone.

~

Arun and Rasha took their post-marriage Emirates flight back to Dubai. They landed in Dubai at midnight. There was no Marhaba service this time to whisk them off through passport control, so they battled the serpentine queue at the busiest hour of the airport. Then they waited in yet another long but organized taxi queue to go home.

They were allotted a pink taxi which was usually meant for women who felt more comfortable being driven by a fellow woman at unearthly hours. Men could only sit in the taxi if they were accompanied by a woman. Arun had the privilege because Rasha was with him. A North African lady driver emerged from the cab that was painted baby pink on the top and smelled of strawberry inside. She herself wore a baby pink skirt that covered her ankles, a full sleeve white shirt with a sleeveless baby pink jacket and a pink cap on her headscarf. She lifted their three heavy bags like a mother picks up her newborn—easily but carefully.

'I think this pink taxi service is a great idea. Perfect for women and men can only travel in it if they are accompanied by women,' said Arun after settling in.

'But, Sir, recently the mother of a five-year-old boy had a tough time dragging him into my cab because he refused to get into a "girls' taxi" because he was a man,' said the driver. Hearing this, Arun and Rasha roared with laughter.

They were out of the airport and on the Garhoud Bridge. Rasha felt she had arrived home. In her three-month stint in Dubai, she had already adjusted with the fast-paced life of the city. She was actually amazed at herself. Through the entire flight, she hadn't shed a tear thinking of her mother when she should have because she was a bride leaving home after marriage. Instead, she thought of the groceries that needed to be bought, the clothes that had to be washed and ironed, the final touches that her home décor needed and all the new recipes she would toss up in her neat kitchen.

'Are you thinking of what Surit da told you while saying goodbye?' asked Arun.

'Not really.'

'As far as I remember, he said, "It's perfect if you want to become a culinary expert at the moment, but in the long run, it will be a shame if you waste your talent." I agree with him.'

Rasha did not reply. She was thinking of the cookbooks she had bought from Oxford Bookstore on this trip to Kolkata.

~

Arun put the key into their apartment door and stood still for a moment.

'Oh my god, Arun! I thought you had turned off the main switch when we left. It's obvious you didn't. The light in the kitchen is on.'

Arun stood there confused. 'I...I distinctly remember I switched it off.'

Their mouths fell open when they entered the kitchen.

A magnet in the shape of a red rose supported a huge card on the refrigerator. The card read: 'Congratulations!' Inside it was written: 'We thought the newly weds would be hungry on their first night in Dubai, so here is some food.'

It was signed by four of Arun's colleagues-turned-friends and their wives. The refrigerator was neatly stacked with five aluminium foil boxes that contained pulao, dal, fish kebabs, chicken curry and the authentic Bengali payesh made with jaggery and rice. The huge box from Spinneys that occupied the entire space in the lower shelf had a Tiramisu cake. Arun and Rasha were surprised and touched. But the surprise didn't end there. As they entered the drawing room, there were two lovely Ikea floor lamps with white metal base standing next to the black sofa set that Arun and Rasha had earlier bought from Homes R Us. A beautiful crystal piece in the form of a lotus flower had been added to the centre table and a crystal candle holder stood on their small dining table. A colourful carpet that had been bought with the already existing curtains in mind had been installed on the floor. The bedroom had a new fancy satin bed cover and fresh roses in unusual colours of peach and yellow had been arranged on the bedside tables. A huge gift-wrapped box sat on the middle of the bed with a card on it that read: 'You will need this now, since you will be entertaining us more often.'

It revealed a twenty-four piece ceramic dinner set that had lovely yellow flowers on it. All the plates, bowls and saucers were in square. Rasha just loved them.

Arun sat on the bed. 'No wonder Soumen had asked for the keys to our apartment. He had said that he would keep it clean for us.'

'...And Reema (Soumen's wife) had asked me what I was planning to buy for the house,' said Rasha laughing. 'But I must say, I have never been surprised like this. They are truly lovely people.'

∾

Rasha and Arun had thoroughly enjoyed their simple Kolkata wedding, but Arun wanted to make the honeymoon exotic. He wanted to holiday in a bungalow on stilts on the crystal clear sea in Bora Bora in the French Polynesian islands. But at that moment, he was both cash and leave strapped. So, his dream honeymoon had to wait for some time.

'Till then, we can do with a short weekend honeymoon in Fujairah,' said Arun.

Rasha was sitting on the floor of their sitting room in her bermudas and T-shirt and leafing through their wedding album. Arun was fiddling with the remote jumping from one sports channel to another. He had twenty sports channels and made full use of it by watching football through the night—another of his eccentricities that Rasha only came to know when she started living with him. When the league matches were on, Arun would get two to three hours sleep every night and look as fresh as a dew drop in the morning. Rasha always wondered how he managed that.

'Arun turn off the TV and let's talk.' He obeyed.

Rasha was excited. 'I have heard there are lovely beachside resorts in Fujairah, Ras Al Khaimah and Ajman. When are we going?'

'Let's make it next week,' he said.

'Next week? I need to get some beach clothes then.'

'We can go shopping tomorrow. Can I switch on the TV now? Barcelona will be playing Real Madrid.'

17

THE ROOM THAT Arun had booked in the Miramar Resort on Al Aqah Beach at Fujairah was located so strategically that from the spacious balcony they could see the sea, the huge swimming pool and the rugged walls of the Hajar Mountains that formed the backdrop of the resort. The view was breathtaking. The resort, built over a huge area in Moroccan architecture, subscribed to the minimalistic philosophy and was not more than three-storey tall.

'It takes just two hours by road to reach such a beautiful place. Who would have thought that?' said Rasha, sipping coffee on the balcony and devouring chicken fajita wraps.

Arun looked naughtily at Rasha. 'So let's start our honeymoon. The bed is really nice and the white sheets smell...ummmm.'

'Are you crazy? Put on your swimsuit. We have to go kayaking before the sun goes down,' she said.

Arun grimaced. 'And what else will we do?'

'After kayaking, we will play table tennis by the pool,' she said pointing at the TT board visible from the balcony. A group of girls in bikinis were playing.

'If I can play with them, I am ready,' said Arun.

'I am sure they will play with you if you put on your charm.'

'But I thought people don't get out of their rooms on their honeymoon and only order room service.'

'Really? But if we do that, you will not get to play with those girls. Make your choice.'

'What would you do if I choose the girls?'

'I would absolutely appreciate that. Because I am sure there will be some pretty girls at the tennis courts too, then at the disco and then at the scuba diving class tomorrow, to motivate you.'

'You plan to do all that?'

'The girls, remember the girls,' said Rasha laughing.

'I think you are forgetting I was the TT and swimming champ in college,' said Arun proudly.

'Even better, if we can ask the girls to race with you in the pool.'

True to her words, Rasha did not leave out a single activity on offer at the hotel. They used the room only for sleeping and changing. On the second last and the last night, Rasha lay on the bed exhausted. Her face was snuggled against Arun's chest and feet intertwined in his.

'This is why people should not be living in with their partners prior to marriage. The wife ends up doing all kinds of outdoor activities during day and sleeps through the night on the honeymoon,' he grumbled.

Rasha didn't stir. 'Rasha, at least we can talk, can't we? It's only 10.30 p.m. And this TV doesn't have any interesting sports channel.'

Rasha didn't stir. Arun watched TV for ten more minutes and then switched it off along with the lights and pulled the sheets on himself with a bored expression. Rasha's eyes opened and gleamed in the dark like a pair of fireflies. A few moments later, Arun found himself transported to a world of ecstasy.

～

They settled for breakfast at a corner table with a view of the sea in the main restaurant at Miramar Resort. The huge dining area had high dome-shaped embellished ceilings and beige walls. The cheerful crowd at breakfast included tourists from different parts of the world and UAE residents, mainly Emiratis, Indians, Britons, and a few Arabs from places like Lebanon and Jordan.

'Quick, look the other way. There is someone over here I just don't want to talk to,' Rasha told Arun urgently.

Arun gave Rasha a puzzled look, making it clear that he was not particularly good at that. Rasha placed her shades on her eyes and tried hard to concentrate on her omelette and fried sausages. A lady tapped her on the shoulders. Arun initially thought Rasha would not look up from her breakfast, but she finally did. The lady was fat and looked uncouth in her short floral summer dress. Her head was covered in a floppy sun hat and coloured blonde hair peeped from below the hat. The hair looked peculiar with her dark Indian complexion.

'Hi Rasha, how are you? What a strange coincidence to meet you in Fujairah.'

'Yes. It's really strange,' said Rasha tersely. Arun thought she harped on the word strange a bit too hard.

'Do you live near about or have you come holidaying here all the way from India?' She laughed, but it sounded more like a screech.

'I live in Dubai. This is my husband Arun,' she said introducing him halfheartedly. 'Arun this is Konika Chatterjee. She used to work with me in *Kolkata Daily*.' 'What are you doing here?'

'I came to Dubai for an interview in the Bollywood magazine *Silver Screen*. But I don't think I will take it up because I met Kasim here at a pub. We hit it off instantly and now he is going to Delhi with me. That's where I work now. I will travel to the US with him after I get my visa in Delhi. Let me introduce you to Kasim, he is American.'

Kasim was good-looking, was in his late twenties and was an American-born Pakistani, who spoke with an exaggerated American drawl. Rasha tried hard to spot the supposed spark between them. *Or maybe he is a conman having some fun with her before eventually dumping her*, she thought.

Pleasantries were exchanged. 'Why don't you join us?' Konika said.

'I am afraid we can't. We have to check out in ten mins. Nice to meet you. Take care.'

It was as if Rasha had just snipped the conversation with a pair of sharp scissors.

Konika and Kasim settled down at a distant table.

'You really don't like her, don't you? I have never seen you being so curt,' said Arun.

'It would be better to say I hate her. Let's go to our room, I will give you all the details. We have a late check out anyway. I just can't stand the sight of her.'

Rasha walked past Konika without even saying bye to her. She focused all her attention on managing her dress—a lemon yellow maxi trailing behind her.

'She's not taking up a job because she's hooked up with an American who is following her to Delhi and promises to take her to the US, and there is no guarantee he would keep his word. This lady sounds bizarre,' said Arun.

'Bizarre is an understatement,' said Rasha. 'And if I tell you how she is, you will fall out of your chair?'

'Like?'

'When I joined *Kolkata Daily* as a trainee sub-editor, she was a senior sub-editor. As such, life was really hard for me as a trainee because everyone was my boss. I would come back after finishing one assignment when someone, just three-months older to me in the profession, would lay claim to his or her seniority and send me off to another one. There would be days when I would do six different assignments, all of which involved legwork. Then there was so much to write, I would be sitting in the office late into the night and filing stories. But I didn't mind because all this was a learning experience and most journalists have to go through this.

But Konika was the biggest bully of them all.'

'She looks like one,' said Arun.

'We had a column where we interviewed actresses and singers about their favourite holiday spot. This dumb Bengali starlet just gave me two lines about Kashmir and said she didn't remember anything and asked me to write whatever I liked. I hadn't gone to Kashmir. My deadline was in two hours and the copy needed four hundred words. We had only one computer with internet where the seniors were doing important work, so I rushed to the Oxford Bookstore, did my quick research and delivered on time. Some top honcho of Kashmir tourism read the article and really liked it. He called up our editor and wanted to offer the writer of the article a free trip to Kashmir. The editor thought that even though I had written the article, it was a protocol to offer the trip to seniors first. Konika, who was a few years senior to me in *Kolkata Daily*, snapped up the opportunity and went off to Kashmir.'

'Really? That's very unfair,' said Arun.

'I was young and new in the profession and the incident was a rude awakening.'

'No wonder you hate her.'

'Wait, the story doesn't end there. Konika went to Kashmir and fell in love with a houseboat owner and stayed on. Her father came to meet the editor one day to find out why she was sent to Kashmir. When he came to know I had written the article, he actually took out all his anger on me and started screaming at me in the middle of the office. The editor stood by me, but it was really nerve-wracking for me to see a grown man crying and shouting at the same time. Apparently, she had told her dad that she had married the man and then she severed all connections with her family.'

'After that?'

'Konica didn't return and *Kolkata Daily* went bankrupt and

closed down in six months. I had forgotten about her till I met her here.'

'Really, Rasha, bizarre is indeed an understatement for her.'

'I will not be surprised if she actually manages to land in America with that Kasim guy. She is completely capable,' said Rasha.

Rasha spotted Konika in the lobby while checking out of the hotel. This time, curiosity got the better of her.

'Your father had said you had married a Kashmiri…' said Rasha.

'I lived in with him, but we eventually didn't marry. I went back to Kolkata, then took up a job in Mumbai and left again. On a trip to Goa, I fell for a Goan businessman and married him. We got divorced a couple of months ago and I took up a job in Delhi. That's when this offer came from *Silver Screen*. So, here I am.'

'Are you in touch with your family?'

The question made her uncomfortable. She started twirling a blond strand. 'Umm…on and off actually.'

'Okay. Bye.'

'Wait! Where do you work in Dubai?' Konika asked Rasha.

Rasha felt her throat drying up. 'I don't work. I am a housewife.' Her voice was barely audible to her own ears.

∾

The return trip from Fujairah was even more beautiful. Arun took a different route. The road they travelled through had the sea on one side and the mountains on the other. The winding road through the mountains gave a better view of the rocky interface of the Hajar Mountains—that started in Oman and ended in the UAE, forming the longest mountain range in the Arabian Peninsula. The next part of the drive through the desert was equally beautiful and Rasha marvelled at the desert sunset. She excitedly zoomed in with her camera on a couple of camels.

She couldn't wait to download all the photographs on her laptop and relive her short but exciting honeymoon. She was doing just that when she noticed an email from Rania in her inbox. Her elder sister rarely wrote to her and when she did, it would usually be two lines, but this one was a long one. If this email had come earlier, she would have immediately thought about Ansh and got scared, but after the card from him on her wedding, she was a bit relaxed. So she decided her sister must have been missing her.

Rania was missing Rasha, but for very different reasons. The email read:

Dear Rashu,

Hope you had a great honeymoon and are enjoying your life in Dubai. We are all doing fine. We miss you all the time. Ma can't go off to sleep early because she is so used to staying up late for you and Baba keeps sitting on the couch in the living room, hoping you will walk in through the door anytime. I am doing okay, too. But some things have happened recently and I thought it better to send you an email and explain the incidents instead of calling you.

I don't know how to say this, but I have given up my job. There is something I never told you. I was seeing my boss for the last couple of years. He was fighting a divorce suit and we had planned to get married after his divorce came through. But he suddenly decided to drop the case and he is back with his wife and daughter. He is a nice man and I am happy for him. But I could not keep meeting him at work every day, pretending that nothing had happened. So I decided to quit. He understood my dilemma and offered me a transfer, but I did not want to leave our parents alone and go off somewhere to nurse my broken heart. I am sure I will find another job soon.

Of course, I have not told Ma and Baba anything about this. I just told them that I was having problems with my boss so didn't want to continue.

But there is a big problem that Dad has landed in. You remember he had told you that he was planning to invest with a friend in a resort near Canning, which is a few hours drive from Kolkata? I think you had rightly told him that business is something a retired professor should not venture into. But, sadly, he never listened to you. He pumped in all his retirement money into the huge property they acquired for the resort. His business partner had told him that he would get the license by bribing government officials and politicians. But the license never came through and Baba found out that his partner, who is also a real estate agent, has sold the same land to three different people. Baba has moved court against him, but looks like it's going to be a really long-drawn battle where he will need a lot of money to fight his case. With my job gone and Baba's money gone, it's becoming a bit difficult for us to do that and also run the household at the same time. You know I have never earned enough to save a lot. But if you are taking up a job, then it will be great if you can send some money home to help us out. But don't worry, we are doing okay at the moment. Love to both you and Arun.

Didi

Rasha bit her lips as she read the mail thrice over. She felt like telling her dad that he should have hired some goons to fight his case and not gone to court instead to fight a futile battle. But she didn't. She felt like asking Rania how could such a sensible and poised woman get into a relationship with a married man with a daughter. But she held back her fingers on the laptop. Instead, she wrote:

Dear Didi,

There is Rs 50,000 in my bank account in Kolkata. You and I hold the account jointly, so you can access it anytime. Make do with it for the moment. Let me see what I can do. Take care.

Love,
Rasha

She told Arun what had happened. 'Send them money from here,' he said.

'It's your money, Arun, not mine. My egoistic father will not accept it.'

'Hmmmm...then what's the solution? A court case will cost a fortune. On top of that, there is a household to take care of,' he said.

'I will find a job. Won't I get one?'

'You will get loads. But I was thinking of you. You are enjoying your turn at home. Aren't you? I don't want you to be pushed into a job.'

'That's okay. Anyway, it's been four months now that I have been at home. I have had my fill, I guess.'

'Do what you think is right. Whatever you do, I want you to enjoy it. You have had your share of tough times and you deserve to be stress-free and happy.'

'If you are there with me, how can I not be happy, Arun?'

'That's filmy, very filmy,' he laughed.

18

INSTEAD OF GOING through the appointments section of *Gulf News* and *Khaleej Times,* Rasha just went out and bought a copy of the magazine *Silver Screen,* hoping the position that Konica had not taken up would still be vacant. She leafed through the hardcore Bollywood contents of the magazine and felt it was up her street. Given a choice, she would have loved to work in a newspaper, but she could not afford to lose time. She took out the email address of the editor from the back of the magazine and emailed her CV. Within minutes, she got a reply asking her to take an e-test attached with the email. She found the test easy, although she sensed a small knot of apprehension in her stomach when she attached her answers and pressed the send button in her email.

She was asked to appear for an interview the next day. Rasha couldn't decide whether she should wear western formals or ethnic formals. She decided on a cross. She paired black jeans with a simple short white kurta with blue and red kotki work on the chest and on the borders of the sleeves. She slipped her feet into her white flat chappals and hailed a cab that took her to the office of *Silver Screen* in Media City. When she opened her purse to pay the cabbie, she saw, as always, Arun had slipped in two hunderd dirhams more, just in case she needed it. Rasha wondered if it was this thoughtful, protective side of Arun that she found most attractive.

Media City housed the offices of CNN, Thomson Reuters, MBC, AP and BBC. Umpteen media houses, PR agencies and other offices thrived under the silver wings of the giant butterfly statue that stood at the entrance of Media City. But *Silver Screen* was located further down, past the butterfly roundabout, to the right. Rasha entered a fifteen-storeyed building and was guided to the eleventh floor by the security guard. *Silver Screen* was written in silver on a giant-sized embossed film reel on the opaque glass door leading to the office. Two women sat at the reception. One was an Indian, the other an Arab. Both had heavy make-up on. Rasha also ensured that she had her foundation on along with a bit of blush and the right shade of lipstick. In Dubai, there was no stepping out for work or formal appointments without proper make-up, something she would not have adhered to so vehemently in Kolkata.

Waiting on the dark leather settees of the lobby, Rasha felt a tingle of excitement going up and down her spine. She wasn't thinking that she would have to get the job to support her family and her father's battles in the courtroom. Rather, she was thinking of the interviews she would do and the gossip she would be privy to, thanks to her friends in the film industry in Mumbai. It was enough to impress her boss. It was as if she had come to retrieve her real self, the self that she failed to find when every morning she went through every single line of the newspaper, inadvertently looking for grammatical and typo errors.

Rasha knew Bollywood was big in Dubai, bigger than it was in Kolkata. Apart from the fan base that Bollywood stars had among the Indian diaspora and the local Emiratis, most of the top stars had homes in Dubai, and those who didn't, were in the city quite frequently to promote their films, attend events and shows, get beauty treatments done, or were simply on a holiday or to shop. So, joining a Bollywood magazine was after all not a bad idea.

Sabrina Kapadia shook hands with Rasha. She was dressed in an off-shoulder navy blue jumpsuit cinched at her slim waist. From the red inner side of the heel, Rasha could make out she was in a Christian Louboutin shoe. She had never been a brand-concious person, but brand-crazy Dubai had forced Rasha to read up fashion magazines, so she could be up-to-date on the style front.

'Lovely Louboutins,' Rasha said.

She did that even at the risk of sounding like a job hunter out to flatter a prospective employer, but somehow, Rasha had seen that being able to recognize a brand on somebody in Dubai made that person as happy and proud as he would be if you told him you knew that Gandhiji was his ancestor!

'Thanks!' said Sabrina, moving away the bangs from her forehead. She wore her hair in a short, straight, ironed blunt cut and looked more like a model on the Milan ramp than an editor.

In her mind, Rasha installed Sabrina on the editor's chair in *Our Times* or *Indian Chronicle* in Kolkata and she could actually see the employees—from the journalists to the peons—coming down in troops to check her out like one would do with a new white tiger cub in a zoo.

'Let's go to my room,' she said. She took Rasha to a glass walled room that had the most stunning view of the Dubai Marina. Rasha hoped, no…she actually prayed that she would get a job in *Silver Screen* and subsequently a desk overlooking the sea. At that moment, that was all she wanted.

'I can see you have considerable experience in journalism,' said Sabrina.

'But we are looking for a features writer. Your last post was that of a deputy editor. How do you plan to fit yourself in this post?'

'Can't you give me the post of a deputy editor?'

'Sadly, no, because we already have someone at the post, but we can try giving you something like lifestyle editor. But I will have to talk to HR about it.'

'What is the job of the lifestyle editor?' asked Rasha.

'We have a very small team so you will have to do everything—

writing, subbing, working on the pages... When can you join?' asked Sabrina.

'Any day,' said Rasha. 'But how much are you offering me?'

'Dhs 9000 (Rs 1,09,000 approx). That's our scale.'

Although the amount was more than double of what Rasha was earning in Kolkata, but living costs in Dubai were really high; and according to her market survey, the salary she was being offered was rather low.

'That's the salary for a trainee journalist in Dubai, certainly not of the lifestyle editor. I will request you to reconsider the package,' she said politely.

'Okay, we will think about it, but my senior would want to talk to you now.'

She left the room as Rasha's eyes quickly registered a speedboat throttling through the sea leaving a gush of foam behind. Sabrina came back with a lady in her forties. She mentioned her name and post, but she was not audible to Rasha. Rasha decided not to ask again. The lady was on the plumper side, with a shrewd face and was looking quite obnoxious in a pair of capris and a top. She could have been Indian or Pakistani, Rasha couldn't make out. After the usual set of questions on her experience, strengths and weaknesses, the lady came up with a stunner. 'Are you planning to have a baby?' she asked.

On any other occasion, Rasha would have retorted, 'It's a personal question,' but she reminded herself that she was at a job interview, so she smiled sweetly. 'We plan to enjoy our togetherness for a few years before we plunge into parenthood.'

Relief spread over the lady's face as if Rasha had finally given her the map to the gold mine she had been looking for all her life. On the other hand, Rasha tried hard to mask the disgust the absurd question had evoked in her.

If I got pregnant next month, would this lady come back to me and say you said this in your interview, how can you be pregnant now? thought Rasha angrily.

Sabrina whispered something into the lady's ears.

'You want a higher pay package? We can't guarantee that,' the lady said gruffly.

Arun had told her categorically not to short sell herself because many companies in Dubai were stingy with salaries although they had a good turnover. Rasha maintained her firm expression.

'Okay, we will email you,' Sabrina said.

The interview was over. While walking out, Rasha eyed an empty desk that faced a glass wall overlooking the sea. She longed for it more than anything else.

∼

'Good you made your point clear. If this one doesn't work out, there are plenty more out there,' Arun told her over dinner.

Rasha's mind went back to that empty desk as if it was already hers.

'I was thinking of this interview and my first job interview in *Kolkata Daily*. Time teaches you so many things.'

'Why, what had happened at your first interview?'

'I was right out of university. I had passed the written test, which was definitely more gruelling than the one I took for *Silver Screen*. I was sitting in front of Ehsaan Aziz, who was going through my CV.'

'Don't tell me you were actually interviewed by THE Ehsaan Aziz. He is probably the biggest journalist-editor Kolkata has ever had.'

'Yes, I am talking about the same person,' said Rasha.

'I have read his editorials since my childhood. He is brilliant.'

'I guess every brilliant man has a temper and Ehsaan Aziz had one, too. He didn't ask me any questions, but rebuked me for the entire fifteen minutes that I sat in front of him. He went through some of my samples—published and unpublished articles—and had something negative to say about each and every line. Finally, when he was through, I felt like I was the biggest idiot Kolkata had ever produced. I had never felt so dejected.'

'Then how did you get the job?'

'That same evening, I got a call from *Kolkata Daily*, saying he wanted to meet me again the next day. He sat at the same place in a worse mood. I was a bundle of nerves. When he looked up, his handsome face broke into a million-watt smile. He said, "I have chosen you to work in the features department. Your pay will be Rs 3,300. You will be on probation for six months; and if you don't perform, you will be kicked out immediately." I felt the moon had dropped from the sky into my hand. Later, I came to know he had chosen five people out of fifty shortlisted candidates and I was one of them. The pay was paltry, but there was so much pride to be handpicked by Ehsaan Aziz.'

∾

Silver Screen made a formal offer to Rasha with a re-worked package of Dhs 13,000 that she was happy with, although it still fell short of the market rate. But Rasha took it up thinking that it would leave her with enough after covering her father's lawsuit costs and the family expenses, so she didn't have reasons to complain. She just kept her fingers crossed for that desk with the sea-view.

Rasha felt oddly happy that circumstances had cut short her housewife ambitions and she was back in front of a workstation with an internet connection and a phone by her side. Her happiness on her first day at *Silver Screen* knew no bounds when Sabrina showed her to the empty desk she had coveted. It was finally hers. Her eyes feasted on the innumerable white yachts moored in the marina that was surrounded on all sides by tall finished and unfinished buildings.

Sabrina, who was in a mini skirt suit, told Rasha about the welcome lunch she had arranged for her that would be attended by the team. She also told her about her job responsibilities that included doing the astrology page, the recipe page, the TV- and film-listings pages. She would have to put in the captions in the events pages too and also interview a Dubaiite every week asking them about all their favourite hangouts. Rasha tried hard to look eager to excel despite the lack of excitement her job responsibilities entailed.

'Did you go through the links of the stories I had attached with my CV?' she asked Sabrina.

Sabrina rolled up her eyes and put her fingers to her forehead and her thumbs to the temple as if she was trying hard to shoot down a migraine attack. She let out a long sigh.

'No, never got the time.'

Lunch was at an Italian restaurant that spread out to an open-air area. They all sat on the lawn to enjoy the January sun. The lawn was surrounded by restaurants, all of which had outdoor seating arrangements. The chairs were filled with office-goers grabbing a quick lunch or relaxing over shisha. Sabrina had invited Priya Jayaraman, the fashion editor, Dimpy Arora, the deputy editor, Jessica Brandon, the designer and two people from the marketing team. It was an all-women team.

Gorging on pasta and pizza, the conversation moved to where each of them had the best pizza ever.

'It has to be authentic Italian pizza,' said Sabrina.

'Where do you get that in Dubai?' Rasha asked.

'I won't be able to tell you that, but I always have it in Italy,' said Sabrina.

'There is this small restaurant on 42nd Street in New York. I prefer it there,' said Priya very matter-of-factly, as if 42nd Street was just around the corner.

'Have you ever tried the Tom Yum Pizza? It's different, but it's amazing. It's a Malaysian special. I always try it whenever I am in KL,' Dimpy said and turned to Rasha. 'What's your preference, Rasha?'

'I love the spicy korma pizza at Pizza Hut, Kolkata,' Rasha said. She had half expected everyone to sneer at her lopsided native taste buds, but all nodded, managing to incorporate the Indian pizza in the conversation along with the authentic and exotic international varieties.

'I have this wedding to attend in Abu Dhabi this evening where Sushmita Sen, SRK and a whole lot of stars are coming. I am wearing a Cavalli, but I can't decide on my diamonds,' said Dimpy.

'Make sure you wear loads of diamonds. All the top Indians from UAE will be there. You have to look important,' said Sabrina seriously, as if Dimpy had a meeting scheduled with Sonia Gandhi on matters of national importance.

Rasha felt like saying, 'How can diamonds make a journalist look important?' but instead she asked, 'I know there is an anarkali style of salwar kurta in vogue these days, but now there is something called a qawalli too. How does that look?'

Deathly silence fell over the table and everyone looked at Rasha like a Martian had just landed.

'She meant a Roberto Cavalli-designed dress, Rasha,' said Sabrina, breaking the silence. For the first time in her life, Rasha felt like hiding under the table out of sheer embarrassment. She felt like a fish out of water with her mismatched flat sandals in the middle of branded high-heels.

Interlude

• • •

It had now become a daily ritual. After scouring the job sites and newspaper advertisements and sending her CV to every possible place, Rasha would set off for Dubai Creek. It took her twenty minutes to walk to the waterfront. She would sit at a bench overlooking the water ogling at the state-of-the-art yachts anchored there. Rasha had always dreamt of taking Arun out on a romantic trip on a yacht. But her dream had long died. Her finances were in such a state that she was struggling to keep her head above the water, renting an expensive yacht was not an option.

She looked at the air-conditioned water taxis and the quaint wooden boats—the abras, the traditional means of transport of UAE—plying the waters. A to-and-fro water taxi ride cost six dirhams (₹72 approx.) and an abra ride even lesser. The tourists on the abras seemed to be enjoying thoroughly. Rasha felt better, she could still afford an abra.

The blaring music from a Lexus, that had docked in the parking space just behind her, interrupted her thoughts. She instinctively looked at the car only to look away with a jolt. Sabrina was disembarking from the car with two foreigners—one lady and one gentleman. The last thing Rasha wanted now was an encounter with Sabrina Kapadia. If they came face-to-face, chances were Sabrina would be bound and gagged by her and thrown into the depths of the Dubai Creek with a huge rock tied to her feet.

Thankfully, Sabrina did not notice her and headed for a huge white yacht standing at a distance. Rasha went back to her cocoon of peace, watching the abras. The great white yacht retracted the anchor and set sail, taking Sabrina in it and Rasha's woes too.

Part 5

Time Stands Still

• • •

19

SABRINA STOOD NEXT to Rasha's desk, indulging in her only ungainly habit—biting her nails. She looked nervous. 'I don't know what will happen? How will we bring out the edition?' she said.

Rasha looked at her calmly. 'We still have two more days. We will do it, don't worry.'

'Are you sure?'

'Yes, I am,' Rasha said confidently.

'You will stay back and finish the work, right?'

'The work will be finished,' said Rasha, in a cold voice.

'Thank you sooooo much. Hugs! Hugs! Hugs!' Sabrina said, hugging Rasha.

During any crisis, Sabrina Kapadia started to behave like a teenager about to have a panic attack in the examination hall. But once the crisis passed, she would snap back to the Milan-model mode, and walk around the office as if she owned the world. So right now, while Sabrina looked and behaved like a lost adolescent, Rasha sounded like the reassuring mother in complete control of the situation. It was another matter that Sabrina was the one at the helm of affairs at *Silver Screen,* and in the last ten months, Rasha's responsibilities hadn't grown beyond the ones delegated to her on the first day—the horoscope, recipe, TV listings pages et al.

Any interview or feature idea Rasha came up with was quickly shot down by Dimpy Arora and Sabrina let her deputy editor take the decisions because she abhorred any kind of brainwork. Sabrina was out for meetings most of the day and left the running of the magazine completely to Dimpy, who in turn was kept busy with her endless 'networking calls' that resulted in relentless gossip in her high-pitched tone. This way, Dimpy ensured the whole office got a slice of the entertainment too. An entire week would pass by like that and Sabrina would only take interest in the magazine on the deadline day. She would be critical of the disorganized Dimpy for not doing her work properly and then divide all the pending work between Rasha and Priya. Not to mention that even during this desperate bid to meet the deadline, Sabrina would get up from her desk at least fifty times to make trips to the washroom, to the pantry, to chat with people from other magazines housed in the same building, to take endless calls and to redo her make-up. As a result, the deadline of 6.00 p.m. would be shamelessly flouted week after week. If the magazine managed to reach the press at 10.00 p.m., it would be considered a job done well.

In the midst of all this, Sabrina could not care less if Rasha's talent was being utilized or not, although she would frequently ask her feature ideas and pass them off as her own to her bosses. Rasha discovered this when she found the printouts of her emails lying on the printer one day. Dimpy, on the other hand, was talented, but was all over the place. Dimpy was a film fanatic, who could rattle off dates, anecdotes, link-ups in Bollywood like a numeric table. From day one, however, she was clearly insecure about Rasha. She ensured that Rasha only interviewed starlets and wannabes, while she reserved the big stars for herself. Rasha preferred to bide her time instead of getting into a face-off with Dimpy.

And that time finally came. Dimpy claimed her husband had got a job in Delhi, so they were moving in two days. In reality, everyone knew that his company was one of the first to be hit by the wave of recession that had taken off like a tsunami from the doors of the US-based Lehman Brothers in September 2008 and had lashed on the shores of Dubai by the end of that year. Dimpy's husband had been sacked and he was moving back to Delhi with his entire family. Like many others who frantically job-searched while their wives held fort, Dimpy's husband couldn't do that because that would have meant downgrading from their four-bedroom villa on Jumeirah Road to a one-bedroom apartment that he was not willing to shift to. He preferred to move to his three-bedroom apartment in Noida than to a so-called cubby hole in Dubai.

Since the time Dimpy had broken the news, Sabrina began to fret and Rasha smiled in her heart. But Dimpy was not the only worry. Page designer Jessica Brandon had said that she was going to the UK for the weekend to see her ailing mother. Rasha had actually found that odd because Jessica had earlier told her that despite staying just miles away from London, she met her mother only on Christmas. Rasha thought it was unlike her to spend all the money and travel to London just to meet her mom and that too for a couple of days. And she was proved right. Jessica emailed that she was staying back in London to look after her mom, but when the incessant calls from different banks started coming in, the HR of *Silver Screen* realized that Jessica had taken out Dhs 500,000 (Rs 60,00,000 approx) from her nine credit cards and had fled the country!

So, *Silver Screen* was in a spot with its designer gone and deputy editor leaving. And Rasha thought it offered her the best opportunity to swing into action.

'Priya can make the pages and I can help her,' she told Sabrina.

'Really? Does she know page making?'

Sabrina was the editor of a Bollywood magazine and yet had not watched a single Hindi movie in her entire life, a fact she proudly told her teammates, everytime there was some discussion on Hindi films. She was also completely ignorant of the talent her team had. Priya was a brilliant journalist with considerable experience. She had also been a deft animator and software wiz, a dress designer for Malayali films and her planning and organisation skills bordered on OCD. Of course, Sabrina knew none of that.

'We will divide the editing work between us,' Rasha said.

'Great! Great! I have a lunch appointment and will be back in an hour.'

Rasha knew an hour could extend to three, but it did not make any difference, because Sabrina was anything but hands-on. She considered delegating work as her birthright.

Rasha and Priya got down to frantic rewriting of the endless interviews and features that had been sent by Sabrina's brother, Soham Kapadia, who ran a small office in Mumbai, hobnobbed with the stars and sent pages and pages of grammatically incorrect, staid interviews, which Rasha, Priya and Dimpy had to set right. With Dimpy gone, the harrowing job had to be done by just the two of them now. How much Soham got paid for his tonnes of garbage was a closely-guarded secret. Sabrina made sure she handled the billing and budgeting. Although the team called her 'The Delegation Damsel', this was one job she absolutely refused to delegate to anybody. She had once got extremely miffed with Dimpy when she offered to do it for her.

It was evident that Soham and Sabrina knew Bollywood stars well because they ensured that some of them walked into their office often or attended *Silver Screen* events. The effects lingered on for months and earned Sabrina ample brownie points from her star-struck bosses. Hence, her failure to do exclusive stories or edgy interviews for the magazine was never questioned. In truth, what Soham sent over, Rasha could edit with her eyes closed because everything fell into the same mould. But the copies were fraught with so many mistakes that a moment's lapse of concentration would result in one being overlooked which would be promptly circled by Sabrina's red pen and Rasha would be hauled up for it.

However, Soham was prolific, so Sabrina was satisfied with her team taking on the rewriting job and not doing much original writing. Rasha should have been completely frustrated with the arrangement but wasn't yet. She convinced herself that if one could walk away with a salary just by subbing and doing inane pages, one shouldn't have any reason to complain. She was happy to be home on time, go out on dinner dates with Arun, and generally not worry that she had some star to chase that evening. But she knew she was becoming indolent. So, when Dimpy left, she was determined to shake herself up and show *Silver Screen* her true self.

Sabrina came back in two hours and asked for an update on the situation.

'We are fine. All copies subbed and Priya is sitting with the designing, although it will be better if you can arrange for a freelance designer,' said Rasha authoritatively. 'The only problem is that we have four blank pages and we need a really good feature or interview there.'

'Oh God! Email Soham. Tell him to send us something immediately,' wailed Sabrina.

'...Unless I do a story,' Rasha said.

'Story? You have a story?' asked Sabrina, as if Rasha was talking about some hidden treasure which she was not supposed to know.

'Yes, Zohaib Khan is shooting in Dubai for his latest film and he is shooting in the aquarium at Dubai Mall today. He is going to shark-dive there,' said Rasha.

'Wow! How did you know that? Zohaib Khan is so cute. You know him?'

'Yeah, kind of.'

'Can you get photographs of his shark dive and an interview with him? It will be awesome.'

'Let me try.'

∾

With two hits in a row, in a matter of a year, Zohaib Khan had become a name to reckon with in Bollywood and also a frequent visitor to Dubai, since most of his films were shot there. But on that particular day, he had a lot on his mind. For starters, he was about to be interviewed by his best friend Rasha Roy, who was completely capable of telling him off by saying, 'That's a stupid answer!' Secondly, he was about to swim with four hundred sharks and sting rays in a tank which held ten million litres of water and had a glass frontage as long as 32.8m, through which all his fans would be peering if they came to know he was in there. He was tense.

The night before, he had sneaked out of his hotel room in Park Hyatt and spent it at Rasha and Arun's cosy apartment, chatting late and then sleeping in Arun's pyjamas in their bed while they slept on the sofa-bed in the living room. They talked about that fateful night when they were both kidnapped and how Saleem bhai had come to their rescue. But a certain detail about that incident had been inadvertently erased from all discussions—the detail that Rasha had never discussed with Arun. After the clarifications that morning at Rasha's home, Zohaib also never brought it up.

Rasha told him that Ansh Ramchandani's third victim, Surit da, had married Gia and was now getting ready to don the mantle of fatherhood. Zohaib told her that he later found out Vineet Agarwal, her supposed stalker from Tantra, was behaving so weirdly that night because he was out to buy condoms! She was on the floor in peals clutching a cushion for support. She had never mentioned anything about an interview at that time to Zohaib and now she was dropping in at Dubai Mall, after calling him on his local number to inform him of her plans.

Zohaib put on the scuba diving gear as he listened intently to the instructor. He was understandably glad that the man would be accompanying him inside the water. As the cameraman took his position with his underwater camera, Zohaib dived.

The Dubai Aquarium was a marvel in itself. It was not only

one of the largest tanks in the world, but also had the world's largest viewing panel with 33,000 living creatures swimming inside. Rasha was standing on the first floor balcony with Forever 21 and New Look behind her and the glass fascia of the aquarium in front of her. She usually loved to spend hours standing there, watching the sting rays swimming in schools, creating symphony in the water. But now she was a bit tense. She had always seen divers getting down in cages to feed the sharks, but Zohaib would be going down without the cage. She hoped everything would go right. She spotted Zohaib inside. He was wearing a black wet suit and yellow flippers with black-and-yellow rimmed diving goggles.

Zohaib comfortably reached the floor of the aquarium and was walking on it in his flippers as a group of small grey fishes with yellow tails surrounded him. He passed through the arch of a rock, touched the large white flower-shaped corals and dodged a huge sting ray that passed by him nonchalantly. A small crowd of teenagers had gathered now because news had travelled that Zohaib Khan was shooting there. Zohaib waved to his fans from behind the glass. Young girls in the crowd squealed in excitement. Then the unthinkable happened.

In his bid to climb the long jutting rocks on the right side of the aquarium, Zohaib lost his footing. He tumbled on a sharp piece of rock. Instantly, two Tiger sharks, each about 3.5 metre long, made a dash for Zohaib. With a wave of his hand, he tried to fend them off, but one had closed in on him. The diving instructor, who was behind Zohaib, instantly rushed towards the sharks with a long stick in his hand. He grabbed Zohaib by the waist and darted towards the surface. But the sharks followed them and one even lunged at the instructor's feet. Rasha could see two more safety divers swimming towards them. Seeing them, the sharks became a bit reluctant and finally stopped tailing the men.

The gathered crowd hit the panic button and the girls who

were earlier screaming with glee were now screaming in horror. Without wasting any time, Rasha ran to the area where Zohaib would be exiting the aquarium. Security tried to stop her, but they sensed the urgency in her voice and let her go. When she reached Zohaib, he was getting his arm bandaged and looked pale.

Seeing Rasha, he managed a smile. 'They are saying Tiger sharks don't usually attack. I don't know what happened.'

'I guess they also wanted a piece of the famous Zohaib Khan,' said Rasha.

His smile became broader. 'You want to do the interview right now?'

'Relax, Zohaib. Let's have lunch at Ping Pong downstairs. Then we can talk.'

They sat on the terrace of Ping Pong that overlooked the Musical Fountain and the Burj Khalifa.

'I am impressed. You have already got a hang of what readers want to read and you are talking accordingly.'

Rasha closed her notepad and bit into a dimsum.

'I guess having a journalist as your best friend helps,' smiled Zohaib.

'Can we order some more dimsums? Don't be stingy, Zohaib.'

'If my old friend thinks I am stingy, then it's good.'

'Why?'

'Then I haven't changed at all.'

He ordered two more plates.

A teenager and her mother approached their table and asked if they could pose with Zohaib for a picture. He happily obliged. The camera was thrust into Rasha's hands. Rasha's heart swelled with pride as she clicked the picture.

∾

Back in the office, sitting at her desk, Rasha wrote:

Headline: **Shark attack on Zohaib Khan**

Introduction: **In an EXCLUSIVE interview to *Silver Screen*, the actor recounts his experience of shooting inside the aquarium at Dubai Mall.**

She felt the adrenaline rushing through her veins and pouring into her muscles, giving her a feeling that she was getting ready for a bungee jump—a feeling that she had not experienced for a very long time.

It was 8.00 p.m. when Sabrina walked into the department. After her brief appearance following the two-hour lunch, she had vanished only to resurface just then.

'Good! Good! You are staying back late,' she said.

The only thing that made the editor of *Silver Screen* genuinely happy was someone staying back late at work. Of course, she didn't know if the person was staying back to make international calls home or to actually work. Sabrina did not enquire if Rasha got Zohaib Khan's interview. She would do it only on the deadline day.

'Wow! Great story, Rasha. We should have given this article six pages instead of four,' said Sabrina at 3.00 p.m. on the deadline day. Of course, with so little time in hand, redoing the pages was out of question.

~

For the first time since she had joined *Silver Screen*, Rasha felt really proud of her work. However, it was not possible to extend the article since time was at a premium. Then, between her innumerable sojourns to the washroom, cafeteria and other people's desks, Sabrina glanced through the pages. But she did not express any kind of satisfaction when the pages went to press at 7.00 p.m. Rasha stayed back, organizing the next week's edition, although Priya had already left. She lived with three single girls in an apartment in Discovery Gardens and it was her turn to cook that day.

When Sabrina came back from the smoking room at 9.30 p.m., Rasha was leaving. 'Oh, wow! You are still here. I am impressed,' she said.

Rasha wasn't surprised that Sabrina was happy about her staying back late. Sabrina, of course, hadn't noticed that they had finished closest to the deadline that day and they even had an exclusive story.

Rasha popped a question. 'With Dimpy gone, who will be deputy editor now?'

'We will have to get someone.'

'Why aren't you giving me the post?'

She looked at Rasha like she had asked the most outrageous question.

'You have been doing only the horoscope and recipe pages for the last one year. You have not proved yourself yet.'

Rasha felt like saying, *It's because of your stupidity*, but didn't. She realized that it was a mistake on her part to buy peace with the jealous, over-reactive Dimpy and bide time. She should have gone for the kill from day one.

'We need someone more experienced for the post anyway,' said Sabrina.

But you have only two years experience and you are the editor. I have lot more experience than you, she felt like saying, but remained silent yet again.

'Don't worry, I will ensure you get a good raise in the upcoming appraisals. Keep up the good job,' said Sabrina, sensing Rasha's discontent.

∾

When Rasha stepped out of the office, it was almost 10.00 p.m. and being a strictly commercial area, Media City looked desolate. Rasha saw the yellow light on the top of an empty cab and signalled it to stop and hopped in. At that time of the night, it took her twenty minutes to reach home in Karama, but on most days when she left office at 6.00 p.m. it would take her an hour because of the heavy traffic. Most people in her office lived in closer locations for the convenience of travel, but Rasha stayed put in Karama for one reason—the bustle and food reminded her of home.

'Where in Karama, Madam?' asked the cabbie, as he steered the car through Sheikh Zayed Road, the main artery of Dubai.

'Opposite Burjuman Mall,' Rasha said, looking up at the tall residential and office buildings lining both sides of the road.

Every time she travelled through this part of Dubai, she was as mesmerized as she was on the day she had landed in the city. Her eyes lingered on the Emirates Towers, her favourite building on Sheikh Zayed Road. The two asymmetrically-shaped towers were an architectural wonder and housed a hotel, an exclusive mall, restaurants and offices. She looked up at the thirty-nine storey World Trade Centre that was the first highrise to come up on Sheikh Zayed Road in 1978 and was modelled on the original one, destroyed in the 9/11 attacks.

The shrill ringtone of her mobile phone made her jump out of her thoughts. It was a missed call from her mother, reminding her to call back. She called home every night without fail. Rania seldom spoke to her. She hadn't found a job to her liking yet, but she had joined an NGO that worked towards meeting the simple needs of people in their old age. Like others in the NGO, Rania spent time with the elderly, reading out newspaper to them, paying their electricity and phone bills, taking them to the doctor or buying them medicines. Rasha was happy that Rania was at least doing something worthwhile and it didn't really matter that she wasn't earning money. Her dad often tried to give her updates on the court case because he felt she deserved to know since she was funding it. Rasha hardly understood the nitty gritties, but she figured this much that it was complicated and would take time.

'You are going back so late? Is it safe?' her mother asked on the phone.

'Yes, Ma. It is very safe. Much safer than Kolkata.'

In her fourteen months in Dubai, she had almost forgotten the street-savvy skills she had mastered in Kolkata. She didn't have to deal with protruding elbows in the backseat of auto rickshaws, lewd comments on the streets, bottom pinching in buses and metros or even cabbies misbehaving and threatening to dump her in the middle of the road. The same Indians who dared to misbehave with women in their own country were strangely civil in this foreign land.

'What language are you speaking, Madam?' the cab driver asked after she hung up.

'Bengali.'

'Oh, you are Bangladeshi?'

'No, I am from West Bengal, which is in India. Bengal and Bangladesh were together before the partition.'

'My grandfather also lived in India, but moved to Pakistan after the partition,' he said.

Rasha had not met a single Pakistani till she came to Dubai and, like many of her generation, believed that they would be as hostile in their face-to-face interaction with Indians as they were in Kargil or Kashmir. Now she knew—starting from food to clothes to hospitality to family bonding—no two communities had as much in common as Pakistanis and Indians.

'I came here in 1970 and Dubai started developing in the early 80s. I have seen it all. I have lived in the deserts with the bedouins and I can speak the kind of Arabic they spoke.'

He uttered a few Arabic words with more pronounced guttural sounds. Rasha could not make out any difference because she didn't know any Arabic at all.

'Is your family in Pakistan?' Rasha asked.

'Yes. I have three sons, a daughter and my wife. Daughter is married and has two sons. Two of my sons are engineers and one is in the plastic business.'

'Don't you want to go back?'

'Yes, I really want to but...' He had a distant look in his eyes. 'I am not sure if they would be happy if I returned. They are so used to life without me. I have built a two-storeyed house in my village and I really want to live there. But I am not sure they would be too happy if I just go there and do nothing. My income ensures a lot of luxuries for them.'

'That's not true, bhai saab. I am sure they will be happy if you go back. Your sons are settled anyway.'

'I hope so.'

'Drop me in front of Burjuman, bhai saab. I will walk it from there. '

'No, Madam. It's too late. I can't drop you there. Tell me which turn to take and I will drop you at your doorstep.'

'And, Madam, keep my number. If you need a taxi anytime, just call me,' he said after Rasha got off the cab.

Rasha keyed in his number and saved it as bhai saab. She stood on the sidewalk, her eyes trailing the taxi till it turned the corner. She wondered if like bhai saab, her family too would be unhappy if she decided to leave it all and go back to Kolkata one day. She felt a bit ashamed of even entertaining thoughts like that.

20

RASHA'S SQUARE-SHAPED DINNER set with yellow floral designs was out from its resting place in the kitchen cupboard. She had cooked prawns in Thai green curry, jasmine rice, pepper chicken and custard. Her menu was much too simple compared to what was usually served at their Bengali friends' homes. There would be anything between ten to fourteen dishes, but Rasha knew she wouldn't be able to stretch herself to conform to Dubai's hosting standards, so she acknowledged her limitations and always kept her menu limited. Despite the minimalistic spread on the table, the appreciation from her friends was always bountiful.

Ankita and Hiran Bagchi sat on their drawing room sofa sipping wine bought from the Dubai duty-free shops. Arun hadn't bothered to get a liquor license because their friends in Dubai were strictly social drinkers and there was never a need to buy liquor continuously for which a license was needed. People were equally happy with coffee, lassi, juice, or even a can of Coke, so the sparse supply of liquor was good enough.

The other two guests for the evening were Soumen and Reema Sengupta. While Soumen worked as an architect in Arun's company, Reema was a housewife and an amateur photographer with a kitty full of awards and photographs published in the *National Geographic*. She was the one who had done the rounds of Ikea and Lifestyle with Rasha, helping her decorate her home. She was the one who had taught her how to clingwrap and refrigerate food, how to pressure-cook prawns to make them soft and supple, how to put dry flowers in the closet to keep them smelling fresh and how to click good pictures on manual mode.

Ankita Bagchi, by then, had fought her inner demons and managed to like Rasha immensely. They bonded over shared experiences of star interactions and media lingos. Rasha could feel Ankita missed her days at *Winds of Change* immensely. With her daughter grown up and having a life of her own, Ankita had become restless, whiling away her time, shopping and socializing. For this cozy do at Rasha's home, Ankita wore a simple white salwar kurta. She sat with both feet up on the sofa in a drawing room that was three times smaller than her own. She looked utterly at ease. Except for the solitaire on her finger, she had no jewellery on. She managed to look so stylish in such simple clothes that Rasha gaped at her. *Ankita di could give Sabrina a run for her money*, she mused.

Ankita, on the other hand, was thinking of what Rasha had told her the day before.

'It's been a month and they have still not managed to get someone for the post of deputy editor. I know you have been an editor before, but it would be a good opportunity if you are thinking of reviving your career. As such, the editor doesn't do much, so you will be the decision maker,' she had said.

'Will I be able to do it?' asked Ankita, looking questioningly at Reema and Rasha.

The men had gone for a smoke to the balcony and Ankita took the opportunity to finally have their girl-to-girl talk.

'I don't see any reason why you can't. You have all the experience,' said Reema.

'But it's been such a long hiatus. So much has changed from the time I was an editor,' said Ankita.

'But the basics of journalism remain the same, right? You have to know how to report, write and edit. I am sure you have not forgotten that,' said Rasha.

'I still have to think about it,' Ankita said. Reema and Rasha glanced at each other.

～

Rasha was not having a great day at work. After slogging her head off for the last one-and-a-half months and ensuring *Silver Screen* looked current, exclusive and smart, she had managed to secure a good appraisal for herself. In fact, she had even begun to think of Sabrina as one of the better bosses. But all that had changed that morning when she came to know that Priya's increment letter had come. She asked Sabrina about her own.

'Oh! Rasha, I am so sorry I forgot to send your appraisal to HR. I am soooo sorry. But we will have another one in three months and I am sure you will get a good hike. Please, please forgive me.'

Rasha was so angry that she could feel her insides boiling in rage.

'They haven't given me any increment too,' grinned Sabrina, trying to appease Rasha.

When Sabrina—who had an influential father with the biggest jewellery business in town and who spent all her money buying bags, shoes, perfumes and holidays in exotic locales—talked about not getting an increment, Rasha's rage got worse. Her own responsibilities at home had increased from the time she took up her job at *Silver Screen*; and more than anything else at that moment, she badly needed a pay hike.

Rania had altogether given up her job search and was totally engrossed in her NGO work. Whenever she needed money, she withdrew it from their joint account, where Rasha sent money every month. Her dad had appointed a more expensive lawyer, who had assured him that they would win the case. Of course, he couldn't say when. Rasha was supporting a household of three with one full-time and one part-time maid and maintaining a Maruti Esteem with a driver. Every day she felt the need to earn a bit more to meet the escalating costs back home and in Dubai too. Since she also had a career, she believed in sharing the household costs with Arun. Although he thought that was unnecessary, he didn't stop her, knowing it was important to her. Arun never asked Rasha about how much she sent to her account in Kolkata every month. On the contrary, knowing how forgetful she was, he continued to slip in a few hundred dirhams into her purse to ensure that she always had enough cash with her.

Rasha sat seething at her desk. The phone rang. It was one of her contacts from Bollywood TV Channel.

'We are organizing the Bollywood Awards in London. We want to invite you there to cover it on behalf of *Silver Screen*,' he said.

Rasha wasn't sure about her luck at that moment. She felt there was a high possibility that Sabrina would end up going to London herself or sending Soham instead. She got up from her desk to get some coffee and clear her mind when she saw Ankita. She was in a well-cut white shirt and Rasha was sure it was branded, although she could not tell which brand it was. She wore a pair of fitting black trousers and carried a Louis Vuitton bag. Rasha was about to giggle as she looked at her feet. Ankita was in a pair of Christian Louboutins. She had lost even more weight since the first time Rasha had met her and looked striking. Her Prada sunglasses were strung around her neck. The Cs of a pair of Chanel earrings pompously occupied her earlobes. She had both looks and brands to flaunt. She made each and every head turn at *Silver Screen*.

Rasha had told Ankita never to tell Sabrina that she knew her because that would ruin her chances of getting a job in *Silver Screen*. Sabrina wouldn't at all want one of Rasha's friends in a decision-making position. So, she walked past Rasha without making eye contact and went inside Sabrina's room. Moments later, Sabrina came out and introduced Ankita Bagchi to Rasha and Priya as the new deputy editor joining from that day. Rasha heaved a sigh of relief.

After work, Rasha sneaked into Ankita di's Mercedes in the underground parking and they giggled like two schoolgirls, who had pulled a fast one on a hated teacher. They laughed till they were breathless.

'Let's catch a quick mocktail at Barasti, then we can head home. I would have loved to have beer, but no question of drinking and driving,' Ankita said.

'You can have your beer and I can drive.'

'When did you get your license? You never told me.'

'Yesterday.'

'How many tries?'

'Third try. Don't worry, no one can beat your record of making it at the first attempt.'

Barasti at Le Meridien Mina Seyahi was packed with after-office revellers, mostly Britons, with a few Indians thrown in. The wooden flooring of the pub extended to an open-air area with a thatched roof that had a view of the Atlantis. The beach could be accessed from the pub. Had they arrived earlier, Rasha would have definitely gone off for a stroll down the beach, but the sun had already gone down and the sea had merged into darkness. They sat at a corner table and ordered their mocktails.

'I am sure you know that when they opened the Atlantis last month, so many stars from Hollywood came down for the huge inaugural bash that was covered by media from all over the world. Shah Rukh Khan was actually staying in a 10,000-square-feet suite where he even threw a private party,' said Rasha, looking longingly at the lights of Atlantis in the distance.

'When Priya and I suggested that we should try to unearth every single detail of what the stars were doing there, Sabrina said we should not step out of office since we were understaffed. She attended the inauguration and the after-parties, but did not write anything about anything. She just went around telling everyone that she had dinner with Priyanka Chopra. Can you imagine I had to ferret out information from articles in *Mumbai Mirror* and *Mid Day* to write on the Atlantis opening? It was so frustrating. Now I have this offer to cover the Bollywood Awards in London. I don't know whether she would let me go or not.'

'Now that I have joined, I don't see any reason why you can't go. I will see to it that you go,' said Ankita.

'By the way, make sure you don't end up calling me Ankita di in office. You don't know me, right?'

Rasha started laughing again, that hysterical schoolgirl laugh.

∾

Prior to Ankita's joining, Rasha had functioned like a one-woman army at *Silver Screen*. And to her nightmare, Sabrina did become more hands-on. She often sat down to edit the copies that her brother sent. 'I think this is not good enough. Can you rewrite this piece? I will take a look at it after that,' Sabrina would say. Rasha could see more work piling up, as Sabrina rejected more and more copies and pictures asking her to rework the writing and look again for pictures.

'I have an event to attend. You are staying back and finishing everything, I am sure,' Sabrina would say.

If Rasha nodded in the affirmative, she got hugs, hugs, hugs and if she didn't, Sabrina would come and stand by her desk with a serious expression.

'I think you should stay back. There is so much to do.' That was the only refrain she knew.

Ankita Bagchi changed all that. She never flouted the deadline of 6.00 p.m. She shared Rasha and Priya's rewriting load and was a brilliant planner and organizer. Rasha was elated that she had finally found the quintessential deputy editor. She even took on the mundane work of horoscopes and recipes from Rasha.

'I think you should start writing now. Start with a great job in London,' Ankita said.

∾

Rasha's three-day London trip was hectic, but she enjoyed every bit of it. She chased the stars at the rehearsals, got both red-carpet and backstage scoops and talked to each and every star attending the award ceremony.

No photographer had travelled with her from Dubai, so she had to grab a Bollywood TV photographer in London, who promised to give her the stills after the awards. When she finally spotted him after the event, Rasha actually jumped into his car, made him drive her to the hotel and fed him dinner, while all the photographs were being downloaded on her laptop. She stayed awake till 4.00 a.m. filing stories for the internet edition, almost missed her flight and then landed in Dubai armed with four hundred exclusive pictures and unlimited scoops for the magazine. She went straight from the airport to the office only to be greeted by a rude shock.

As soon as she stepped inside her office building, she could sense something was amiss. *Silver Screen's* umbrella company published twelve more magazines, which were housed in three floors of the same building. She first went to the tenth floor, where the cafeteria was also located, and peered through the glass door. She was greeted by several empty desks and the occupants of the other desks looked forlorn. She took the stairs to the eleventh floor. On the left side of the elevator were *Silver Screen* and two smaller magazines. On the right side were the offices of four other magazines. Rasha could not see a single soul through the glass wall on the right. She could feel her heart in her throat.

She opened the opaque *Silver Screen* door, half expecting

emptiness there too. To her relief, all her colleagues were at their respective desks, although the cluster of desks to her right and left were empty. She knew the Lebanese girl, who sat on her left and worked for the Arabic magazine, and often left chocolates for her on her desk. But she strangely could not recall the name of the girl who sat behind her and worked in the gourmet section. Rasha had never interacted with her. In fact, she found it weird that she actually didn't know the name of the girl who sat behind her for nine hours every day, five days a week.

She placed her small travel bag below her desk and the handbag on top of it. She turned towards a sullen-faced deputy editor.

'How was it?' asked Ankita.

'Very hectic, but fruitful. What happened here?'

'A lot. You should be glad you were not here. It was very hard for us.'

'What happened?'

'They had to close down six magazines because they couldn't bear the overhead costs anymore. HR just told these people to leave the office as soon as they came in to work yesterday. It was a horrible scene. Some were crying, some were shouting angrily and trying to break office property. Security had to be called in. We sat in the middle of all this, trying to work.'

'It must have been horrible,' said Rasha

Rasha now looked at Ankita with fearful eyes. 'Now, what happens to us?'

'Sabrina has scheduled a meeting today at 3.00 p.m. We were waiting for you.'

The meeting was attended by Sabrina's bosses and the HR, so she was carrying her notepad and a bunch of printouts and was exuding her usual air of authority. She sat at the head of the table in the meeting room.

'I know unpleasant things happened in the office yesterday, but the management didn't have an alternative,' she said.

Rasha thought of her home in Gariahat and her parents watching *Debi* on TV in their airy living room, basking in the security of their daughter's job in the Middle East.

'We are also going through a tough time. The advertisements are dwindling.'

She thought of the court case and the land that her father so desperately wanted back.

'And people are not buying anything more than necessities.'

Rasha could visualize Rania sitting with an old couple somewhere in Kolkata, reading out a book to them.

'But the good news is *Silver Screen* is still making profit. But we cannot be complacent. Our circulation is dipping rapidly. So, we have to work harder to ensure better sales even if that means staying back late in office every day.' The last nine words of the sentence were said in a commanding tone.

So, *Silver Screen* was not folding up. Sabrina's voice had never felt so pleasant to Rasha's ears. When she came back to sit at her desk, the view of the Marina looked a little bit more tranquil than usual.

∾

That meeting was probably Sabrina's last involvement with the magazine. Ankita took over like the captain of a ship and navigated the boat through choppy waters with her intelligent marketing strategies and feature ideas. Sabrina also made her contribution by staying outside office, attending endless meetings throughout the day and on deadline day, she was so busy—with what, no one knew—that she didn't have the time to go through the magazine anymore. A few months down the line, the team knew that Sabrina didn't go through the magazine even after it was published. Not even through the editor's note that was diligently written by the deputy editor and went with Sabrina's stylish photo and name.

But she began to worry about one thing. Rasha, Priya and Ankita were now writing so much for the magazine that Soham's copies were being given less and less space. And that meant her brother was earning less and less from his crappy articles.

'I think this story is brilliant, you should take it,' Sabrina sometimes told Ankita.

Ankita would answer with finality. 'It's full of fluff. There is nothing new in it.'

'As you wish,' Sabrina would meekly say. Few weeks later, she would again mention how she still thought the article was great. Ankita would continue to disregard her suggestions.

Months passed, but the recession hung on *Silver Screen* like the sword of Damocles. Circulation did not dip further, but it did not pick up either and the advertisement prices had to be slashed. Of course, Rasha did not get her increment because all increments and promotions were on hold. In a situation like this, she was glad she still had her job.

By the end of the year, there was one promotion that did not face any recession problems though. Sabrina Kapadia became editorial director. She took everyone out for a lavish dinner at the Japanese restaurant, Zuma, and later even dropped Rasha home in her brand new red Ferrari.

21

'HOW COULD YOU tell Tania that I decided to publish that story when I was the one to repeatedly tell you not to publish it? It is a completely speculative story and Tania can sue us for this. You said she wouldn't come to know if it is published in Dubai. But see, the magazine hit the stands yesterday and today morning her secretary called you. And you passed the buck to me. How could you do that?' Ankita shouted.

She was trembling with anger. Sensing the possibility of this outburst, Sabrina had quickly summoned her to the meeting room, so the rest of the office would not have any inkling of what was happening. Rasha and Priya had also been called in because they had to be in the know-how of things.

Sabrina looked at Ankita guiltily. 'Since she doesn't know you, she will not be that mad. Don't worry, this will pass. Just don't accept any phone calls from Mumbai.'

Tania Sharma was Bollywood's No. 1 actress, who was having a very public affair with a top director. Sabrina had gone for a holiday to Mumbai and some of her friends, who belonged to Tania's circle, told her that she was an alcoholic and often turned abusive. Apparently, in a fit of rage, she had thrown an ashtray at her director boyfriend that led to his hospitalization. Sabrina wanted to make the story the cover feature. Ankita felt it would be suicidal to publish such a speculative story without any proof. Priya and Rasha fully agreed with Ankita. But, suddenly, Sabrina became extremely adamant and ensured the story went on cover.

'If you are the editor of the magazine and you have written

the story, why didn't you have the guts to say it's yours? Why did you have to give my name?' fumed Ankita.

'I told you this will pass. It's not going to be an issue, trust me. Just don't take any calls from Mumbai for a couple of days. That's all,' said Sabrina with a no-big-deal expression.

She was being politely dismissive in the way elders often are with obstinate teenagers. But her words did not do anything to dab away the red flush on Ankita's face.

'But do you still think we should have published the story?' asked Rasha, looking at Sabrina.

'Are you guys ganging up against me? Yes, it is a brilliant story and you will see how the sales of the magazine go up. Which is what we need right now. So stop giving me ethical bullshit.' Sabrina stormed out of the room.

That was the third time in a month that Ankita and Sabrina had had a serious altercation; and on all occasions, Ankita was right. The first time they had locked horns was when Ankita wanted to publish pictures of Kareena Kapoor and Saif Ali Khan shopping at Mall of The Emirates. Ankita and Rasha's common friend Reema had gone to shop there and captured them through her powerful zoom lens. The entire team, except for Sabrina, thought those looked like lovely paparazzi pictures where the couple was pictured shopping together, holding hands and obliging autograph hunters. But Sabrina said that Kareena and Saif would not like those photographs to be published, since it was their private moment. Ankita argued that there was nothing private about shopping at a mall, but Sabrina stuck to her decision.

The second time was when Sabrina promised to be back on a Monday from her holiday to close the magazine, so that Ankita could leave for her own to Kolkata the same day. Sabrina called up on Monday morning to give her standard excuse that she had missed her flight and asked Ankita to go for her holiday the next day.

Ankita left the closing of the magazine to Priya and Rasha, which was satisfactorily done, and took her scheduled flight to Kolkata. The moment she came back from her holiday, she was summoned to Sabrina's room and reprimanded on her irresponsible behaviour. When Ankita pointed out that Sabrina was being irresponsible by missing the flight, all hell broke loose.

Ankita's anger had been building up throughout the month and the Tania incident was like the last nail in the coffin of their already brittle relationship. It was clear that Ankita's editorial judgment and Sabrina's editorial judgment were at loggerheads, but putting the blame squarely on her shoulders for something that she had not done was something Ankita could not deal with. After splashing her face with cold water, Ankita managed to leave her anger in the washroom and even switched on to a jovial mode at the party in the evening.

Both Ankita and Rasha were invited to the opening of a boutique on Jumeirah Road and the event was attended by every fashionista in the Asian community of Dubai. Rasha really liked the owner of the boutique, a twenty-something Pakistani girl called Husna Siddiqui, who rubbed shoulders with Dubai's swish set from dawn to dusk, but remained pleasantly unaffected by her own wealth. Rasha wore a brown Marc Jacobs dress that her school friend from the US had passed on to her when she stayed with her in Dubai on her way to Kolkata. Her friend had worn it at a couple of parties, but couldn't repeat it any further, so she gave it to Rasha, who, of course, didn't mind. She paired the dress with brown Kurt Geiger high heels. Wearing flats was a style debacle in Dubai. Rasha had to finally give up her comfort to conform to fashion. She had to practise walking in her heels at home to make her Dubaiisation complete.

Ankita was in a Stella McCartney dress and she carried a Birkin bag. Although there were quite a few people who owned

Birkins in Dubai, but the super-expensive bag never failed to catch attention. Only Rasha knew that Ankita had bought the Dhs 36,000 (Rs 4 lakh) Birkin at a price of Dhs 15000 (Rs 1 and a half lakhs) from a Pakistani lady, who was leaving Dubai because her husband's real estate business had collapsed. The ladies at the party showered Ankita with endless compliments. Thanks to her years of socializing, she knew almost all those who mattered in the city and she introduced them to Rasha. After finishing the round of formal greetings, Rasha and Ankita were checking out the clothes in the boutique when they spotted Sabrina. Although Sabrina knew that Rasha and Ankita would be attending the party, she did not tell them that she would be at the party too. But then why should she have? She was, after all, the editorial director, the two words she often repeated to flaunt her authority, whenever she failed to command respect with her work.

She quickly glanced at Ankita's Birkin and her hand automatically clutched her 2.5 patent black Chanel bag. It was expensive, but not expensive enough to hold a candle to the Birkin. She was in the same pair of Diesel jeans and Calvin Klein shirt that she had worn to work that day. She greeted Husna first and then hugged Rasha and Ankita and rubbed cheeks with them saying: 'Muah! Muah!' as if they were meeting after ages. Looking at their smiling faces, no one could imagine what had transpired in the meeting room at *Silver Screen* that same morning.

They were served fresh orange juice and canapés when they had settled down on a majlis, an Arabic floor seating arrangement, inside a white gazebo. The large and comfortable cushions had small diamond shapes woven in red, black and white threads. The centre of the majlis had an expensive Persian carpet. The majlis had been laid out on the lawn of the two-storeyed villa that had been entirely converted into a boutique. Rasha rested her computer-stiff back on a cushion and nibbled on the snacks on offer. The dainty canapés did little for her after-work appetite, but she knew that she could not expect more. Unlike in Kolkata, food was definitely not the mainstay of any event in Dubai, networking was.

'Look at that lady there,' said Ankita, pointing to a stylish woman standing at a distance.

'Just two months back, she was like a queen bee at every party. Wherever she stood, people would just buzz around her. Now she is standing alone.'

'Why? Why has her status suddenly changed?' asked Rasha with interest.

'Her husband lodged a complaint against her for adultery. You know it's a punishable offence here, right?'

Rasha nodded.

'She was jailed for a month, so was the man she was having an affair with. I am not too sure, but I think the case is still pending in court and her husband has filed for divorce. After this whole saga she has become like a leper in the Dubai social circuit. No one wants to be seen with her.'

Rasha looked shocked. 'Gosh, how scary!'

'And that lady over there...' said Ankita, gesturing with her eyes to a lady in yellow skinny pants and animal-print top.

To Rasha, her attire looked quite ridiculous, but she was sure Sabrina would snub her saying that that was the most fashionable thing to wear at the moment. Actually, after her Cavalli faux pas, Rasha never opened her mouth when it came to clothes.

'She is the rising star now.' Ankita finished.

'Why?'

'Her family owns a hugely successful Indian supermarket chain in the UAE and the Middle East. They always had the money, but only recently did they upgrade their home from the supposedly not-so-cool Sharjah to upmarket Jumeirah. So, finally she can be accepted with open arms by her high-society friends.'

All that while, Sabrina's ears caught every word that Ankita uttered, but she did not show any interest in the conversation.

'They have a lovely collection. Are you planning to pick up something?' Sabrina finally asked Ankita.

Rasha gulped. Picking up a Dhs 4000 (Rs 48,000 approx) piece didn't require much thought for both Ankita and Sabrina, but for Rasha, a Dhs 500 (Rs 6000 approx) item was expensive enough and a Dhs 4000 dress a distant dream.

'Maybe I will pick up something and wear it on my holiday to Turkey next week,' said Ankita nonchalantly, before snapping, 'How come this collection interests you, you never wear ethnic clothes?'

'I wear sarees to weddings sometimes,' said Sabrina brushing aside the sarcasm that was lurking in Ankita's smirk and then added, 'Oh, I forgot you will be off for four days next week, right?'

She continued her attempt to get even with Ankita. 'The economic downturn doesn't affect you, eh? Still shopping and holidaying big time.'

'Yes, of course. My lifestyle will remain the same even if *Silver Screen* folds up tomorrow,' replied Ankita. Her words had a trace of arrogance.

Sabrina took the snub in good spirit and kept grinning, although Rasha had a sinking feeling in her heart.

Husna was standing nearby and she latched on to the word Turkey. 'Who's going for a holiday now?' she asked.

'I am,' said Ankita.

'Oh, lovely. Make sure you take the cruise on Bosphorus and the hot-air-balloon ride in Cappadocia,' she said.

'What about you? Any holiday plans?' Ankita asked Husna.

'I travelled to the USA, Paris and China this year. I think I now need to concentrate on the boutique.'

'See how some people are unaffected,' said Ankita, looking at Sabrina.

'...by what?' asked Husna.

'By the recession,' said Ankita.

'But, Sabrina, you have not gone anywhere this year? Are you so worried about the recession?' Ankita was innocence personified. Rasha thought Ankita had a brilliant future in Bollywood.

'Yeah, everyone told me this is the wrong time to start a business. But the clientele I am targeting is not the kind who would stop dressing up because of a recession,' said Husna.

Looking at Ankita and Sabrina, Husna sensed the undercurrent of animosity. She tried hard to change the direction of the conversation. 'Rasha, did you holiday anywhere this year?'

'Yes, we went to Petra in Jordan and also did a quick trip to the Zighy Bay resort in the Musandam Peninsula in Oman.'

Apart from shopping, travelling was the favourite Dubai pastime and if one could throw in the name of an expensive resort, like the way Rasha did just now, it added value to the conversation.

'I think Zighy Bay is just amazing. When I had gone there last year, I met actress Tania Sharma. She is such a nice person. She joined us for lunch. She was so down-to-earth and unpretentious,' said Husna.

The mention of Tania Sharma cast a shadow on Sabrina's and Ankita's faces and made Rasha uneasy.

Then Husna dropped the bomb.

'By the way, who did the cover story this time? I think it is in very bad taste. I really like Tania and I think she is a good actress. You guys have only quoted sources and have gone on to allege that she is an alcoholic and is abusive. That's not fair.'

'Truth is very unkind, Husna,' Sabrina said cooly.

Rasha could see the smug expression on Ankita's face from the corner of her eye.

'Will you quote me and write that I think she is the most wonderful celeb I have met. That's also a truth, isn't it?' said Husna.

But suddenly Husna seemed to have second thoughts about the conversation and her expression changed.

'I guess by supporting Tania, I am messing up the chances of my boutique getting some coverage in your magazine. Please don't mind, Sabrina, I do get emotional sometimes,' she said with feeling.

Sabrina nodded, but Husna was too late. The damage was done.

~

Next day, Sabrina came to office with only one agenda—she had to prove she was the boss.

'We are not going to cover the boutique. It's my wish.'

Ankita looked up from the computer. 'Is it because Husna spoke her mind? If we are running a magazine, we have to accept criticism.'

'You will do what the editorial director says and not question me every time I say something.'

Ankita opened her mouth to say something, but didn't.

After lunch, Ankita called everyone, including Sabrina, to the meeting room. 'I have emailed you my resignation letter. I am quitting from today.'

'It would have been nice if you had stayed on, but it's entirely your decision,' Sabrina said curtly.

Rasha had seen this coming because of the circumstances that preceded the decision. But she hadn't imagined it would be that very day. Ankita was her senior, a good friend and an extremely committed and relaxed worker. She enjoyed walking into *Silver Screen* every morning and seeing her smiling face. Rasha thought about the difference the absence of that smiling face would make in her life. But a bigger shock was in store.

Priya took them to the cafeteria after work. 'I am putting in my resignation too. My parents have fixed a match for me in

Kerala. I am getting married. Now that Ankita is leaving, I don't want to go back to the nightmare of working with Sabrina again. I could have continued for three more months, but now I want to take a break.'

Rasha managed to congratulate her heartily, but she could feel the knot in her stomach crawling up to her chest and tightening like a noose around her neck.

'Rasha, you should start looking for a job too. With us gone, it will be hard for you to work with Sabrina,' said Ankita.

Something snapped inside Rasha's brain. When she spoke, she could hear her own rude voice, but she had no control over her emotions.

'You were not working here when I joined *Silver Screen*. So, I will find my own way. You don't have to worry about me,' she said stubbornly.

She instantly knew her words had not gone down well with Ankita. She just shrugged. But Ankita completely failed to see the hurt that Rasha was trying to disguise with her words. Ankita didn't serve her notice period and discontinued going to the office from the next day. But just like the economic downturn ravaging through Dubai, Rasha's last conversation with Ankita ravaged their relationship. Rasha met Ankita at common friends' homes, but their interactions were formal and, at times, even awkward. She apologized to Ankita, but it made things worse. She started looking through her at parties, making the strain in the relationship evident to all.

At work, however, Sabrina transformed into a new person from the day Ankita left. Her first move was to call Rasha aside and tell her imploringly, 'I hope you are not planning to turn your back on me.'

'Don't worry, I am staying,' Rasha replied like a schoolgirl, who was being asked the question by her first crush.

Sabrina held her hands tightly. 'Thank you sooooo much. Hugs! Hugs! Hugs!'

'How do you plan to run the magazine now?' asked Rasha.

'We are looking for two people, but nobody for the post of deputy editor. I will be more hands-on now.' Rasha cringed.

Rasha's hands were full like never before and to Sabrina's immense happiness, she stayed back late and took on the entire bulk of work that Priya and Ankita did. For the first time in her life, Sabrina sat at her desk for long periods, going through copies and trying hard to meet the deadline. She was extremely sweet and understanding towards Rasha, even helping her with mundane work such as picture research and TV listings. She stayed back in office too and ordered pizzas for both of them. Rasha was naïve enough to think that Sabrina had changed. She was so horribly wrong.

~

'You will finally be able to take a breather now. We have found our two people,' said Sabrina after two months.

She looked stylish in her harem pants and frilly top, a look that Rasha thought she herself would never have managed to pull off. She was standing with her arms folded, resting her derriere on Rasha's desk. Rasha noticed that Sabrina's nails, which she had bitten frantically after Ankita and Priya left, had grown back and were painted in a deep orange colour.

'Who are they?' Rasha asked.

'They are amazingly talented people. One of them is Soham's wife Xena. She always wanted to be a journalist and had earlier helped me with some writing too.'

'Does she have experience in journalism?' asked Rasha.

Sabrina gave her a how-can-you-ask-this-question look. 'She has done her graduation in the US,' she said proudly. 'Just like me.'

Rasha wouldn't give up. 'Has she worked somewhere before this?'

'Yes, of course, she was working in the marketing department of my dad's business. She is going to be the fashion editor.'

'And who is the other person?'

'She is a very talented young girl from Mumbai. She is joining as the features writer.'

'And is she family too?'

Sabrina sensed Rasha was now mocking her. She stopped leaning on her desk, stood straight and switched back to her authoritative mode. 'She is the daughter of a distant aunt, whom I have not met in a few years, if you call that family.'

Rasha's eyes scurried to the lone sailing boat in the Marina. She felt lonely.

Soham's wife Xena Kapadia was a nice person and a far more able writer than her husband. The features writer, twenty-five year-old Alina Shah, was a sweet girl with good organizational skills but zero writing ability. The day the two of them joined, Sabrina's attitude towards Rasha did a complete volte-face. Rasha's opinions were quickly brushed aside and Sabrina started treating her on an equal platform with the inexperienced Xena and Alina and that became unbearable for Rasha.

However, if ever any mistake was made or any news missed, Sabrina would haul her up. 'You should have taken care of it. They are newcomers, how will they know?' This dichotomy absolutely irked Rasha. It was now amply clear that Sabrina had only been syrupy to her till she got her own coterie in place.

Arun was very supportive. 'Things are getting better. Companies are opening up for employment. You will find something. They don't deserve you,' he told her one day.

Arun had gone through a tough time too. The real estate business had been hit hard and people had been given termination letters in bunches. But Arun's company had tried its level best not to retrench, although they had to opt for a pay cut. Now that the storm had passed, they had also been given their increments, however small that was.

Hearing about Arun's increment, Rasha thought she would bring up her own with Sabrina. The editorial director scheduled their meeting at the office terrace.

'Don't expect an increment. It's not going to happen because we are still not making good profit. And, anyway, I have been keeping a close watch on you for the last few months. Your writing is horrible, you can't edit properly and you are disorganized,' said Sabrina.

Rasha looked Sabrina in the eye. 'I know what I am, Sabrina. It was because of me you could publish the magazine when nobody was there. You cannot take away my self-confidence. I know I am damn good.'

'Arrogant! You are so bloody arrogant! You think you are the best.'

'I am. Whether you like it or not. I know why you suddenly think I am so bad. You want to prove your sister-in-law is better than me.'

'She is. She is the best journalist on this floor. That's what my boss also thinks.'

Rasha started laughing. 'A journalist with three months experience, who confidently writes "Amitabh Bachchan's father's name is Teji Bachchan". You had also seen it and sent it to press. If I had not corrected it to Harivanshrai Bachchan, it would have been published like that.'

This infuriated Sabrina even more. 'You are bad at your work and on top of that you wear that I-am-the-best attitude on your sleeve. We have been nice enough not to ever say you can't even speak proper English. Your diction is not right. It's…it's…so Bengali.

Now, I don't want to take this conversation any further.'

When Rasha went back to her desk, from the terrace, Sabrina had already read her emailed resignation. She quickly sent her the reply:

Heyy Rasha,

Hope you are doing great. I am sooooo sad you are leaving the company. I am gonna miss you like anything. With great sadness, I am accepting your resignation, but I respect your decision. Please get in touch with HR for the formalities.

Thanks,
Sabrina Kapadia
Editorial Director

Rasha was trying hard to write her story, but she truly couldn't give wings to her thoughts. Sabrina tiptoed behind her and asked her to follow her to the cafeteria. She got two mugs of coffee for each of them.

'I discussed with people higher-up but maybe they did not value you, so they asked me to accept your resignation.'

Rasha's composure had returned and so had her sense of humour. 'Really? I am surprised people higher up even know me. I thought only one person brought out *Silver Screen* and that is Sabrina Kapadia.'

'You are getting angry, Rasha.'

'Why are you looking so glum? You should be happy I am leaving. Isn't that what you wanted?'

'No! No! Not at all. You are not a bad worker.'

'You first decide how you want to classify me.'

'Rasha, you will have the exit interview…'

'That explains the cups of coffee. You needn't worry, I will not write anything against you.'

'Thank you sooooo much. Hugs! Hugs! Hugs!' She got up to hug Rasha with a radiant smile. Rasha stood up robotically to accept it.

'You also do me a favour, Sabrina. Don't bother to give me a farewell party and follow it up with a lavish gift. It will be nice if you can do away with this hypocrisy.'

Part 6
In the Midst of Mayhem

◆ ◆ ◆

22

THE SECURITY GUARDS at the airport were trying hard to straighten out the muddled formation of the four queues leading to the passport-control counters. More passengers poured in from flights that had just arrived, making the task harder for the guards. Some passengers even started having who-entered-the-queue-first altercations. Rasha was probably the only passenger standing in the middle of all this and smiling. Arun noticed that she was drumming her fingers on the slim leather folder that held her passport and visa. He knew this was Rasha's effort at suppressing the excitement that was assaulting every nerve in her body. She was raring to explore Egypt.

During their time after college, Arun remembered, Rasha always carried a book with her to read in the metro, bus, tram, cab, wherever. And most of the time, the topic would be Egypt. Even now, as Arun glanced over her shoulders, he could see the tip of James Patterson's *Murder of King Tut* peeping from her handbag, a book that she devoured on the Egyptair flight. Once on their way back from a movie at Globe Theatre on Lindsay Street in Kolkata, Rasha dragged Arun to the Indian Museum and into the mummy room.

'You should have taken up history and then studied Egyptology,' Arun had told her.

'Then it wouldn't have remained a hobby. It is so much fun this way,' Rasha retorted.

If there was one place Rasha earnestly wanted to visit in this world, it was Egypt.

Rasha and Arun were pleasantly surprised to see a man standing with their names on a placard right next to passport control. The queue at the exit had become even more chaotic and people were standing impatiently as they were allowed to go one by one through the green channel.

'This is peak season, so it will be a bit crowded everywhere. I hope you don't have anything to declare and you are not carrying too much cash,' the man said.

They were carrying quite a bit of cash, but they had divided it between them and had kept the money in different corners of their respective handbags.

'Why? Will there be a problem if we have cash?' asked Arun.

'Yes, sometimes they create problems. But don't worry. Just tell them you are not carrying much. I will go through the other gate and wait for you there,' he said pointing to the car park.

Rasha stepped out of the airport into the January sun and closed her eyes and inhaled the Egyptian air.

'Am I in Egypt? Pinch me,' she said.

'I think I would like to do that when we reach the hotel,' said Arun.

Rasha didn't reply. She was staring at something with the kind of expression one would have if they saw a ghost.

'Obelisk! An obelisk,' she shouted, clutching Arun's arm.

Arun followed her eyes and saw a very tall pillar, but couldn't fathom the reason behind Rasha's excitement.

'These were the marvels of Egyptian architecture. This is a monolithic stone monument that has a tapering end like a pyramid, so you can imagine what effort it would have taken to install it.'

Arun nodded as he looked admiringly at the obelisk. 'I can see that I don't need to hire a guide. I already have one with me,' he said.

The man, now waiting for them in the car, introduced himself as Adel Abbas. A bit on the plumper side, Adel had curly hair and fair complexion. He wore spectacles, a tie and a formal shirt and trousers. He worked with the travel agency through which Rasha had made all her bookings.

'I will take you to your hotel now,' said Adel in impeccable English.

'It's great to meet you, Adel. How long have you been working with this travel agency?' Rasha asked as the car started rolling out of the airport car park.

'Three years, Ma'am,' he said politely.

'So you always wanted to join the tourism industry?' she asked.

'Not really. I studied Economics and wanted to get into banking, but it didn't happen. But I make a fair amount here and the tips are good.'

'Would you have earned more if you had worked in a bank?'

'Yes, I would have, Ma'am.'

'Are you married?'

Now Adel looked a bit uncomfortable.

'I am sorry if I have asked you a personal question,' Rasha said.

'No, no, Ma'am. Actually I can't get married right now even if I want to. Marriage is expensive. I don't have that kind of money. Also, I will have to rent an apartment since our two-bedroom apartment is shared by my parents, my two younger sisters and my elder brother. Rents are very high. I will have to earn more to get a new place. I will have to wait.'

'How old are you? I am thirty, Ma'am.'

'How long will you wait?'

'I really don't know. I am saving, but I have to look after my family too,' he said, letting out a sigh.

'Sorry to be so curious, but do you have a girlfriend?'

To this Adel smiled shyly. 'Yes. We are childhood friends. She is a part-time teacher.'

'How old is she?'

'She is twenty-six, Ma'am.'

'I thought girls get married early here.'

'Not in Cairo, Ma'am. If you want to marry the man you love, then you will have to wait, otherwise you can go for older men with money.'

'She doesn't even know when she will marry you. No pressure from her parents?'

'Yes, it has been very hard. When she was twenty-two, her mother fixed her marriage to a forty-three-year-old widower. But she refused. Now she is too old, she will have to wait for me.'

'How can she be too old at twenty-six?'

Adel shifted a bit uncomfortably in the car seat and shrugged.

It took them more than an hour to get out of the traffic bottleneck at the airport. It was clear that no one followed traffic rules in Egypt. All men at the steering wheel were aggressively trying to bully their way through. This created a huge mess on the road that the traffic policemen found impossible to handle. But Rasha and Arun felt they had arrived home. 'This is so much like Kolkata,' Arun laughed.

'Ma'am, where are you from?' asked Adel.

'We are from India,' Rasha said. She had been categorically told by her friends in Dubai that it was safer to say she was from India, otherwise she would run the risk of being fleeced everywhere if she said she was from Dubai.

'There, Ma'am, there's the Nile,' said Adel, as the car advanced towards a bridge. Rasha tried hard not to let her disappointment show. The Nile of her imagination and the Nile in front of her were clearly at odds. This was not the wide blue river where the pharaohs' majestic boats plied. Rasha's thoughts went to the Vidyasagar Setu in Kolkata and the view of the Ganges from there. The muddy and polluted water of the Ganges lacked the blue tint, but it could rival the mighty Nile any day with its breathtaking view.

The Nile looked slimmer and calmer than Rasha had read in history books. From the point where she was on the bridge, she could see only shabby buildings. Then her eyes went to the pot holes on the bridge and old semi-broken Fiats and Ladas bouncing through it. The real-life Egypt looked anything but grandiose. Rasha thought it was peculiar how everything about Cairo took her thoughts back to Kolkata. The two cities were in fact so similar— the teeming millions, the hustle and bustle, the mad traffic—only Cairo looked like the Kolkata of her childhood—dirty and drab.

'Most of the buildings look like they have not been painted for a long time...' said Rasha.

'People don't paint them to evade tax, Ma'am,' said Adel.

'Here's your hotel, Ma'am,' he said, as the car pulled up in front of a freshly painted white building with a huge lobby.

Rasha had chosen a five-star-hotel right in the centre of Cairo and she liked their spacious room with a view of the street on one side and the hotel pool on the other.

She sat cross-legged on the sofa in the corner of their room and began cutting an apple with a knife. Arun leaned on the bed to take off his shoes and socks.

'Why are you having an apple now? Let's go for lunch. I am famished,' he said.

'Wait, I will have to write down everything that Adel told me, otherwise I will miss out something important. He was my first interview,' grinned Rasha.

'I guessed as much,' said Arun.

FROM THE DAY she put in her resignation at *Silver Screen*, Rasha's career hit the proverbial doldrums. Arun, for once, was wrong. Rasha couldn't find a job in Dubai, something that he had assured her she would. She went through umpteen job advertisements in the newspapers and on websites, but could not find a single job worth taking up. The few that she was offered gave her posts that did not suit her profile or offered her pay that undermined her abilities. She found a few freelancing opportunities that required her to write articles on cars, watches and jewellery. She diligently wrote and sent them on time. After she delivered the write-ups, some magazines even failed to pay her. She nagged them with phone calls for months, then she finally gave up.

She got through the tests and interviews at a newspaper that offered her a good pay, but the post of a sub-editor, the designation she started her career with. She felt like grabbing the salary, but her ego stopped her from taking up the post.

Then she came to know through a friend that a newly launched magazine was looking for a senior editor. She promptly called and went over for an interview. She waited for the editor at the plush meeting room when the marketing director walked in carrying the printout of her CV and asked her a set of inane questions.

'The editor would like to meet you. She is a style icon of Dubai,' said the marketing director and left.

The stylish editor was dressed in a bang-on-trend short, black skirt and beige lace top. She shook hands with Rasha. Thanks to the botox jabs, her skin looked taut and young, but her hands were a dead giveaway of the age she was so desperately trying to hide. Rasha could see through a lip job and a mild nose job too. Although Rasha herself had blow-dried her hair, something she ended up doing more often in Dubai, to look presentable, she thought she should have opted for more stylish clothes than the pair of jeans and white shirt she was wearing. She wasn't sure if she looked the part, pitted against the fashionable editor.

'Criminology graduate. Ah! That's interesting,' the editor said.

This triggered off something in Rasha and she foolishly started talking about her experiences in covering crime. The editor listened with a straight face.

'How will this help our lifestyle magazine?' she asked when Rasha had finished her animated explanation.

'You are looking for a senior editor, right? I have extensive rewriting, editing and decision-making experience.'

From the look on her face, Rasha understood that the editor had already lost interest. She pushed the magazine towards Rasha. Rasha opened the first page and tried very hard to conceal her astonishment. The name of the magazine and the name of the editor were the same! When she looked up, she knew that she had not been successful in her efforts at concealment.

When Rasha left the office, she told herself: *I should have put on my American accent. I should have mentioned her Gina shoes the moment I noticed them. I should have told her about my writing experiences in the fashion industry.* Then her thoughts moved in another direction. *Maybe I am being over-confident and over-expectant*, she thought. She could feel that self-doubt had started eating into her confidence.

Her expectations soared after her meeting with a British gentleman, the editor of a community magazine that had been recently launched. He not only had the gift of the gab, but was a treasure trove of experience gathered in Dubai and London. Sitting with him at Seattle's Best Coffee at the Media City food court,

Rasha didn't realize when the minutes ticked by and it became an hour. The man knew about Bollywood and was also interested in knowing about Rasha's encounters with the stars. She was enjoying an invigorating conversation after a long time, but she also hoped the conversation would translate into a job offer.

'I am really impressed with your resume. It will be great to have you on the team. Although we are not hiring immediately, I will try to push for a vacancy,' he finally said.

In the next couple of email exchanges, he said he was still trying to create a vacancy for her and in the final one he dashed her hopes. He said he could not give a timeline and she would have to wait.

Every time Arun told her that people waited much longer to find a job and it had been only six months for her, Rasha flared up. She was aware her own confidence had reached a nadir and no amount of pep talk from Arun could perk her up.

So many times she could hear Sabrina's words ringing in her ears, 'You are an obnoxious worker, Rasha.' The words especially resonated around the empty house when Arun left for work and Rasha was still lying in bed.

It was 1.00 p.m. on a Sunday morning and Rasha was still languishing in bed. She had this overwhelming urge to call up her mother and cry. But she was afraid to do so. Rasha hadn't told them that she was jobless. She didn't want to fuel their anxiety. A cursory look through her bank accounts had told her that her family could subsist on it for at least eight months, if any unexpected expense didn't crop up. But it had. And Rasha was pretty sure it was her father's doing. With much pride, he had told his lawyer last month that his daughter worked in Dubai. The lawyer immediately asked for a cheque of Rs 30,000 to cover miscellaneous costs. And this month, he wanted Rs 20,000 more. A month was left before her account would diminish to the last penny and she would have to borrow from Arun. She felt frantic and restless. She thought she had to hear her mother's voice to calm down her nerves. She picked up the phone to dial the number, when the phone rang in her hand.

'Hello Rasha, this is Vinita Sajnani. How are you?'

'What a pleasant surprise, Mrs Sajnani. I am fine. Thank you.'

'Listen I want to invite you to my daughter's wedding. It's at the Armani Hotel. Give me your address and I will post the card. You will have to come.'

Rasha gave her address and hung up. Mrs Vinita Sajnani was one of the few who kept in touch with Rasha after she quit *Silver Screen*. A Harvard Business School graduate, she was the brains behind the success of the retail giant Sajnani Group. She was a mild-mannered, sophisticated lady whom Rasha admired immensely and Mrs Sajnani liked her too.

'Arun, you are invited too. But I don't know if I am in the mood to go,' said Rasha, opening the invitation card made out of red handmade paper with designs in gold on it. The card had been couriered to her along with laddoos packed in a red-and-gold box.

'I think we should go. I don't want to give up the opportunity of seeing the Armani Hotel. Also, Rasha, all the big shots of Dubai will be there, so it's a good opportunity for you to network,' said Arun.

Rasha wore her favourite blue crepe saree with a zardozi border and Arun looked dapper in a Ted Lapidus suit. In her Ritu Kumar saree, Aldo golden heels and Salvatore Ferragamo clutch, Rasha finally felt at one with Dubai's fashion frat pack. They had to earlier email their passport copies because of the strict security at the venue. When they arrived, Rasha and Arun's name were ticked on the list that also had their passport copies pinned to it. Although it was the handiwork of none other than fashion wiz Giorgio Armani, Rasha found the décor at Armani Hotel a bit Spartan and way too minimalistic next to the flamboyance of Dubai. But she had to admit that the combination of white, black, grey and browns highlighted with muted lights, created a signature effect.

The Swarovski-studded lehenga of the bride and the gold-embossed sherwani of the groom were a complete mismatch with the décor, but the couple looked happy and everyone else next to them looked equally happy. There were, at least, twelve hundred guests at the reception, all decked up in their best and making the most of the opportunity to network. As Rasha had expected, the entire *Silver Screen* team was there in their full finery. Looking stunning in a grey gown, Sabrina rushed to Rasha as soon she set eyes on her.

'Oh, wow! You are here too. Great to see you,' she said, as she brushed her cheeks against Rasha's.

Rasha could not bring herself to reciprocate the action. In fact, she felt more like an iceberg.

'So what are you up to these days?' asked Sabrina casually.

'A lot of things,' said Rasha coldly. 'You'll have to excuse me. My husband is getting bored. I need to join him,' she said, making it clear that she did not want to further the conversation.

But there was someone else Rasha was genuinely happy to see.

'Oh, Rasha, it's so good to see you. I have been missing you so much,' said Susanna, hugging her warmly.

Susanna White had joined as the page designer of *Silver Screen* after Jessica Brandon fled to the UK. Susanna was a pretty twenty-five-year-old girl with brown hair and a figure to die for. She was also from London, but she was the opposite of Jessica. She was extremely close to her family—her parents visited her twice a year—and she was enamoured by her nephews and nieces. At work, she would be talking to Rasha about them most of the time. Susanna was simple, friendly and fun. In Rasha's last days at *Silver Screen*,

Susanna and Rasha always had lunch together and when Rasha sometimes told her what Sabrina was doing to her, Susanna would look at her appallingly.

'But you are so hard working. How can she say all this?' Susanna often told Rasha.

Rasha felt guilty that apart from a few messages on Facebook, she hadn't called or met Susanna after she left her job.

'You have done justice to this red gown,' she told Susanna.

'You always compliment me,' said Susanna. 'Listen, I would have called you. You had told me you are interested in covering hard news. I might have a contact for you.'

Rasha's face brightened. 'What contact?'

'Not so fast, babe. Meet me tomorrow at Paul Café at JBR Walk at 8.00 p.m. I will give you the details there,' said Susanna.

Rasha looked out of a glass wall of the Armani Hotel located on the thirty-ninth floor of one of the world's tallest tower. Dubai had never looked so stunning.

∽

'Aren't you feeling much better after attending the wedding?' asked Arun, as he switched from one sports channel to another. He also had the laptop open in front of him, where he was tracking the scores on livescore.com.

Rasha was in her pyjamas, sitting next to him on the couch, removing her make-up with a wad of cotton. 'Yes, I am glad I went,' she said.

'By the way, thanks, Rasha.'

'For what?'

'Because of you, I got to see the Armani Hotel. I really liked the Italian fare.'

Rasha smiled. 'Did you see the necklace around Mrs Sajnani's neck? Must have cost a few million dirhams,' she said.

'Yes, I noticed. But she is so classy, she carried it off perfectly. Sabrina was looking stunning too.'

'When did I say she wasn't?' Rasha looked away gloomily. Arun realized this was one name he should not have brought up in the conversation at that moment.

Their fights were always triggered by something Arun said. Rasha most often failed to see the humour in his words these days and she reacted otherwise. Sometimes he spoke without thinking, like he did right now, and that infuriated Rasha. He, in turn, got infuriated by Rasha's sloppyness. Nowadays, she did not bother to fold her clothes and keep it in the cupboard. Arun hated seeing all her clothes strewn around their bedroom when he came home from work. He sometimes folded them himself and sometimes he urged Rasha to do it. She thought why it was such a big deal to him that everything had to be perfect at home, and they ended up arguing. But he was determined to avoid a squabble at the moment because Federar was about to play Nadal on TV.

He quickly changed track. 'You are meeting Suzanna tomorrow, right?'

Rasha nodded absent-mindedly.

~

JBR Walk was crowded on Thursday evenings, but Rasha always liked the ambience there. Built at the foot of the tall buildings of Jumeirah Beach Residence, The Walk had an old-world charm with cobbled sidewalks and gaslight-shaped lighting. All the restaurants had outdoor seating arrangements. Rasha enjoyed the sea breeze, as she sat on a bamboo chair outside Paul and sipped her coffee. Susanna had said she would be late because Sabrina wanted her to stay back and finish some work. Rasha had smiled wryly after she hung up.

'I am famished. Can we order food first?' said Susanna as she plonked herself on the chair opposite Rasha.

Rasha complimented her black crochet top. 'Got it for just Dhs 40 (Rs 490) from Top Shop. Great deal, no?'

'You always manage to get great deals. I have to go shopping with you.'

'But I think you will like the deal I will talk to you about now.'

'Stop playing with my curiosity and come out with it,' said Rasha.

'You always told me you admired a particular magazine that is published in the US and is hailed as one of the best in the world…'

Rasha looked at her wide-eyed.

'My boyfriend's American friend was working for them as the Middle East and Africa correspondent. He is relocating to the US and is frantically looking for someone to replace him. Here's his number. I think he will like you.'

'Susanna, I really don't know how to thank you.'

'And I really hope this works out for you. Isn't this what you always wanted to do—write in-depth features of international relevance? But right now, we are going for a swim in the sea.'

'It's dark, Susanna,' said Rasha alarmed.

'So what? You sit on the beach if you want. I am swimming.'

They crossed The Walk and headed to the beach. Susanna took off her jeans and top revealing a chic animal print bikini.

'You sit here with my clothes and bag. I will be back quickly.'

Rasha sat on the beach, hoping Susanna's boyfriend's American friend liked her enough to consider her for the job.

∽

Mike Stevens didn't have an office in Dubai and he operated from his home in the Marina. He arranged to meet Rasha at the Marina Mall food court. Susanna had spoken highly of Rasha Roy. He hoped she would be extremely good because where he worked, there was no place for mediocrity.

He was dressed in informal khakis and a T-shirt while Rasha was in a formal black trouser, a semi-formal frilly top and had blow-dried her hair. They exchanged greetings and then discussed Rasha's experience.

'Can we work on it this way? I hope you know about this Russian woman who's hit the headlines because her Pakistani husband has fled the country with her three sons and she is fighting a battle to be reunited with them. I have been assigned to do an interview with her. You do it. Let me see how you fare.' Rasha nodded in agreement.

A week later, Rasha was sitting at the same table and Mike sat opposite her in the same khakis, but in a different T-shirt. She was in formals, but hadn't bothered to blow-dry her hair.

'This will do. You have covered all the aspects. You have managed to speak to the guy in Pakistan as well. You have also done a separate feature talking to Consular authorities in Dubai and Russia. Now can you do another one? We want a feature on Emirati women, how they are progressing in all walks of life. Talk to successful women. I have heard five Emirati women are training to be pilots soon and there are women working in the police too. Find out about them.'

Three weeks later, Rasha sat at the same table in a pair of jeans and T-shirt with no make-up and her hair tied in a ponytail. Mike wore the same Khakis and a white shirt. He didn't praise her. 'This will do,' he said with a straight face.

Rasha couldn't be sure if he liked her story.

He now ran his hand through his blonde beard. 'The youth in Egypt are apparently a ticking time bomb. The unemployment rate is at an all-time high.'

'Yes, I know,' said Rasha. 'The quality of life is very low in Egypt and there is very little opportunity for the youth.'

'Good. Our hunch is that the ongoing Tunisian Revolution might have an impact on them. Can you go to Egypt and get me a story? It will be an all-expenses-paid trip.' Rasha couldn't believe her ears.

24
~

JUNEID HUSSEIN WAS a freelance photographer whom Mike had contacted to help Rasha with her project. Rasha's brief was to go as a tourist and do her research for the feature. She could, by no means, tell anyone that she was a journalist. So when Arun wanted to come along, the whole idea worked out perfectly. The idea of a husband and wife touring Egypt was any day more inconspicuous than a lone woman exploring the city.

Juneid had spoken to a few young people, who were willing to talk to Rasha. She told him that she wanted to travel by public transport to get a feel of the city. So they took a micro-bus to go to the apartment of her interviewee, who lived next to the Khan Al Khalili market near Islamic Cairo. The micro-bus looked very much like an outdated Maruti van, just a little bigger, with seating arrangements made in four rows. The white paint on the body had chipped at numerous places and there were dents all over the bus. The bus creaked and croaked as it advanced. The springs in the seat had also given away, making the ride uncomfortably bouncy. The bus was occupied by twelve people, nine men and three women, including Rasha. She drew quizzical glances since very few tourists took the micro bus. Juneid told her that Egypt's public transport system was a nightmare and the teeming millions had to depend on the metro and these micro-buses from private operators to move around. Taxis were expensive and he warned her to be careful when bargaining on the fare, because the cabbies always tried to dupe tourists.

A young girl in her twenties in a pair of jeans and T-shirt

was getting off the bus when something happened. Suddenly she started screaming at a man in Arabic. The man coolly looked away. She was clearly angry, but finally walked away. Rasha asked Juneid what had happened.

He looked embarrassed.

'What happened? Tell me,' she said sharply.

'The man had touched her backside and she was abusing him for doing that.'

The man was sitting in front and had now turned around and was looking at Rasha. She glared at him. No one else in the bus had reacted when the lady was shouting.

'This is a growing problem in Egypt, sexual harassment of women on the streets. But that lady is Christian. If she had covered herself like Muslim women do, she would have been safer.'

This comment irritated Rasha. 'I don't agree with you. Women in Kolkata face harassment like this all the time. It doesn't matter if they are in jeans or in salwar kurtas or in sarees. It doesn't really matter to perverts.'

'You will know better,' Juneid said and clammed up.

Rasha thought of her innumerable harassment experiences on different modes of public transport in Kolkata, but she shuddered when she thought of her worst experience ever. A man touched her breasts on the bus. She slapped him hard. He started shouting at her in defence. While most of the men and women remained passive, the only person to come to her aid was a poor female fishmonger, who was returning home from the local market.

She took off her torn slippers and threatened to beat up the guy. 'I saw what you did to didi,' she had said. The man did not say a word more and got off at the next stop.

Rasha and Juneid left the micro-bus on the main road, walked past the entrance of Khan Al Khalili market and entered an alley. This place was located in the old part of Egypt and was crammed with both tourists and locals. The slender road they walked through had houses on each side that looked old, but the Islamic architecture was resplendent on their walls. The alley reminded Rasha of North Kolkata's architecturally rich but dilapidated houses that had not been repaired for decades because of lack of funds. In Kolkata, they were torn down to make way for apartment buildings, but in Egypt, it seemed land sharks hadn't smelled blood yet.

They stopped in front of a two-storeyed house that had an arched doorway and wooden windows with beautiful carvings on them. Juneid rang the door bell. A beautiful girl in her late twenties opened it. She was wearing a long flare skirt that covered her heels, a white-full-sleeve T-shirt with a sleeveless denim jacket on it. Her hijab matched the colour of her jacket. Her skin was spotless like porcelain, lips pink without any hint of lipstick and her dark eyes twinkled with intelligence.

'Please come in,' she said. They took the short flight of stairs to a room upstairs. The room was sparsely furnished. It had a three-seater sofa on one side and floor-seating arrangement on the other. A colour TV along with a DVD player stood on one side. The yellow walls of the room were in desperate need of painting, but vibrant curtains in maroon and yellow made up for the dull walls. The bright January sunlight was streaming through the window.

As Rasha sat down on the sofa, she extended her hand, 'Hi! I am Zubeida.'

Zubeida El Taha was a graduate in history, but she had never found the job she wanted. To while away her time, she took up blogging and her blog soon became the mouthpiece of women in Egypt. But it also landed her in serious trouble. She had been arrested a few months ago for writing controversial articles on her blog. They blocked her blog and asked her never to write again.

'But I haven't stopped. I am writing under a different name,' she smiled.

'Aren't you scared they might trace it to you again?' asked Rasha.

'After what I went through in prison, I am not scared of anything anymore.' She showed her hands. The nails on her thumb and index finger were gone. Rasha could feel the goosebumps on her own arms. 'They tied me up for days and experimented with all kinds of torture. After my release, I was so weak that I could not get out of bed for a month,' she said.

'What about your family? Do they support you?'

'My parents fear for me. But I tell them, someone has to think of freedom, you cannot live in fear all the time.'

'So you think blogging will bring freedom?' asked Rasha.

'It will at least reach thirteen million internet users in Egypt and help create an opinion.'

Rasha felt she hadn't seen a more fearless and articulate woman in her entire life. She wished she could borrow some courage from Zubeida. Zubeida posed for Juneid's camera. 'Who knows, if my picture comes out in your magazine, I might get arrested again. But I have to let the world know about our suffering. For a bigger cause, one has to sacrifice.'

Rasha took Zubeida's email id and they left her house. They walked out of the alley. 'Do you want to check out Khan Al Khalili since we are on this side?' Juneid asked.

'That's a good idea,' said Rasha.

They entered the bazaar through an arched entrance. The narrow lanes of the bazaar were buzzing with tourists. They were haggling over lanterns, sheesha, spices, handicrafts, papyrus and anything Egyptian. The narrow space made the jostle even more acute and shop owners added to the ruckus as they loudly summoned all and sundry to their respective shops. Rasha had told her friend Reema, who collected refrigerator magnets, that she would get her one from Egypt. She spotted some in one shop and went for a Nefertiti bust.

'Sixty Egyptian pounds madam. It's made of real copper,' the salesman said.

Juneid started laughing and said something to him in Arabic, then he turned to Rasha. 'Give him eight and take it.'

When Juneid laughed, Rasha noticed he had a child-like face that looked mature because of the thin beard. His lean body and short hair made him look younger, but he was in his thirties.

'Do you want to try a special pomegranate drink at one of the restaurants here?' he asked.

'That would be great.'

Rasha and Juneid sat down at a table outside a restaurant in Khan Al Khalili market. Very few chairs were empty. There were foreigners all around trying out sheesha and local Egyptian food. Rasha could not spot a single Indian.

'This drink is amazing,' she said. 'Now tell me, Juneid, are you married?'

'Don't try to make me a subject of your feature,' he said guardedly.

'Okay, no problem. I will not ask.'

'No, I am not married. I am facing the same problem as most Egyptian men. Although I make a lot of money in my international assignments, but since I am a freelancer, most girls' parents think my income is unstable. I also don't want to waste my hard-earned money on a costly wedding. I am trying to become a permanent photographer of the magazine and move to the US.'

'That will be better, I suppose.'

'My brother is there. He went to college here, but never got a proper job. He works as a driver in a private car renting company, but he earns good money. His wife and children and my parents are well off here because of him.'

They took a taxi back to the hotel where Rasha was supposed

to join Arun for lunch. The cabbie initially asked for two hundred Egyptian pounds. When Juneid started talking in Arabic, he settled for fifty. Rasha asked Juneid to join them for lunch, but he said he had work and left.

~

Arun had gone to explore Egypt on his own. 'When you walk around this city, you get the impression that it is poor,' he concluded.

'It is. Twenty per cent of Egyptians live under poverty line and most of the country's wealth is siphoned away by corrupt people in important positions,' said Rasha.

'Then I think Indians and Egyptians should sit together. They will have a lot to discuss on corruption,' said Arun.

'I am sure they can give each other some interesting tips too.'

'We will see the pyramids of Giza tomorrow, followed by the museum. You can do your interviews in the evening unless, of course, you find some of your subjects in these places.'

The goosebumps that had disappeared when Rasha stepped out of Zubeida's home returned when she stood in front of the Great Pyramid of Cheops. The sheer magnitude of the structure was absolutely overwhelming. She and Arun climbed up on the humongous blocks of rock and Adel clicked their photograph. Adel had arrived right on time to take them to the pyramids and he warned them that it would not be a good idea to go all the way inside the pyramid because the tunnel was too small, claustrophobic and one had to go a long way on hunches.

'But we have come all the way to experience that,' said Rasha.

'Your wish, but it is very uncomfortable.'

Rasha and Arun bought the tickets and stood in the serpentine queue. All the people who came out looked breathless and flushed. When they both crossed the gate to go inside, she saw a lady drinking water in gulps from a bottle and panting.

'Is it that difficult?' Rasha asked.

'We can still decide not to go,' said Arun.

'Are you crazy? We will go.'

Since the main entrance had been sealed, tourists went in through the robber's entrance, a tunnel dug on the side of the pyramid. They crossed the sandy area and walked through the narrow entrance. Light filtered through the entrance as they walked on a wooden plank, then the roof became lower and they walked with their heads down. A few feet down, the roof dipped suddenly and they went on all their fours. Suddenly, it became pitch dark. The tunnel was around two and a half feet in width, a column of people were going in on their hunches on one side and a column was coming back from the opposite side.

Rasha was crawling inch by inch and sweating profusely.

'Are you okay?' asked Arun. Panic gripped her because she felt she couldn't breathe. She tried hard to be brave and said a feeble yes and hoped the tunnel would end. But it went lower and lower down and became even narrower. Rasha's panic rose as she could sense the breathlessness of the people on their way back. They finally reached a large dark room. She supposed the stone sarcophagus of King Khufu was in the middle, but she was desperate to join the file that was going back and didn't look at the sarcophagus. She desperately needed air. She crawled really fast and felt like pushing past the lady in front, who was going rather slowly. Finally, she could see a glimmer of light. She got up on her wobbly feet and rushed into the sunshine. Even Arun was red in the face. Adel stood there, holding a bottle of water. Rasha gulped and gulped and couldn't talk for ten minutes. Her head started reeling and she thought she would faint. Arun wasn't talking either. Twenty minutes elapsed and then Arun finally spoke. 'I never told you I suffer from claustrophobia.'

'What? Why didn't you?'

'Because it was your dream to go inside a pyramid.'

~

The rest of the day was spent at the Egyptian Museum. 'If you have to see the museum properly, it will take you months. But I can arrange a professional Egyptologist to be your guide at the museum,' Adel said.

'Yes, please' said Rasha.

Tahia Gabba was sitting in front of the majestic red building of the museum on the square cemented area that had shrubs sprouting from the middle. She wore a pair of jeans with a black full-sleeve, high-neck T-shirt. She had a sleeveless sweater on top. The colour of her hijab matched her bag, a style statement most young Egyptian women liked to make. She wore sunglasses. The museum was teeming with tourists, but Tahia skillfully navigated through the crowds and took them to the most important statues and artefacts. She deciphered hieroglyphics for them, as Rasha intently hung on to her every word and feasted her eyes on the statues of Ramesses II, Nefertiti and Hatshepsut.

'What's special about this?' asked Tahia standing in front of a statue.

'It has the face of a woman, but the face has a beard. It has to be Queen Hatshepsut, the only woman who ruled Egypt as a Pharaoh,' said Rasha.

'Remarkable,' said Tahia. 'Not many tourists know this,' she said.

Rasha beamed at Arun with child-like pride.

They had to buy separate tickets to visit the mummies and Tutankhamun's treasure room. Although photography was prohibited in the mummies' room, some insensitive tourists continued clicking the mummies on the sly. Rasha was looking at the mummy of Hatshepsut, when she heard someone talking in Bengali.

'See, that mummy's second toe is just like mine. It's so much shorter than the big toe.'

Rasha looked up to trace the face of the voice. The face was typically Bengali. Rasha's eyes first went to the vermillion on her forehead, then to the white and red bangles on her wrist—the shankha and pala—a tradition rarely followed by married women in modern Bengal. She was in a simple cotton printed salwar kurta, standing next to her husband, who had oiled hair and the trademark Bengali pot belly. Rasha smiled at her. She smiled back shyly, but they didn't speak.

Sitting at a coffee shop next to the museum, Rasha's mind was still wandering through the corridors of Tutankhamun's majestic home, when she was brought back to reality by the television on the wall. They were showing news on the developments in Tunisia and all eyes were glued to the TV. Tahia had brought them to an authentic Egyptian café, a favourite hangout of the youngsters in Egypt. Not many tourists knew about it. Four guys on a table next to the TV screen started saying something loudly amongst themselves. Most people in the café were in their twenties. Some were sitting with laptops in front of them. There were two love-struck couples sitting in one corner. The number of men was definitely higher than women, but all were listening to what the boys were saying and were catching the news in between. Before Rasha could ask Tahia what they were saying, hush descended on the café as everyone trained their eyes on the entrance. Rasha turned around to see two Egyptian police officers in black uniform and sunglasses walking in.

They stood there for a few minutes, automatically halting all activities at the café. They spoke to the café owner, who quickly turned off the TV. They took a look around and left. The four young men paid their bills hastily and left after them. Everyone else resumed their activities, but now all spoke in low voices, clearly showing the advent of the police had left its impact.

Rasha asked Tahia in a whisper, 'What were those guys saying?'

Tahia looked around and brought her lips close to Rasha's ears. 'They were saying, if those guys in Tunisia have the guts, we have it too?'

'Do you feel there is a possibility of an uprising?'

Before Tahia could answer Rasha's question, she greeted a man standing next to her and gestured him to sit with them.

'Meet Abdul Ziada,' she said.

Abdul was in his twenties and he had been long occupying a corner seat in the café working on his laptop. He placed the folded notebook on the table and sat opposite Rasha.

'This lady here was asking if there is a possibility of Tunisia happening here?' Tahia said to Abdul.

Abdul's face hardened. He looked squarely at Rasha.

'Can you keep a secret?' She nodded.

'Come to Tahrir Square tomorrow.' He excused himself and left.

'What did he mean?' Rasha asked Tahia. She shrugged, a bit unsettled. 'I really don't know.'

'Who is he?'

'He is an Egyptologist like me. And he is my husband.'

'You got married really early. I was told that young people don't get married early because of high living costs.'

Had Rasha not been in the reporting mode, she would not have asked such a personal question, but in this case, she had to, for her feature.

She noticed Tahia's face had clouded. 'Er...We haven't had a formal wedding yet,' she said.

'Then are you engaged?'

'No, actually...I don't know how to say. Umm...we had an urfi marriage last year. It is not a formal registered marriage, but it is marriage that is approved by Allah.'

'I didn't get you,' said Rasha.

'This marriage does not give me any rights of child support or alimony in case of a divorce. But Abdul and I are not leaving each other, we are sure of that. We will register our marriage when we have enough money. Till then, urfi allows us to share marital bliss.' Tahia smiled shyly.

'I get it. So have you rented an apartment or do you live with your parents?' asked Rasha.

'No, no. I told you I am married because you are an outsider. Except for his parents, nobody knows about our marriage. Neighbours won't approve of it.'

'Then marital bliss...?' asked Rasha.

'We manage,' said Tahia, looking at Arun and making it clear that she would not reveal any more.

Adel joined them after lunch. He took them to the citadel, better known as the Mosque of Mohammed Ali. At the entrance of the mosque, there were people handing out blue robes to women who were not aptly dressed to enter the mosque. In her full-sleeve shirt and jeans, Rasha passed the inspection of the lady in command and she was not given any robe to wear. The breathtaking interiors of the mosque were worth gaping at for hours and Rasha and Arun couldn't take their eyes off the beautiful chandelier that hung from the centre of the conical ceiling of the mosque and extended in circles through the entire red-carpeted prayer room. They stepped outside to click photographs of Cairo that unfolded in front of the Citadel, including the three pyramids of Giza visible at a distance.

'What are those dilapidated buildings?' said Rasha, training her lens on the buildings that looked like rat holes ready to tumble down any moment.

'Those are the slums,' said Adel.

'People live there?' she asked in surprise.

'Yes,' said Adel.

'Where's Tahrir Square?' she casually asked Adel on their way back.

'It's close to your hotel. We will be passing it on our way, Ma'am.'

Tahrir Square looked snazzier than the rest of Egypt. It was a huge roundabout with almost seven lanes. It had a round manicured lawn in the middle. Some women sat there chatting, while their children played around them. Cars zipped by from all directions.

'That's the Mogamma building. It has a number of government offices. That way, can you see the museum, Ma'am?'

Rasha craned her neck from the fast-moving car to catch a glimpse of the museum that had mesmerized her in the morning.

'That's the American University of Cairo and that is the National Democratic Party Headquarters,' said Adel, trying to be the perfect guide.

Rows of palm trees stood mutely on all sides of the square.

25

ARUN'S EYES WERE thick with sleep, but he still managed a slit and looked at the table clock on his side of the bed. It said 10.00 a.m. He turned on his stomach and swept his left hand below his pillow in anticipation. His hand touched something. He pulled it out. It was a big red envelope along with a Galaxy Chocolate. The card inside read:

> Dear Arun,
>
> Happy Birthday!
> Thanks for being a wonderful husband.
>
> Love,
> Rasha
> 25.1.2011

Rasha opened her droopy eyes when Arun kissed her. She kissed him back and pushed her nose in the hollow of his chest and closed her eyes again. They both were still revelling in the memory of the lovely time they had had the night before. Dinner at the Nubian Village restaurant at the Grand Hyatt in Cairo was quite an experience. Rasha had to admit, sitting at one of the tables at the restaurant, that Nile did look extraordinary in the night. The reflection of the dazzling lights of downtown Cairo on the longest river in the world made the view ethereal and the delectable Egyptian spread made Arun's pre-birthday celebrations exotic.

Post dinner, they aimlessly walked around the streets of Cairo, savouring the sights and sounds of the lively city. When they stepped inside the gates of their hotel at 3.00 a.m., the traffic on the road and the people thronging the sidewalks made it look like it was only 9.00 p.m. The lobby manager on night duty told them that Cairo never retired for the night.

It was past 10.00 a.m. when they finally woke up. The cars were still honking with the same intensity, but the voices seemed louder than usual. Arun pulled the curtain back and stood there for a few seconds. His expression soon changed from that of surprise to that of shock.

'You must see this, Rasha,' he said urgently.

Rasha sat erect on the bed, dropped her feet into her slippers lying on the carpet and scampered to Arun's side. The scene instantly reminded her of the famous, or rather infamous, political-party-led processions in Kolkata that brought the city to a halt.

Streams of people were walking on the streets, wriggling between cars and gushing like a torrent over the footpath. Traffic had come to a standstill. Some people were adding to the noise pollution levels by keeping their fingers pressed to the horn. Some had abandoned their cars and joined the crowd that comprised mostly young Egyptian men. Some of them were talking to passers-by, and from what they could gather from the hotel window, it seemed they were urging them to join the procession. Some tourists were standing on the pavements at the risk of being engulfed by the thousands marching past them. Everyone was headed in one direction.

'Isn't Tahrir Square that side?' said Rasha pointing to the right, her mind running back to Abdul Ziada's words the day before.

Arun nodded. 'Let me call up the hotel lobby and find out what's happening,' he said.

The information he gathered made them quickly shower and dress up. They had a banana each as they had no time for an elaborate breakfast. Rasha hastily called up Juneid. He said he would meet them in half an hour at the gates of the Egyptian Museum.

They asked the lobby manager for directions to Tahrir Square. 'It's close by, but I think it will be easier if you follow the crowd.'

When they stepped outside, traffic hadn't moved an inch. Some tourists were vigorously training their handycams at the crowd in the hope of catching something unique in Egypt. Rasha carried her own camera, which was anything but a professional one. It was a dependable Canon with a 30X optical zoom. It would stand her in good stead if she needed it.

As they approached Tahrir Square, the stream of people started swelling up in all directions. Rasha swiftly turned around as she heard a familiar Bengali voice. It was the same lady she had seen at the museum the day before. The lady smiled at her again.

'Are you from Kolkata?' she asked the lady in Bengali, at the risk of sounding clichéd.

The lady looked at her as if she had finally found her soulmate. Her smile spread from ear to ear and she nudged her husband. 'They are Bengalis.'

'Any idea what's happening?' Arun threw the question at the gentleman in Bengali again.

'No idea, but I am pretty sure nothing good is happening. I spoke to my travel agent and I am flying back to Kolkata tomorrow. I think you should do the same. By the way, where do you live in Kolkata?'

'Alipore,' Arun said, not elaborating that they were residents of Dubai at the moment.

'You?'

The gentleman extended his hands to shake Arun's. 'I am Gourab Banerjee from Bhawanipore and this is my wife Rupashree.

'I am in the garments export business and my business partner lives in an apartment in Tahrir Square. We are going over to his place to get a better view of the whole proceedings. He says this might be something serious.'

Rasha's reporter mind began to tick. 'Is your partner Egyptian?' she asked.

'Yes.'

'Can we join you in some time at the apartment?'

Gourab hesitated. 'Yes, sure. You want to come with us now?'

Rasha thought Juneid would be waiting for her.

'A little later, maybe. Give me your number, I will call you.'

They exchanged numbers and Gourab and Rupashree proceeded towards the apartment, while Arun and Rasha turned towards the museum.

'Journalists can be opportunistic and shameless,' said Arun.

'That's the only way they can survive,' Rasha laughed.

∾

Tahrir Square had become unrecognizable. There were no cars on the busy thoroughfare, only people standing around. Rasha had seen crowds like this only at Mamata Banerjee's meetings at the Brigade Parade Ground in Kolkata. But as more and more people joined the crowd from all directions, Brigade began looking dwarfish next to Tahrir Square. Rasha and Arun found it hard to inch their way through the bulging crowd to the Egyptian Museum. But they somehow managed. True to his words, Juneid was standing there.

'What's this?' asked Rasha.

'I guess it's an effort at an uprising. Seeing me standing here, some people asked me to join them.'

'Okay, let's start work. You will have to help me interview some of the protesters here, if they don't speak English. Then get some good pictures that reflect the mood at the square. We will file a story today.'

Juneid didn't like the fact that Rasha was giving him

instructions. 'You don't have to worry about my job. You think of yours,' he said sharply.

'Okay,' she said coolly.

Rasha charged like a bull into the crowd and moved in every direction in her quest for information. She spoke to at least ten people that included college students, factory workers, bankers, doctors and a couple of housewives, all of whom resonated the same feeling—the time had come to demand change. They refused to continue a life of perpetual struggle for a livelihood and basic comforts. They all believed that the Jasmine Revolution of Tunisia had arrived in Egypt.

Rasha and Juneid quickly went to a cyber café and sent their pictures and article. Mike Stevens wrote back: 'Keep us constantly updated and stay put. We are uploading your story in the online edition right now.'

Ten minutes later, when she clicked on the website, she saw her story and byline.

As Rasha walked back to Tahrir Square, the murmur of voices had transformed into a thousand drums rising and falling in its pitch. People were shouting, 'Erhal, erhal (Leave, leave)', for President Hosni Mubarak. They looked possessed. But a smile was dangling from Rasha's lips and she was mentally high-fiving herself. She felt she had finally arrived in the land of the Pharaohs.

∾

'How many people do you think there are?' Rasha asked Anwar Said.

'Could be a million, could be two,' he said.

'Could be just 10,000 and we are just over-estimating,' said Juneid cynically.

Gourab Banerjee had taken the January 26th flight to Dubai and then the Emirates flight to Kolkata, but he had gifted something invaluable to Rasha—the eight floor apartment of his business partner, Anwar Said.

Unlike the deprived millions in Egypt, Anwar was wealthy and was flourishing in his garments business. Like Gourab in Kolkata, he had other business partners in Delhi, Mumbai, New York and London. His huge three-bedroom apartment was occupied by his family, comprising of his wife and their two teenaged daughters. His apartment was furnished with expensive couches, teakwood chests and the two-door refrigerator in the kitchen was stuffed with necessities that would be sufficient for them to survive if the revolution at his doorstep did not allow him to step out for groceries. Egypt had given him more than he wanted in terms of wealth and happiness. He was just setting off for a quick vacation to Sharm El Sheikh with his family, when Tahrir Square happened. He junked his holiday plans and since then had been sitting in his balcony through night and day. He was extremely hospitable to Rasha and Juneid, who had been clicking and writing from his perch and even using his fax machine to file reports, since the internet had been promptly identified by the people in power as the perpetrator of the revolution and had been shut down all over Egypt.

The revolution had been anything but peaceful over the past three days. From Anwar's eight floor balcony, Rasha could see the ruling National Democratic Party headquarters up in flames, army tanks all over and the soldiers trying hard to disperse the crowd with teargas and stones. Ever since the revolution had begun, Rasha only hit the hotel bed to pass out for the night. The rest of the day was spent either at Tahrir Square or on Anwar's balcony. Six days had gone by like that. On the seventh day, the atmosphere at the square was far more relaxed, in fact, it wore the ambience of a fair.

The army had finally pledged its friendship to the people and were just silent onlookers. The fear of death and bloodshed had given way to temporary triumph. As darkness descended on the square, the guitars came out from the tents; and men, women and children, irrespective of their class division, sat around in groups and sang. Rasha and Arun sat in front of a tent listening to the lilting melody tinged with pathos and anger.

∾

'Rasha, my twelve-day leave comes to an end on February 3. What do you intend to do? If this goes on forever, we can't stay on,' said Arun. Rasha was still looking for that exclusive story that would make her name Google-worthy. She wanted to tell Arun that she would like to stay on in Egypt looking for that story. But she knew that Arun would be too worried to leave her alone in a country collapsing into anarchy at the moment.

They were about to leave for the hotel when an army officer walked up to the group they were sitting with. The atmosphere stiffened. Spotting the officer, they quickly blended into the darkness of a tent. It was a small plastic tent, the kind that Rasha had seen so many times on the beaches of Dubai. It barely had room for one person, but the two of them managed to huddle on the fleece blanket that was neatly laid out on the floor. Tents of every kind had cropped up in Tahrir Square in the last one week. There were the makeshift plastic ones, the gazebo-turned-tents, the professional camping ones and the kind in which Rasha and Arun were huddling together now.

The music had stopped and Rasha and Arun could hear the Arabic exchange between the army officer and the people. The voices started shifting to a distance. A young girl with lovely curly hair, in a pair of jeans and a pink-and-black hand-woven sweater, peeped into the tent. The flag of Egypt unfurled on her shoulders like the Superman's cape. She had told Rasha her name in the morning, but Rasha could not recollect it, having asked the names of at least fifty people that day. Along with the rest, she had jotted the girl's name down somewhere in the notebook that was in her handbag.

'It's safe, you can come out. See what's happening,' she said.

Rasha's eyes followed the direction in which she was looking. She was dumbstruck. A clearing had been created on the street and some young men were playing football with a few soldiers.

'The army officers said that they would gift us a tank if our men could beat them at football.' She laughed.

That night, Rasha's fingers flew on the keyboard of her laptop as she sent Mike her account of the football match between the army and the civilians. When she retired for the day, she just wanted the night to pass off quickly so that she could be at Tahrir Square at the crack of dawn. In her hotel room, she missed being a part of the revolution like a nicotine addict misses the puff. The journalist in her had finally woken up from a long slumber.

26

'JUST HOLD MY hand, hold my hand, you will not feel the pain.'

Rasha wasn't sure if she had woken up or if she was dreaming. She opened her eyes and could feel the conical ceiling reeling above her. She felt agonizing pain on the right side of her forehead and closed her eyes. She touched her forehead and felt something wet. Something wet was sticking to her eyes, so she struggled to open it.

'I am holding her, do it now.' She heard the voice again.

She felt a sharp prick and lost consciousness.

When she came around again, she felt less dizzy. She could move her head slightly to one side to witness the mayhem that was unfolding around her. There was a lady lying on the floor next to her with blood on her face and another lady was on her left with a bandage on her arms. People were running around in white coats with bandages and wads of cotton. She could hear screams of pain all around. She looked up at the conical ceiling. The place looked like a mosque, but the activities around her made her feel that she was in a hospital. She tried hard to piece together the sequence of events to comprehend why she was lying on the floor of a mosque in so much pain. She touched the soreness on her right side and felt a bandage. Her next thought was of Arun. She could not see him. In her anxiety, she tried to get up, but failed.

She felt the gentle touch of a hand on hers and turned around, hoping to see Arun's face. Rasha's first interviewee in Egypt, fearless blogger Zubeida El Taha, was kneeling next to her and looking at her kindly.

'Arun, where's Arun?' said Rasha.

'I don't know who you are talking about. I spotted you when the horse jumped on you, and brought you here.'

Everything came back to Rasha in a flash. From Anwar Said's apartment, she and Arun had gone for their routine stroll in Tahrir Square defying the curfew, like the rest of the people in the country. They never imagined the scene would turn so ugly, so fast. Some people came in buses armed with knives and firebombs and charged into the crowd, wrecking havoc. The army stood there as mute spectators as the battle between the supporters of the regime and protesters ensued. Rasha and Arun were running for the cover of Anwar's apartment when a firebomb exploded close by, hurling them to the ground. The last thing Rasha remembered was that she was trying to get up when the hooves of a horse closed in on her.

'Where did a horse come from?' asked Rasha.

'Mubarak's men came on at least twenty horses. And two camels,' said Zubeida.

'You have got around ten to twelve stitches. I hope they have done a good job. There should not be a scar on this pretty face,' she said.

'But Arun, I need to find Arun,' said Rasha urgently.

'First, check if he is here. This mosque is the only makeshift clinic we have, so everyone hurt is being brought in here,' said Zubeida.

The thought of Arun being hurt filled Rasha's heart with fear. But she wanted to find him first.

'Can you do me a favour? Can you call Juneid here? He will be able to help find Arun.'

'I can't, telephone connectivity has been disrupted,' she said.

~

Juneid was on the other side of the square, trying to chronicle the events through his lens. He was so absorbed in getting pictures, and afterwards helping out his wounded countrymen, that he had actually not missed Rasha and Arun. The fighting continued well into the evening and extended to the night. Juneid alternated between taking pictures and helping out some of the fifteen hundred wounded people.

It was 2.00 a.m. when he saw a man, bleeding profusely from the nose, being carried away by four men to a tent. The maroon sweater and jeans looked familiar. When he recognized him, he rushed towards the four men carrying him.

'Arun, Arun! Are you okay?' he said, as they entered a tent.

Arun looked at him with dazed eyes and managed to squeeze out the word, 'Rasha…' from his lips.

'Where is Rasha?' asked Juneid sharply.

'Find her,' Arun said in a whisper.

Arun had no clue how long he had been lying there unconscious. He had seen the horse closing in on Rasha and had jumped up to push it out of her way. He had managed to lessen the impact, but he wasn't sure if it had hurt Rasha. The man riding the horse had hit him with something heavy. When he regained consciousness, he could not see Rasha and felt the bile building up in his throat.

Juneid sat next to Arun in the clumsy tent as the sound of bombs, firing and screaming provided the background score.

'I will find her. You stay here and don't go anywhere,' he said resolutely.

When Juneid came out of the tent, Tahrir Square still resembled a battlefield. He started looking in each and every tent and looked everywhere the wounded lay. He checked in Anwar Said's apartment, in case she had gone back there. But she hadn't. Juneid went back to the square and saw his cousin, one of the architects of the Facebook group seen as being responsible for the revolution. The young boy told him about the secret location of the mosque where they had created a makeshift clinic.

'I am taking someone there right now. You come with me,' he said.

Inside the mosque, Juneid scoured each face, looking for Rasha, but couldn't find her. As more and more wounded people crowded the mosque, Juneid stood there thinking of a possible place where she could be.

~

'Are you looking for me?'

Even before he turned around, the voice filled his heart with relief. Before she could ask him, he blurted out, 'I will take you to Arun.'

Rasha had emptied her bed to accommodate someone in a more critical state than herself, but her head was still throbbing and reeling, which was why Zubeida had forced her to stay in the mosque despite her repeated requests to go look for Arun.

'You wait here with her. I will get a car and Arun,' Juneid told Zubeida.

She looked at him doubtfully.

'I will manage,' he said firmly.

'Be careful, they are still setting cars on fire there,' said Zubeida.

Juneid stepped out into the shadows and walked down an alley for quite some time before he reached a taxi stand. There was a lone man sitting inside a taxi. As the man was about to protest, Juneid opened the door and sat inside.

'Here's your chance to do something for your countrymen. Start the car.'

The man did not say a word and started driving. They parked the car in a by-lane next to Tahrir Square. Arun was sitting inside the tent in escalating pain and worry.

'I have found her. Let's go,' said Juneid.

He helped Arun to his feet and walked him to the alley where the taxi was waiting. Arun was breathless by the time they reached the taxi. After navigating through a number of dark lanes and broad roads devoid of people, they reached the mosque. Tears streamed down Rasha's face when she saw Arun in the cab. She sat in the car and hugged Arun as the taxi started rolling again and picked up speed. It took a right turn into a crowd. A dozen men armed with knives and bottles stopped the taxi. One of them came to the front window and said something to Juneid. He replied in Arabic. The exchange became heated as the men surrounded the car. They looked at Rasha and Arun as if they were some newly acquired species at the Cairo Zoo. However, once their inspection was done, they let the taxi pass.

'Who were they?' Arun asked.

'Pro-government men. They didn't want to believe you are just curious tourists who got caught in the crossfire. They wanted to know what you guys were doing there when all the tourists have left Cairo. I said your passports were stolen from your hotel room, so you could not leave till your embassy issued new ones. They were finally satisfied.'

∿

A bandaged Rasha and bleeding Arun made quite a sight when they stepped into their hotel lobby. The lobby manager ran to their aid. Some members of the staff looked at them with questioning glances and whispered among themselves.

When Rasha looked at herself in the bathroom mirror, she was horrified by the sight. Her blood-stained clothes and swollen face looked scary. Arun wasn't sure if he had a broken nose because, even after downing two painkillers, the pain hadn't subsided. Rasha used the hotel phone to inform Mike about the incidents. He was concerned and asked her to catch the next flight to Dubai.

It was dawn when they both pulled the sheets on their chest

to get some rest. Arun planned to pack in the afternoon and catch their scheduled evening flight back home. The painkillers had definitely helped Rasha, because she had already gone to sleep. Arun struggled with his pain for sometime till he, too, managed to doze off.

∿

They both woke up to loud banging on the door. 'Open up! Open up! This is the police.'

Arun felt an arrow of pain shoot up his nose into his head when he got up to open the door. Rasha couldn't get up from bed, she was petrified.

There were three men in police uniform at the door. 'Who is the journalist here?' asked one of them.

'Journalist?' Arun said. 'Nobody. I am into real estate and this is my wife.'

The police officer's eyes narrowed, as he looked at Rasha past Arun and then his eyes settled back on him. 'What happened to you?'

'We were passing by Tahrir Square yesterday when someone attacked us.'

The police officer laughed. 'You would go there only if you are a journalist. Stop lying. Tell me the truth,' he demanded.

Arun was vehement. 'Not us. We are tourists. We didn't get a flight home so we are still here.'

'Really?' he said mockingly.

Arun quickly added. 'But we are leaving today evening.'

'Show me your passports.' All this while, Rasha was sitting motionless on the bed, unable to figure out where this was leading to. Arun took out their passports from his bag and gave it to the police officer. The other two police officers had lost interest by then and left the scene.

'From Dubai,' he said with renewed interest, flipping through the passport.

'So how much cash are you carrying?'

At that moment, Arun had thousand Egyptian pounds with him. All the dirhams were in Rasha's bag.

'Five hundred Egyptian pounds,' Arun said.

'I am sure you are not going to spend all that by today evening. Can I have it?' he said unashamedly.

Arun took out the money from his purse and gave it to him.

'Have a safe flight,' said the police officer, returning their passports. He smiled crookedly and left. Rasha and Arun heaved a sigh of relief.

Five minutes later, the banging on the door was louder.

'Open up. This lady inside is a journalist. You were lying. She has been writing reports from the business centre. I will have to take your passports.'

Rasha felt like banging her head against the wall. On two occasions, the internet connection on her laptop gave her trouble and she had filed her stories from the business centre in the hotel. Someone must have seen that.

Arun looked at Rasha angrily. She stared back at him feebly. 'This is downright harassment. Can you prove my wife has written reports from the business centre?' Arun said unwaveringly, as he opened the door.

The police officer gave Arun the you-are-going-too-far look, and spoke in a commanding tone. 'I want you and your wife to come with me to the police station. I am waiting for you outside, don't take more than five minutes.' He banged the door shut.

Rasha found it hard to slip on her sweater through her bandaged head. Instead, she threw on a jacket on her shirt. She had heard the police had not been nice to the international journalists, who were thronging the country. She worried about this trip to the police station.

The police car they were in was as shabby as any other four wheeler in Cairo. When they reached the police station, they were asked to wait outside on a cold bench as the officer went inside with their passports. There were two European men at the police station, but Rasha didn't dare to find out if they were journalists. She just hoped that in the midst of all this, the Cairo police would not get the time to Google her name, because every single report she had filed from January 25 was on the net. If they did, she could give up all the hopes of getting her passport back. Like the rest of Cairo, the walls of the police station too had plaster peeling off everywhere. There was an outside area with a bench, where they were sitting, and an inside room where the police officer was. There were other rooms too, but all the doors were closed.

Half an hour later, the police officer came back. 'You are not flying today that's for sure. We need to ask you a lot of questions,' he said looking at Rasha. He went back inside without a word more. Rasha's palms turned sweaty thinking of the missing nails on Zubeida's hands.

She thought that she had to let Mike know what was happening. She was not sure how the police would react if they saw her on her mobile, so she plunged her hands into her handbag and tried to send a text message surreptitiously.

Before she had finished, another police officer came out from the room. 'Rasha Roy?' he asked.

Her hands dislodged from the mobile with a start and she looked up. 'Come with me,' he said.

'Where?' Arun asked.

'Don't ask questions. I will be back in a minute. Just follow me,' he said in a low voice.

Rasha and Arun looked at each other, not sure if this was a good sign or a bad one.

However, they didn't get a chance to think further about their own situation as their eyes went to the young woman who was walking in through the doors of the police station, led by an elderly woman. The young woman's face was smeared with tears and kohl. Her cheeks bore scratch marks that looked like she had been clawed by some wild animal. Her left eye was half closed because of injury. She had swollen and bleeding lips and disheveled hair. She was finding it hard to walk and was leaning heavily on the elderly woman. They spoke to a police officer in Arabic, who asked them to sit next to Rasha and Arun.

'What happened?' Rasha asked the girl in a low voice.

She looked at her with eyes that had turned red and puffy due to constant crying.

'I was raped by a mob last night.' She broke down.

'Where did this happen?' asked Rasha.

'I was dragged to a bus in Tahrir Square,' she said.

'Give me your phone number,' Rasha said urgently.

The girl stared at her blankly.

'Give me the number quickly. I mean no harm. I will call you and explain.'

The girl blurted out her number and Rasha scribbled it on her notepad under the cover of her handbag.

'Let's go,' said the police officer. Rasha looked at the girl one last time and, a trifle reluctantly, followed him outside clutching Arun's arms.

'Come with me,' he ushered them to a car. They climbed in.

'So you are an undercover journalist?' the police officer asked. Rasha kept quiet.

'It's interesting. Your passport says you came to Egypt on January 22. Did you know the revolution would start in a couple of days?' he asked in a sarcastic tone.

Rasha thought that in circumstances like that, it was best to keep one's mouth shut. She tapped Arun on his thighs, as he was about to say something. He felt the tap and recoiled.

'So when is your flight?' asked the police officer.

'In an hour,' said Arun.

The police officer's face became thoughtful. Arun had the urge to ask him where he was taking them, but decided against it.

'So, how is life in Dubai? I have heard people have a lot of money there.'

Arun thought it would be rude not to answer. 'Yes, it is a rich Emirate.'

'And you? Are you rich?'

As a reflex action, Rasha clutched her dirhams-filled bag. 'No, we are not rich. We are just middle class,' said Arun.

His face turned thoughtful again and Arun was pretty sure he was plotting on extracting some cash from them.

'Where's your hotel?'

Arun told him.

'Have you packed?'

'Almost.'

'Okay, I will take you to your hotel. Get your things.'

This troubled Rasha. She wasn't sure if he wanted to make their belongings his own. But at that point, they didn't have an option but to follow his orders. They dumped everything that was lying around into their bags and were ready in ten minutes. Rasha just managed to send a message to Mike and Juneid from her phone.

∾

They set off again to their unknown destination. The police officer drove for another half an hour and finally jammed on his brakes.

'We have reached,' he said.

Rasha and Arun could not believe their eyes. They were in front of the Cairo International Airport.

The officer smiled and handed them their passports. 'Egyptian police is not all that bad, Madam.'

Rasha looked at him awkwardly and smiled. Arun thanked him profusely.

They ran inside and headed straight to the check-in counter. Only ten minutes remained before their flight was scheduled to take-off.

The man at the counter looked at them annoyed. 'You are too late. Boarding is over. I am afraid you can't fly today.'

REEMA'S LAST TELEPHONIC exchange with Rasha took place a couple of days before. After that, she had lost touch with her. Sitting on the couch of her Bur Dubai home and watching Tahrir Square unfold on the 40-inch screen on her wall, Reema was getting worried. Soumen was in China for work and her inability to share her anxiety with someone made her even more restless.

She knew that the relationship between Ankita and Rasha was still frosty, but the only person she could think of calling at the moment was Ankita.

'Ankita di, I don't know if Rasha and Arun have managed to board their scheduled flight because I have lost touch with them. But I am going to the airport to wait for them. If you are not too busy, will you come with me?' she asked her over the phone.

'Yes, of course. My car's gone for servicing, so can you please pick me up?'

Reema hung up, smiling. She was happy that her effort at breaking the ice between her two closest friends had not been futile. She quickly slipped on her Juicy Couture velour hoodie and track pants and put the keys into the ignition of her Pajero. In no time, she was driving down Palm Jumeirah and knocking on the door of Ankita's villa. Ankita was in a pair of jeans and a T-shirt. She hadn't bothered to put on any make-up. She hopped into the car.

'Have you been following Rasha on the net?' she asked Reema, who nodded in the affirmative.

'She has been brilliant. I am really glad that she got this opportunity. She is an absolute reporter at heart,' said Ankita.

Reema sped through Sheikh Zayed Road and Garhoud Bridge and reached the airport in no time. It didn't take her long to find a parking space.

'The flight is late,' said Reema, looking at the flight update board at the Dubai International Airport. 'Let's have coffee.'

The two ladies settled in two chairs at the Starbucks corner.

'I hope Rasha and Arun are okay,' said Ankita, with concern.

'I have always shared a special connection with Rasha, but things weren't in the best of state between us after I left *Silver Screen*. But I have realized that we both were victims of circumstances and there is no point being bitter about it,' she said.

Reema was pleased with herself.

'The flight's arrived. Let's go,' she said.

They stood at the waiting area of the arrival lounge. An hour later, they were still waiting in trepidation.

There was no sign of Rasha and Arun. Reema called their mobiles repeatedly, but there was no reply.

'Have they not come? Let's wait for ten more minutes, then we can go to the enquiry desk,' said Ankita.

'There, there…there they are,' said Reema.

'My god, what happened?' said Ankita, as both started waving frantically to Rasha and Arun.

A sensation of relief swept through Rasha's body as she spotted her friends.

'You both look awful. What happened?' said Ankita.

'It's a long story,' said Arun.

'What happened to your phones?' asked Reema.

'No charge,' Rasha said with a tired smile.

∾

As Rasha put the key through the lock of her Karama apartment, home seemed the most peaceful and safe corner in the world.

Reema and Ankita stayed on for some time, helping Rasha and Arun settle down.

'We will come over tomorrow morning with lunch and hear everything,' said Ankita.

'Reema, can you take me to Welcare Hospital tomorrow? I need to check my nose. It might be broken,' Arun said.

'Yes, sure,' replied Reema.

Once they were gone, the first thing Rasha did was put her phone on charging. It instantly beeped twice. The first message was from Mike.

It read: 'We have got in touch with our contacts in the Egyptian police department. Hope you can catch your flight on time.'

The second one was from Juneid.

It read: 'I am going to her place tomorrow. Hope you have reached safely.'

Rasha had used the satellite phone on the flight to make two calls. One was to the girl she had met at the police station and the second to Juneid. The girl had just left the police station after filing her report when Rasha caught up with her. It took her some time to convince the girl about the interview and the picture. On the one hand, the girl wanted the world to know about her plight, but on the other hand, she was scared of the backlash from the society. She had said she would think about it.

The second call was to Juneid. 'If we can get this story, it will be a world exclusive. See if you can get the photograph.'

The pain on the right side of her forehead woke her up early next morning. Arun was already up and had made two steaming cups of tea. He came to the bedroom with tea and Rasha's favourite McVitie's biscuits. He drew the curtains back to let some sunlight in.

'I think there is a message on your phone. I heard it in the middle of the night,' he said.

'How is your nose?' she asked.

'Hurting, but not unbearable,' said Arun.

Rasha reached for her phone. There was an email sitting in her inbox. It read:

Hi Rasha,

I have decided I will give you the interview. Call me.

Afifah

Rasha had not even asked the girl her name at the police station. She had thought her name was beautiful, but looking at her email now she was in a journalistic dilemma.

Should I make Afifah's misfortune my golden opportunity? she thought. She was not sure.

Epilogue

~ℰ~

'I love this. Thank you so much, Rasha,' Susanna said, rolling a three-feet-long rectangular papyrus.

'I am glad you like it. I really don't know how to thank you for giving me the contact of Mike Stevens. It's been a life-altering experience,' said Rasha.

'Come on, Rasha, don't be so formal. Check this out. I got you this bag from my holiday in Phuket,' said Susanna, taking out a brown leather bag from a plastic packet.

'It's lovely,' said Rasha, running her hand through the soft leather surface.

Susanna lifted a sushi to her mouth with her chopstick. Rasha was using her fork, because she felt clumsy around chopsticks. A lovely breeze was blowing from the sea and everyone was enjoying the February sun on the terrace.

The ambience of the terrace hadn't changed at all in the last one year. Only the circumstances had changed from the last time Rasha sat there. Susanna had asked her to come down to the office for lunch. Initially, Rasha wasn't too keen, but finally she gave in. Now sitting there on the picturesque terrace, she was glad that Susanna had given her the opportunity to change the last memories of her favourite haunt in office.

'So what next?' said Susanna.

'I have been called to New York next month to meet the editors and attend a workshop. I will be meeting Afifah too,' said Rasha.

'That's great. I am glad that the human rights group is taking her to the US. The girl deserves some peace.'

'Yes, that was my condition when I did the story,' said Rasha.

'*Really? You ensured this?*'

Rasha nodded. '*And Mike pushed it.*'

'*You are just amazing. Anyone else in your place would have treated it as just another story,*' said Susanna.

Afifah had no clue as to what she was getting herself into with that interview, but I had. So, it was my duty to ensure her safety,' said Rasha, inadvertently touching the scar on her forehead.

Susanna finished her bento box and sat back. '*How are your parents and sister? I must send you my niece's birthday pictures. They had a fairytale-themed birthday.*'

'*You must. As for my parents, they are fine. My dad's finally won the court case. My sister is working on the resort project with him. I hope things turn out fine.*'

'*That's good news. I am sure they will. But I have some news for you.*'

'*What?*' said Rasha a bit alarmed.

'*I am getting married in June and you are attending my wedding in London along with Arun, and I am not taking no for an answer,*' she said in one breath.

'*And you took so long to tell me this,*' said Rasha, getting up from her chair and hugging Susanna. '*I can't imagine how beautiful you will look dressed up as a bride. Of course, we will come.*'

'*Now, now, who's come to visit us?*'

Rasha didn't have to turn around to add a face to the voice. She knew who it was.

'*Hi Sabrina, how are you?*' she said.

'*I am fine. I am fine. What brings you here?*' she enquired.

'*Lunch with Susanna obviously,*' said Rasha, looking fondly at her ex-colleague-turned-friend.

Sabrina settled down on a chair opposite Rasha and brought out her pack of cigarettes. Her blunt haircut had changed into a Rihanna-like pixie crop and her attire was faithful to fashion trends. But she had the same boots on—the ones she wore on the day of that fateful meeting *with Rasha.*

'You haven't been shopping much lately. Old ones.' Rasha looked at her boots.

'Yeah, been too busy at work, no time to shop,' said Sabrina.

'I will be back from the washroom quickly. Please excuse me, ladies,' said Susanna.

Once Susanna was gone, Sabrina uncrossed her legs, exhaled cigarette smoke, and leaned towards Rasha across the table.

'I have been intending to tell you this for a long time, but never managed to. Thanks for not writing anything against me in the exit interview,' she said in a conniving tone.

Rasha smiled. 'You are welcome,' she said.

Sabrina leaned back, crossed her legs and went back to her characteristic I-own-the-world attitude. 'So, what are you doing these days?'

Rasha took out a magazine from her handbag and laid it on the table. Afifah's picture was on the cover with Rasha's byline. Afifah had already become a familiar face to people following the revolution in Egypt. Nevertheless, Rasha didn't expect someone as current-news challenged as Sabrina to know about her.

Sabrina's yellow-nail-polished hands reached for the magazine. Her jaws hardened. She flipped through a few pages disinterestedly as if she was going through a leisure magazine at a beauty salon. Rasha knew the cover had the desired impact on her when she started chewing the nail of her little finger, something Sabrina always did when she was under stress.

'No, no, don't. The nail polish will chip,' said Rasha.

This irked Sabrina even more. She raised one eyebrow, took a long puff from her cigarette and tried her best to act indifferent. 'So, you are freelancing for them?'

'No, I am their Middle East and Africa Correspondent.'

Sabrina froze.

'And they have called me to New York next month to meet the editors

and attend a workshop,' Rasha delivered the coup de grace.

Rasha got up to leave and as she looked at Sabrina, she almost felt sorry for her. She took one last glance at the Marina. A solitary speedboat was cutting through the waves and disappearing into the horizon.

Acknowledgements

Quoting Charles Dickens' famous line from *The Tale of Two Cities*, I have to say, 'It was the best of times, it was the worst of times for me.' I was dealing with extreme pain and intense happiness all at the same time. Twenty-four days after I lost my brother Anirban Mukherjee to cancer, on 31 March 2010 my son, Vivaan, was born.

I have to thank Vivaan, first, for holding my hand firmly and taking me through the emotional roller coaster I was experiencing at that time. He helped me take the decision to finally sit down and write this book.

Thanks to my husband Jaydip Sengupta, for believing in me, pushing me constantly and giving direction to the book.

I would also like to thank my ex-colleague and dear friend, Roshni Mukherjee, for having all the confidence in me. Thank you Rajasri Sawant for taking care of my son when I was writing.

Thanks to my parents, Anjali and Niroj Mukherjee, for letting me fly and to my in-laws, Ruby and late Satyabrata Sengupta, for loving me unconditionally.

I owe much to my family for supporting me in all my endeavours. Thank you, Subhadip Sengupta and Sathi Dey Sengupta. Thank you, Anita and Dhiresh Guha, Pratik Sengupta, Sudip Sengupta, Supriyo and Moonmoon Sengupta, Sumit and Lipika Dasgupta.

Thank you, Dibyendra Nath Mukerjea and Aarti Kothari, Ronita Roy and Dr Parthib Basu, Chirag Basu, Subhendranath and Subhra Mukherjee for your encouragement. Thank you, Snigdha Roy, Ashok and Ratna Mukherjee.

A big thanks to Dr Amiya Banerjee, Dr Sipra Banerjee, Anamika Banerjee, Arun and Anima Basak, Anita and Ake Lonnberg, Suprakash and Indira Chatterjee, Dr Santanu Das and Anubha Das.

I owe much to my Dubai friends who are my new family. A big thanks to the Kars (Chandrani and Sankha), the Bhattacharyyas (Sujata, Gautam and Ruhi), the Bhowmiks (Ashis, Sumita, Avantika and Ahiri) and the Das's (Sanjib, Moumita and Ryan). Thank you, Moyna Sen, Rohan and Nilafer Alvares, Harsha Lulla, Jigna Bhatt, Rekha Kuldeep, Nirmala Natarajan, Mahalaya Banerjee, Salam Al Amir and Lekha Menon.

I am blessed to have friends who have always been there for me. Thank you Sunayana Sarkar, Indrani Das, Rajasri Saraswat, Ellora Bhattacharya, Sreeraj Mitra, Saroni Roy, Saswati Dutta Gupta, Dr Tumpa Mukherjee, Shyamali Bose, Bappa Mazumdar, Samit Chanda and Pabitra Das. Thanks to my late brother's friends, Bhaskar Das and Debabrata Basu.

I believe teachers have the most influence on a person's life and mine is no different. Thanks to Professor Prasanta Ray, Dr Surajit C. Mukhopadhyay, late Jashodhara Hanafi, and my tutor, Prodosh Sen. Thanks to late Abhijit Dasgupta for being a great teacher at the workplace.

And most importantly, thank you, my commissioning editor, Kausalya Saptharishi. If you hadn't picked up my manuscript from the thousands that are sent to Rupa Publications every year, I wouldn't have been writing this acknowledgements page today. Thank you editors Sneha Gusain and Barnasha Baruah for polishing my manuscript and making it shine.